THE WEIGHT OF BLUE

J THOMAS WITCHR

NATBEN PUBLISHING

Contents

FOR MIM

1.

If it had been a film, the ferry would have gone down in a full-blown cinematic disaster: people screaming, luggage flying, and, at the crucial last moment, a hero leaping through a curtain of smoke to save a young damsel in distress.

At least, that's how Rafe Cardoc would have directed it if the scene were in one of his films.

I hadn't noticed any young damsels on board. And if I hadn't been standing on the top deck, staring at the water and feeling a bit sorry for myself, I might not have noticed anything wrong at all. Just a bump. A slight tilt beneath my feet.

We were somewhere between Sainte-Maxime and Saint-Tropez, gliding across the gulf aboard the ferry La Belle Sirène. The sea lay still beneath a postcard-blue sky. The passenger deck bustled with business types and a few sunburned tourists, while delivery vans, trucks, and cars of all types, including mine, were secured nearby.

The day was too beautiful to feel dangerous, and I was still trying to figure out what was happening as more people began gathering on the top deck. The ferry listed a little more, and even the half-inebriated passengers noticed something was off. Still, there was no sense of panic.

An announcement came over the speakers, first in French and then in English. Calm. Almost unsettlingly so:

"Mechanical failure. Please proceed to the lifeboats."

The majority of the crew stood stunned and hesitant, as if waiting for someone to tell them what to do. Then a young crewmember stepped forward and took charge. He looked no older than sixteen, thin, with shaggy red hair. An oversized navy jacket hung awkwardly from his narrow shoulders, as though it belonged to someone else. Despite his youth, he seemed the only one with a plan.

He began to direct the crowd toward the lifeboats, and I was pulled along. The deck tilted again, but there still didn't seem to be any need for urgency. There were plenty of lifeboats, and in the distance, I could see more boats approaching, everything from broken-down fishing vessels to luxury yachts.

Then the tilt grew sharper. A few passengers grabbed the railing. Someone muttered something anxious in French. I felt the first real spike of unease, and feelings shifted from inconvenient to frightening in a heartbeat.

A shrill, urgent cry cut through the air. Heads turned.

A heavyset woman in a floral blouse barreled toward the lifeboats. Her perfume, a dense, powdery cloud of cheap fragrance, reached us a moment before she did. She ran with the determination of someone who had spent her entire life assuming disaster was personal.

"Non, non, non, le ferry va couler, je le sais!"

I didn't understand the words, but the meaning was obvious. She intended to be first into the lifeboat, and I was in her way.

I tried to sidestep, too slow. At six-foot-three and just under two hundred pounds soaking wet, I wasn't much of a barrier. She plowed into me like a freight train, sending me spinning like a human pinball into a hard collision with someone else.

I was cursed in French, though it wasn't my fault, and shoved again. I lost my balance and went down face-first, throwing out both arms to keep from smashing into the metal deck. My right wrist crumpled like tissue paper, and a sharp stab of pain shot up to my elbow.

Before I could get to my feet, a razor-sharp stiletto heel stabbed into the inside of my thigh. I sucked in a breath, catching a strong whiff of garlic mixed with perfume.

Hands grabbed my shoulders. A deckhand with a sunburned nose shouted something urgent in French. Another crewman, older, with thick forearms and a faded mermaid tattoo, rushed over and hauled me upright. The deck tilted even more beneath us.

They hustled me toward the lifeboat. Madame Floral Blouse was already seated, clutching her handbag to her chest as if it held the crown jewels. She glared at me as though getting in her way were my fault, then looked away with a dismissive sniff.

The irony was that there was no reason to hurry. It took another thirty minutes before we were safely away: ten minutes to finish loading, and another twenty while the crew argued about the proper way to use the levers to lower the boat into the water.

Once the boat finally settled into the water, a dispute broke out over how to start the engine. Two crew members shouted heatedly in French, gesturing wildly and seeming on the verge of a fistfight before, at last, they managed to get it running. I couldn't shake the feeling that I had stumbled into a scene from an old Marx Brothers film.

We puttered out a short way from the ferry and heard a small explosion. We watched La Belle Sirène lean farther into the sea. The rear cargo gate dipped under. I caught one last glimpse of my car before it disappeared into the gulf.

The young red-haired crewman touched my shoulder and said something insistent in quick, breathless French.

"I'm sorry," I said, still shaken. "I don't understand."

He blinked, searching for the word. "English?"

"I'm American."

Recognition flickered across his face. He nodded once, then gave a small shake of his head. "Ah. American." He hesitated, then managed, carefully, "Very... bad. I am sorry. Such a pity."

I thought he was referring to my wrist, which I was cradling against my stomach as it began to turn a vivid shade of purple.

"I'm hoping it's not broken. I'm hoping it's just a sprain."

He looked at me, puzzled, then shook his head. "Non, non. I meant the Ferrari. I saw you drive it on board. Beautiful. Very expensive."

I understood then that he was not all that concerned about my wrist. I realized I could have been sprawled at the bottom of the lifeboat, broken and bleeding, near death, and he still would have been more distressed about my shiny car.

The rest of the ride to shore was mercifully short. At the pier, someone in a reflective vest noticed my wrist and flagged down an ambulance crew. One of the attendants, a stocky, impatient man, stuffed me into the van with more efficiency than sympathy.

At a small clinic near the ferry office, an austere, unfriendly woman handled my wrist like a side of beef. I never found out if she was a doctor, a nurse, or just someone who had wandered in off the street to practice medicine. When I complained, she spoke to a nearby woman in French, and they laughed. I suspected something crude.

She fit a brace firmly around my wrist and half my arm. I hadn't realized she spoke English until she addressed me in a tone sharp enough to school a misbehaving child: "You have a fracture. It's not serious, but it is a break. You'll need to keep it supported for several weeks and do your best not to knock it against anything."

She gave me a small bottle of pain pills, and she fitted me with a sling as well, decorated with Looney Tunes characters. She explained that the cartoon sling was the last one they had. More likely, it was another joke at the expense of the ugly American.

The same ambulance took me back to the marina. Once I arrived, reality set in. Everyone else waited, shaken and subdued. A few were wrapped in foil blankets that crinkled when they moved, making them resemble misplaced astronauts.

After a twenty-minute wait, we were herded into a low building near the water. It looked like it had been built for school field trips and disappointing lunches. Bottled water and crackers were set out. No ice.

A balding man with tired eyes and a rumpled suit stopped in front of me and asked for identification. I handed him my passport. He scribbled something on a clipboard and told me, in a mixture of French and English, that someone from the ferry line's insurer would contact me within forty-eight hours.

"For now," he said, handing me a short form, "please fill this out and leave a contact number."

I wrote illegibly with my left hand. I saw him staring at my Looney Tunes sling. I thought he almost smiled, but I could have been mistaken. He didn't look like someone who smiled a lot.

I left my name and my new cell number. I was a little reluctant about writing it down. I'd been stingy about giving it out. I'd changed my old one when I left California. I didn't want my former bosses tracking me down.

I pushed the door open and stepped into the evening air, squinting against the sun's last glare. Across the cobblestones, a small cluster of the crew from La Belle Sirène huddled together, looking like a group of cats who had just been told their favorite fish had gone bad: solemn, stiff, and staring at nothing in particular.

Before I could slip past them, the young red-haired crewman came barreling over. He'd apparently forgotten that my French was almost nonexistent. He launched into a rapid-fire explanation, words tumbling out at lightning speed, his hands slicing the air as if he were conducting an invisible orchestra. I managed to catch only a few fragments, voiture and perdue, and figured he was still expressing concern about my missing car.

I didn't have the heart to tell him the truth. I hadn't even liked the car that much: a sleek Ferrari Roma Spider, red as a cardinal's robe and twice as sinful. It looked fast, even standing still. It had cost a fortune, a huge chunk of everything I'd saved during my years working at Sweet Angel Productions.

But the car wasn't me. I'm not James Bond. I don't drive fast. I don't charm women. I trip over the word hors d'oeuvres, and I own three identical beige sweaters.

I'd bought the car to impress a girl I'd met in Barcelona, jet-black hair, impossibly long legs, and a personality that could swing from serene to cat-crazy in a heartbeat.

We'd traveled together for a while. Nothing intimate. Separate rooms. Her idea, not mine.

In Florence, we wandered cobbled streets, watched kids play soccer near ancient walls, and lost hours in the Uffizi, mesmerized by Botticelli and da Vinci. We shared gelato by the Ponte Vecchio and got delightfully lost in the Boboli Gardens, letting the maze of hedges and fountains steal time from us. We even took a tiny riverboat down the Arno, drifting slowly through the city as the afternoon sun dappled the water.

In Pamplona, we witnessed the running of the bulls: white shirts, red sashes, pounding hooves, adrenaline thick in the air. My companion urged me forward, and I was tempted, but common sense, or perhaps cowardice, kept me behind the barriers.

Inside the bullring itself, the blood sport, as Hemingway called it, thrilled me less than it did her. Her eyes shone at the kill, and later she gave me a kiss on the cheek and a wave of her fingers and drifted away with a matador. Or maybe a picador.

The car didn't do much for my love life. Maybe I should have bought a bull instead.

2.

I'd envisioned myself driving along the coast in my fancy new car, my Spanish girlfriend beside me, her hair whipping in the wind. So much for great expectations. No girlfriend. No car. And even if I did have a car, I wasn't going anywhere soon, my wrist felt as if someone were stabbing it with red-hot needles.

It was already getting dark, and the only room I could find near the docks in Saint-Tropez was above a noisy bar called Le Zinc Pourri. My basic French translated the name as "The Rotten Bar." I had to be mistaken. No one would name their business the Rotten Bar. Regrettably, the name fit.

My room was tiny. There was no closet, a single dresser, and a single fragile-looking chair. I was afraid to sit in it.

The bed leaned to one side, as if defeated by gravity. The bathroom down the hall had a shower, but the water ran dirty brown. I decided against using it.

The toilet was an antique, probably from the war years, with a high cistern and a rattling pipe. The single window gave me a view of the roof next door.

My wrist throbbed like a bad tooth. The pills dulled the sharpest edges, but left a dull, persistent ache and a hint of nausea. In the movies, the hero always gets up from his injuries triumphant, but the movies lie about pain. Human beings are fragile, and pain hurts. That's why it is called pain.

The bar below never slept. Laughter and clinking glasses echoed upward. I knew enough French to realize a soccer game was on. Every so often, the crowd erupted so loudly that even my bed trembled.

I was trying to use my thin pillow to block out the sound from below when my phone rang.

"Three hundred thousand dollars!" Calvin Mitchell roared. "How do you lose a car worth three hundred thousand dollars?"

"I didn't actually lose it," I said.

"That's what the insurance people told me when they called. What do you mean, you didn't actually lose it?"

"I know exactly where it is," I explained.

"Where?" Calvin demanded.

"At the bottom of the ocean."

Calvin Mitchell, an early installment in my collection of stepfathers, was eighty, an eccentric genius, a minor alarmist, and, conveniently, my insurance broker. He had despised my Ferrari from the moment he learned of it. Calvin drove a 1989 Toyota.

"Whatever possessed you to buy a car like that?" he asked.

"I liked the seat heaters," I said.

"The seat heaters?" he gasped.

"But they probably don't work underwater," I added.

He was silent for a long moment, then let out a slow, resigned sigh. "You know," he said, "I once thought you might follow me into the business. I thought you had a sharp mind. My three children don't have a brain between them, but you... I thought you could take over when I'm gone."

"I didn't really care for the insurance business, Calvin," I said.

"Yes, well... I see now that it's for the best you didn't."

When he hung up a few moments later, I got the impression he would no longer be my insurance broker, and that his earlier estimation of my intelligence had dropped by several levels.

I swallowed two more pills and stretched out on the narrow bed, the springs complaining beneath me. I didn't think I would sleep, but I did.

Early the next morning, I headed downstairs. A weathered man with curly white hair and no teeth was mopping the floor. He evidently worked long hours because he had rented me the room the night before. He looked ancient enough to have been around since the French Revolution. I thought he was probably the guy who escorted Marie Antoinette up the steps to the guillotine.

I asked where the bus stop was, and he leaned on his mop for a moment as if deeply pondering the question.

"It's very far away," he said finally. "Long walk. You should stay another night."

"Why? Will the bus stop be any closer tomorrow?"

"Two nights, and we give a discount."

I didn't tell him I would have preferred the guillotine.

He reluctantly gave me vague directions and watched me intensely as I left his bar. I wondered if he was giving me the evil eye.

Outside, the streets were waking. Scooters buzzed past, sunlight bounced off whitewashed buildings, and a baker slammed open a shutter, releasing the smell of fresh bread that almost made me forget the throbbing in my wrist. I adjusted the sling and stepped toward the door. Maybe I could survive Saint-Tropez another day.

I bought two pastries and a coffee strong enough to wake the dead. Sugar and caffeine hit hard, and for a moment, my wrist stopped hurting. I felt something like clarity.

Following the man's directions, I walked up the road, past a shuttered market, then left at a crumbling stone wall covered in vines. No bus stop. No taxi. Just the view. The Gulf of Saint-Tropez stretched out below in deep blue, dotted with boats moving like lazy insects. The sea shimmered in the morning light.

An hour later, I began to suspect the bar owner had misled me, probably on purpose.

A warm breeze carried faint church bells. A crooked gate held a handwritten sign: À Louer. For rent.

I pushed the gate open. Uneven stones framed by lavender and rosemary led to a villa with blue shutters and a leaning lemon tree.

A woman emerged from the road below, drying her hands on a dish towel. She was heavyset, with tough, sun-darkened skin and wary eyes. Her face was deeply wrinkled, her hair nearly white, and I immediately wished my very expensive Leica camera wasn't also at the bottom of the ocean, along with everything else.

Some people simply photograph well, and I could see her in the camera's eye, standing before the rocks with the sea behind her. In her strong, narrow face, I caught a glimpse of her Mediterranean ancestry, perhaps mixed with a stray Viking or two.

"What do you want?" she asked.

"I was looking for a bus stop," I explained. "I was told there was one around here, but it seems I've been misled."

"No bus stop," she said.

"Then could you direct me to one?"

"Where do you want to go?" she asked.

I shrugged. "I haven't decided yet."

"You could stay here," she said. "It's for rent."

"Do you own it?"

"Me? No. I rent it for my uncle. He's a professor. Travels a lot in the summer. It's a very nice place."

"I'm sure it is," I said.

"You want to rent?"

"Maybe. Depends on how much."

She named a price, and I whistled softly. "I could rent the Taj Mahal for that."

"It's quiet. No parties. No barking dogs."

"I'm sure it is, but I can't afford that price."

"How much can you afford?"

I offered a fraction of her asking price. At first, she shrugged and looked insulted. When I didn't raise my offer, she cocked her head, sizing me up.

"All right," she finally said.

"All right?" I repeated. "You're taking my price?"

"Sure," she said. "I like Americans."

"You've met a lot of us?"

"They come. They spend. I like their money."

I shrugged. "Who wouldn't?"

And just like that, I had a villa clinging to the sun-blasted slope above Saint-Tropez. I owned nothing but the clothes on my back. My bank balance was disappearing faster than a cold drink in the Mediterranean heat, and my wrist throbbed constantly.

But then every paradise has an entry fee.

3.

I f I'd had the money, I would have stayed in Saint-Tropez forever.

Beaches like melted gold. Sunsets bleeding into the sea. At the bottom of the hill, a small café named Café du Port served pastries so buttery they felt almost criminal. By afternoon, sandwiches and slices of pizza with melted cheese filled the air with warmth and aroma. Outside, the hum of scooters and distant laughter mingled with the tang of salt from the sea.

Days slipped into evenings, evenings into nights that felt infinite. My wrist was healing. My mood was improving. Life was slow, sweet, and aimless.

But along with an entrance fee, every paradise has a snake, and mine was another stepfather named Walter Griggs. In another life, he had signed my paychecks, corrected my posture, and "elevated my potential." I had hoped I was free of him and Sweet Angel Productions, but disentangling yourself from the past isn't always easy. With one phone call, Griggs pulled me back in.

I was sitting in the garden of my rented villa when he called, sipping bitter coffee while bougainvillea climbed the whitewashed walls around me, and the sea flashed like polished steel below. I had made a few friends in the area, and when my cell phone rang, I answered without thinking.

"Where are you?" he asked tersely.

His was not a voice I wanted to hear. I almost hung up.

"France," I said.

"Care to narrow that down?"

"Saint-Tropez. Beaches, sunsets, bikinis. Good croissants."

"What's the closest airport?"

"Seriously, Walter?"

"The closest airport."

"You can't get there from here."

"You're not as funny as you think," he said. "I need you to come home."

Home. I wasn't sure what that meant anymore. After my mother died, I lived with Griggs until I was old enough to move out on my own. He provided the essentials: a roof, food, and tuition. Affection was not included.

He also gave me my first job at Sweet Angel Productions, and six months before, I'd quit. Walked away for good. I'd spent most of my life acting as a buffer between two men, director Rafe Cardoc and accountant Walter Griggs. I kept their egos from colliding long enough to finish films. Some days, I felt less like a bridge between them than a moving target.

I handled the dirty work no one wanted. I did what Rafe or Walter wouldn't.

Rafe was Sweet Angel Productions' crown jewel, the genius with a bullhorn and a God complex. Critics adored him. Students studied his films like scripture. And to be fair, the work was honest and raw, pulled from something deep inside himself.

Walter was the man who kept us within budget, the one who protested over every dime spent. My mother had brought him and Rafe into her company, leaving them with equal shares. The terms of her will forced two egotistical men to work together, but they hated each other and left the rest of us feeling like corn in a grindstone.

Walter was dry, humorless, and often irritating, but I got along with him far better than I ever had with Rafe. Rafe believed his genius excused him from basic human decency. He treated people like disposable props. He yelled, belittled, humiliated, and because his films made money, he was always forgiven.

I forgave him also. Until I didn't.

Our final argument tore through the Culver City studio like a storm, rattling doors and windows. Arguing with Rafe always felt like stepping into a twisted horror movie. The left side of his face bore scars from a long-ago car accident. His lips were forever curled in a sardonic smile. His left eye was cloudy and milky. He wielded his looks like a weapon. Intimidating. Magnetic.

He didn't respond when I told him he was mentally ill and that I'd never work for him again. I'd said similar things before.

But this time, I meant it.

I changed my cell number, closed the condo, grabbed my passport, and took off for Europe. No plan. No destination. Just drifting.

"Your father was making a movie in Georgia," Griggs said, interrupting my thoughts.

That made me sit up. Nobody ever referred to Rafe as my father, least of all Griggs. According to my birth certificate, my father was a short, stocky, alcoholic cowboy actor named Roy Sterling.

Vicious Hollywood gossip told a different story. When my mother discovered Rafe, he was making Disney television movies adapted from a popular children's book series, Mysteries of Moonbeam Meadows, by Augusta Bloom.

As soon as my mother saw the first film, she recognized Rafe's genius and spent the next couple of years trying to lure him to Sweet Angel Productions. Rumor had it she offered him far more than money.

My mother never confirmed anything. If I asked, she deflected, shutting down the conversation before it began. Still, the rumors lingered. Set whispers. Ugly gossip.

When I was finally old enough to watch the Disney movies, they never held much appeal. I had already spent too many hours on soundstages. I knew the smell of hot lights, the way a monster looked before CGI added its scales, how a hero's leap landed on a stunt pad just out of frame.

So when people talked about movie magic, I saw the seams. Green screens. Strings. Tape marks on the floor.

But the films did lead me to the books. I still kept the full set of fifteen Moonbeam Meadows novels in a chest in my condo closet. I told myself they were collectors' items, that one day they might be worth something. The truth was simpler. I couldn't let them go. Those mysteries carried me through the quietest corners of my childhood.

I was the kid folded into the corner of a room with a book in his lap, on the edge of the playground, in a studio hallway, anywhere I could vanish without notice. While other boys shouted and ran, I stayed small and still, living in borrowed worlds. The characters in those pages were old friends. Their adventures felt like mine.

"Aren't they having a war or something in Georgia?" I asked Griggs.

"Not that Georgia," he snapped. "This was in the United States, near a town called Folkston, by the Okefenokee Swamp."

"So not Tbilisi?"

A pause. "I need you to come back immediately. Tell me the nearest airport, and I'll make reservations."

"Let me be, Walter."

"We need to talk about your future with Sweet Angel Productions," he insisted.

"I quit, Walter. Don't you remember? There is no future for me with Sweet Angel."

"Then you need to come back for the funeral."

I sat up straighter. "Funeral?"

"Rafe rented a lightweight Cessna at a local airport near the shoot. You know how he loved to fly. Came in low, clipped the trees. He's dead, Noah."

The words landed softly, almost politely, as if Griggs were reporting bad weather. For a moment, I said nothing. The world seemed to contract around me, the air thick and still.

Rafe Cardoc. Dead.

Of course. Griggs saved the important news for last.

I should have felt something. Grief, anger, relief. Maybe all three. Instead, there was only the dull, empty hum that follows an explosion, the kind that tells you the world has shifted on its axis and a great deal of damage has been done, even if you can't see it yet.

4.

Rafe Cardoc had seven ex-wives. They handled all the funeral arrangements. They didn't dare leave it to Griggs, who would have rented the back room of a local restaurant for the service and arranged a quick cremation afterward.

My flight from France arrived thirty minutes late, and the long trip made my wrist start hurting again, even though I had thought it was fully healed. I took a taxi to my condo, where a limousine was scheduled to pick me up. I barely had time to shower, shave, and change before an impatient driver was knocking at my door.

I wasn't expecting such a big crowd. The parking lot at First Avenue Anglican Church overflowed with cars spilling into the street. When the limo pulled up, a small group of mourners had already gathered on the front steps.

As the door clicked open and I stepped out, a man immediately reached for my hand. I didn't recognize him, though something about his face felt familiar, like a distant relative from an old family photo.

He shook my hand with too much enthusiasm and launched into a heartfelt condolence, then stopped mid-sentence. I caught the flicker of confusion in his eyes as he realized he wasn't supposed to know Rafe was my father.

It was one of those well-known secrets, whispered cautiously and passed around like gossip with a warning label. Everyone knew, or thought they did, but no one ever said it out loud. Not in public. Not to me.

It wouldn't be the last time I saw that look that day.

Even though I'd long since discarded the Looney Tunes sling, I started to regret not buying another, if only so I could shake with my left hand. Instead, people kept pumping my right hand like a handle, and by the tenth handshake, the damage was done. Fire crept up my wrist and into my forearm, lingering there, sharp and insistent, long after each handshake ended.

Inside, the church was packed. Standing room only. But the real spectacle sat in the third pew: all seven of Rafe's ex-wives, arranged in a perfect row, as if choreographed. Each wore high-fashion black: tailored, dramatic, unmistakably intentional. For them, mourning was a red carpet event.

They varied in age and body type. Some younger, some older; some willowy, others voluptuous. But they all bore the unmistakable imprint of Rafe's taste: dark hair, sculpted curves, long legs. They could have been cast from the same mold, touched up just enough to avoid suspicion, a line of glamorous, sculpted Madonnas with a hint of menace.

The minister stood at the podium, holding a notepad as if it might fall apart in his hands. With his neatly trimmed beard and gentle expression, he was perfect casting, but it was clear he had never met Rafe. He kept glancing down at the name as if afraid of mispronouncing it and accidentally summoning the dead.

"We gather here today to celebrate the life and legacy of Rafe Cardoc," he began. His voice was tentative; each word handled like glass. "He was a man of great talent. A man who touched many lives through his work."

He paused, glanced at the notepad again.

"And though I didn't have the pleasure of knowing Mr. Cardoc personally, I've been told he was... a force. A creative spirit. Someone who"—another quick look at the page—"lived life on his own terms."

A soft murmur of polite agreement passed through the pews like a breeze.

The minister continued, offering a string of tired platitudes about legacy, memory, and the unknown hour of death. He was clearly stretching, padding his speech like a student trying to meet a word count.

If Rafe had been alive, he would have walked out in disgust.

At the cemetery, Rafe was laid to rest in a far corner. Cheap seats, in a manner of speaking. The same minister said a few more words, then the crowd slowly began to disperse, trading handshakes and condolences.

I stayed behind, watching the workers lower the coffin and cover the grave with flowers. Some of the arrangements probably cost more than Rafe's beloved classic roadster. He would have appreciated the extravagance.

I'd noticed Griggs a few times during the service, but he was nowhere in sight once the last mourners drifted away. I assumed my limo had already left, but I wasn't in a hurry. Instead, I wandered to another gravesite. One I knew well.

Patricia Alden

Actress. Wife. Mother.

The words were arranged in the order she would have chosen. Actress first. Wife second. Mother last. A woman of contradictions, who thought motherhood was just another distraction in an already chaotic life.

I turned to leave, and a hand touched my shoulder.

One of the ex-wives. Rita Boucher.

A bosomy woman in her sixties, with short dark hair streaked with silver and coal-dark eyes. She might have been Rafe's third or fourth wife. I lost track. Her elegance was effortless but calculated. She carried herself with the confidence of someone who never apologized for being the smartest person in the room.

She married Rafe during her impressionable starlet phase, divorced him less than a year later, went to law school, graduated with honors, founded her own entertainment firm, and became one of the most feared and sought-after lawyers in Hollywood. Behind closed doors, she was often called the Butcher, a takeoff on her second husband's surname.

"I was a huge fan of your mother's," Rita said. "She's one of the reasons I wanted to be an actress. She was very popular for a while. It seems she guest-starred in every show I watched."

"Not to mention several forgettable movies," I said.

"Poor little Amish girl makes good," Rita said.

"You know she wasn't Amish," I said.

Rita widened her eyes theatrically. "I'm shocked. Truly. You mean her bio isn't accurate?"

"Her bio also claimed she played the harp and spoke four languages," I said.

Rita shook her head. "I feel so betrayed. Next, you'll tell me Roy Sterling isn't even your father."

I laughed. "Careful, Rita. That's Hollywood blasphemy. And you know I've had a surplus of fathers. My mother treated marriage as a hobby. Some people knit. She collected husbands. The first I remember was Ralf Lewiston, a Disney animator. He drew little animals on my lunch bags. He'd probably get sued today.

"Then came the insurance guy, and the little, short producer who didn't last but a week. I forget his name..."

She interrupted me. "And then there was Griggs."

"Yeah. Griggs, who gave me a roof and a job. Although he probably gave me the job more to irritate Rafe than anything else."

"And when was the last time you saw Roy?"

I stopped and looked at her. "Why are you suddenly curious?"

"Just making conversation," she said innocently.

I never knew Rita to just make conversation, but I answered anyway. "The last time I saw Roy was at a party given by the Walcotts. He was drunk. He called me the bastard child of his ex-wife."

"Charming."

"A real Hallmark moment."

"And Rafe," she said softly.

"Never accepted. Never acknowledged."

"But everybody knows he's your father."

"I'm not sure he did," I said.

I started walking toward the front entrance, and Rita fell into step beside me.

"Wasn't it a wonderful service?" she said. "I'm sure Rafe would have enjoyed it."

I looked at her like she'd lost her mind. Her eyes sparkled with dry amusement.

"I'm sure he would," I said.

We were both lying.

Her heels clicked lightly on the gravel. "You know," she said, almost to herself, "I'm going to miss knowing Rafe is out there. He was a no-account, skirt-chasing reprobate, but I still cared for him. We all did."

I wondered what she wanted. Of all her traits, sentimentality was not one I ever associated with Rita. She hadn't waited for me just to reminisce.

"I guess he'd laugh at me for getting emotional," she continued. "He'd tell me I was being silly. He'd tell me to move on."

I knew he would have. With that crooked smile and quick change of subject, he'd claim grief was just another inconvenience to step around.

"You know, a reporter once had the nerve to ask me how I could get up in the morning and bear to look at him."

"And what was your answer?"

"I honestly didn't know what he was asking me at first. Under the force of his personality, you kind of forget what he looked like."

"Certainly, it never put women off. They were always chasing him."

She shot me a half-amused sideways look. "What's that I hear in your voice? A touch of self-pity?"

"Maybe a little," I admitted. "Lately I feel like I'm failing Relationships 101."

"What? You want to be more like Rafe?"

"Not exactly that," I said.

"Get it out of your mind. I've watched you grow up. You're nothing like Rafe. To him, commitment and loyalty were empty phrases. Somehow, you've managed to stay clear of all the hypocrisy around you, which still amazes me. When you promise something, you follow through. The right person will come along. If I were only younger—"

Her voice cracked, and her face reddened. "And that's today's advice from the lovelorn."

Silence settled between us. We were both mourning Rafe in our own way, and something told me she had never fully let go of him. I wasn't sure what I felt for Rafe: boss, father, a man I respected yet sometimes intensely disliked, someone who had often violently rejected the idea that we shared the same blood.

Had I loved him? I didn't know. And had his death changed my life in any way? I wasn't sure of that either.

"I just can't believe he died flying," she said.

"The same thing has been troubling me," I admitted.

"He wouldn't have gotten into a plane while drinking," Rita said. "He was the most cautious pilot I've ever known. He checked every gauge, every system—twice. Sometimes three times if he was nervous. He'd ground a plane over a flickering indicator light."

"Or a dirty tire," I added.

"I believe it had something to do with this new movie he was making. It was troubling him more than usual."

"And you know this because...?" I asked.

"We talked on the phone. Often."

"Seriously?"

"It happens like that sometimes. We became friends after the divorce."

"And he told you the newest movie was bothering him? Why?"

"He didn't say," Rita admitted.

"Still, I can't believe anything could bother him enough that he would make mistakes flying."

"I keep telling myself the same thing," she murmured, "but I can't make myself believe it."

"What was this new movie about?"

"Don't you know?"

"I never saw a script. I quit before he started."

"All I know is that it concerns a young woman who was murdered near the Okefenokee swamp back in the sixties. Griggs would have the details. Rafe told me he was writing the script based on some out-of-print book."

"Rafe was writing the script?" I asked, astonished.

"I know. Hard to believe. He wasn't much of a writer."

We reached the gates of the cemetery, and Rita asked, "What will you do now?"

"Right now, I'm going back to Saint-Tropez as soon as I can get on an airplane."

"And will you eventually go back to work for Sweet Angel Productions?" Rita pressed.

I hesitated, then let out a dry laugh. "I'm not even sure there will be a Sweet Angel without Rafe. He was the heart and soul."

"I'm sure Griggs is full of ideas," she said. "You probably won't care for any of them."

I shrugged. "I'm not certain Griggs would even want me back."

"Oh, he will. You keep undervaluing yourself. Do you know what a lensseer is?"

"I don't know that word."

"It's someone who sees things through a camera lens that normal people wouldn't notice. A visionary. Rafe says that's what you are. He says your only problem is a lack of self-confidence."

"Really?" I asked. "Rafe said that. Could my lack of confidence possibly have anything to do with him constantly reminding me how useless I was?"

"Bitterness does not become you," she said.

She reached into her purse and handed me a glossy white card. "My home and office number. If you decide to walk away from Sweet Angel, call me. I might be able to give your career a jumpstart."

I had the odd feeling that offering me a job was what Rita had been leading up to all along.

"Someone out there needs a professional gopher," I said.

She shot me a sharp look.

"Don't be ridiculous. You're Rafe Cardoc's son. You'd start in the mailroom."

5.

When I stepped out of the cemetery, my limousine was gone, just as I expected. I reached for my phone to call a taxi, but another dark blue limousine drifted to the curb. Griggs lowered the back window and looked out at me.

"Get in. Let's get lunch."

"I'm not that hungry."

"Get in, Noah. We need to talk."

I sighed and walked around to the other side. I needed the ride, and I wasn't in the mood to argue under the warm afternoon sun. Griggs and Rafe had always been good at steering me toward things I didn't want to do. Whether out of weakness or habit, I learned it was easier to follow than to fight. Resistance only delayed the inevitable.

Sliding into the back seat, I was surprised by the changes in Griggs. For as long as I'd known him, he'd had a slightly rumpled quality, always in need of a shave and a haircut. Now he looked sharp, and I couldn't believe he was so dressed up just for Rafe's funeral. His suit, maybe Hugo Boss, was elegant and a stark contrast to the wrinkled jackets and coffee-stained ties he typically wore. He even smelled of expensive cologne, and Griggs never wore cologne.

"Don't you look spiffy, Walter," I said.

His face reddened.

"You're a little old for a midlife crisis."

He ignored me and asked instead, "What's the matter with your wrist?"

I was cradling it against my stomach. "Just sore. Too many hand-shakes."

He nodded, storing the information, sympathy optional.

We rode in silence, the hum of the engine filling the space. Just as I thought we might avoid conversation altogether, Griggs reached into his coat and removed a small rectangular box, dark blue with a ribbon tucked beneath the lid. He placed it in my hands.

"Here."

"What's this?"

"Open it."

I hesitated, then did. Inside was a watch, sleek and striking, the kind displayed behind glass in stores where prices are whispered, not posted. Its face was a deep black, punctuated by elegant gold accents that caught the light with every tilt. Needle-thin hands hovered over the dial, precise and deliberate, while on the back, a small inscription was etched.

Happy twenty-fifth birthday, Griggs.

I recognized the watch, a Longines Spirit Zulu that gave split times. I was stunned. Growing up, birthdays had meant almost nothing. No cake. No presents. Sometimes, not even a word of acknowledg-ment. The years passed, the calendar flipped, and life went on. I had learned early not to expect anything, certainly not five-thousand-dollar watches.

"What is this?"

"It's obviously a birthday present."

"Obviously," I said. "But my birthday isn't until the fifth of July, and this is kind of an expensive birthday present."

He shrugged, practiced indifference. "It seemed appropriate. Next month, you'll turn twenty-five. You'll gain control of your mother's trust fund and the shares she left you in Sweet Angel Productions."

"All twenty percent."

"Twenty percent is significant," he said, faintly defensive. "It will provide a steady dividend to supplement the trust."

"If we stay profitable."

His eyes flicked toward me. "And what is that supposed to mean?"

"I can't forget that you own forty percent of Sweet Angel, and Rafe owned the other forty. The two of you clashed constantly yet somehow created something extraordinary. My mother used to say she designed it that way. That friction would produce better work. And she was right. But you've always been careful with money, Walter. Without Rafe pushing you, I doubt you'll spend a cent more than necessary. From here on out, the films won't be art. They'll be echoes."

"Your head is full of smoke," he said calmly. "We will continue making movies. And they will be profitable. Possibly more so."

I didn't like the way he said that.

Griggs directed the driver to Finesse, Culver City's newest magnet for money that wanted to be seen spending itself. Inside, the scent of seared fish clung to the walls, mixed with fresh paint and ambition. Reclaimed wood tables glowed beneath industrial lighting, and floor-to-ceiling windows framed the street like a display case. Look, but do not touch.

We took a secluded table in the back. A single candle burned between us, casting soft shadows across Griggs's face and deepening the lines that never quite moved.

The waiter appeared immediately, and Griggs didn't just ask for a glass of white wine; he ordered a bottle of a specific, expensive sauvignon blanc by name. I had never known Griggs to have a refined taste. He never worried about quality when quantity would do. Sensing my surprise, he shrugged and said, "They do good fish here."

We both ordered salmon. I ordered coffee.

When the bottle and my coffee arrived, Griggs allowed the waiter to pour his glass and took a sip. He nodded appreciatively, but I had the feeling it was less about savoring the taste and more about honoring the ritual.

During my short absence, Griggs appeared to have transformed from a dull, gray accountant into someone entirely different.

He raised his glass to me. "Still not a fan of the fruit of the vine? Even after all that time in France?"

"No."

He studied me, then adjusted his tone. "I probably shouldn't drink either. But wine works better than the pills they give me. Alcohol abuse isn't hereditary, Noah. Just because your mother and Rafe struggled doesn't mean you will."

It sounded like reassurance. Really, it was permission.

Griggs wasn't cruel, but he was distant from ordinary emotion. Everything could be solved by balance sheets and incentives. Apply the right pressure, and people behave predictably.

He would never understand that even the smell of alcohol pulled me backward. My mother unconscious on the couch. Bottles hidden in drawers. The cycle of rehab and relapse, grinding and inevitable.

She had a weakness. I knew myself well enough to fear inheriting it.

So I didn't drink. Not in France. Not anywhere.

Griggs sighed and swirled the last inch of wine in his glass. "Rafe, though," he said quietly. "It would have been better if he'd never touched the stuff. Driving drunk was bad enough. Flying an airplane was insanity."

"I can't believe he would do that."

"You're defending him? After everything?"

"He had many flaws," I said, "but he never would have flown drunk."

"I've read the NTSB and FAA reports," Griggs said. "He rented a Cessna near the shoot. Late flight. Came in low. Clipped the trees. They ruled pilot error, slowed reflexes due to alcohol."

I stared into my coffee.

"What do you think really happened?" I asked.

"I only deal in conclusions," he said. "And those are the conclusions."

"And privately? What do you think?"

He ignored my question and asked instead. "Have you ever wondered why he picked such an ugly fight with you right before production on the new movie started?"

"We fought a lot," I said.

"But this was different. Nastier than usual. Everybody said so."

I shrugged. "Maybe. But he seemed to be hurting more lately. The accident he had as a child took a terrible toll. Not just on his looks, but on his body. And the headaches... they were brutal. The damage you could see on the outside was only part of it."

Griggs nodded. "I do know he was drinking more and taking a lot of painkillers. Not a great combination."

"Rita Boucher says he was troubled by his new movie."

Alarm flickered across his face. "You've been talking to the Butcher."

"I don't think she likes that name," I said.

"You need to stay away from her. She's a menace to our business."

"I didn't realize you felt so strongly about her."

"Just stay away from her," Griggs said.

Our food arrived. The salmon, pan-seared and glazed with something citrusy, was arranged carefully on oversized plates. The baby potatoes were stacked as if with surgical precision. The salad looked assembled with tweezers. Frilly greens and pine nuts were scattered like gold flakes and drizzled with vinaigrette.

Upscale. Pretentious. Trying too hard. Still, the coffee was excellent—dark, hot, and unapologetically bitter. I took a sip and let the bitterness anchor me.

Thunder cracked overhead. I looked toward the heart-shaped window across the room. It was poorly installed, and putty was still visible along the seams. Rain began to fall, slow and steady, streaking the glass.

Another myth shattered.

It does rain in Southern California.

6.

Griggs carved into his fish with a connoisseur's precision, savoring the moment; then he spoke, his voice as clean and sharp as his blade.

"I'm sincere about you coming back to Sweet Angel," he said. "I know your mother would have appreciated you continuing to be a part of the studio she created, and I honestly think we'll make a great team."

I doubted it. He didn't need me. Plenty could do what I did, and do it cheaper. Of course, keeping me around probably made for good publicity, since my mother had started the studio.

I know it said something about my character that I didn't immediately refuse his offer. Back in school, when we studied the Robert Frost poem about the two roads, my classmates voted me "most likely to take the easiest one."

That was exactly what Griggs was offering: guaranteed salary, flexible deadlines, a seat at the creative table. No real power, no real pressure. A soft gig, a placeholder, padded cuffs.

I know how to hustle when necessary. Pull all-nighters, rewrite scripts until my eyes burned, call investors on the second ring, stroke actors' egos until they smiled.

But I'm better at coasting. Let Griggs make the decisions. I'd read his scripts, offer notes he'd ignore, let my name slide into the credits as producer, and collect a check like clockwork.

I could do better. Other doors were open, the kind Rita had hinted at, opportunities with real stakes. But those doors came with long hours and real responsibility. Failing in front of my peers was unpleasant. It was easier to glide along while the world moved beneath me.

"I'll think about it," I told Griggs. I caught the flicker of his thin smile that said he knew he'd won. I hated myself for my weakness, but Griggs was my Mephistopheles, and time had made it easier to accept his Faustian bargains.

"The two of us together will make a real success out of Sweet Angel," he said assuringly.

"And lots of money," I said.

"Of course. That goes without saying."

He turned back to his salad, spearing a leaf with deliberate precision. Another glass of wine gone. At the rate he was filling his glass, he was going to finish off the bottle. I hoped I wouldn't have to carry him out.

"And while you're deciding what you're going to do with your life, there is one small chore you can do for me."

"You want my firstborn?" I asked.

"Nothing so drastic. Go to Georgia. Take a look at your father's movie."

"I'd rather give you my firstborn," I said.

He didn't flinch. "Ann says it's the best thing he's ever made."

"Of course she does," I muttered. "She thought Rafe walked on water."

Ann Giordana once ruled the B-horror scene like a blood-soaked queen: Blood Season, Carnival of Flesh, Dead Highway. Her poster was practically a rite of passage: red bikini, streaked in fake blood, zombies looming behind her like backup dancers from hell. A lot of teenage boys had her poster taped to their walls. I was one of them.

But her voice never worked onscreen, too high, too nasal. By thirty, the offers dried up, and she latched onto Rafe. Script supervisor, costume designer, second unit director, whatever kept her near him. On set, they called her Rafe's shadow. Not a compliment. But she never seemed to care. She was loyal, maybe blindly.

"She assures me the movie is nearly finished," Griggs said. "Ready for post. All it needs is someone to bring it home. She even suggested she might be able to do it."

I liked Ann, and she was solid technically, but I doubted she could finish one of Rafe's films.

"I've got two weeks left on my rental in Saint-Tropez," I said. "Why don't you go?"

"I have pressing business here," he said. "You know I don't travel well. A trip like that and I'd be incapacitated for a month."

I shook my head, but I knew I'd end up going. It always seemed inevitable when Griggs wanted something from me.

"What's this movie about?" I asked.

"You said Rita told you it was a murder mystery. You now know as much as I do, except the movie is based on a book by a former cop named Carol Treadway. No longer in print. Where Rafe got it, I have no idea."

"Who's in it?"

"Ned McDonald, Dylan Welch, and Cassie Rhodes."

Ned McDonald, reliable, gentle, the nice guy who never got what he wanted. Dylan Welch, rebellious, talented, adored by impressionable young women.

Cassie Rhodes? That one caught me off guard. Not an actress, a TV personality, a product of publicity. America had watched her grow up on The Winthrop Saga, playing the perfect daughter. I'd seen the show a few times, mostly when Rafe considered guest actors.

"Rafe cast Cassie as a lead?" I asked.

Griggs already knew my thoughts. Rafe had a history of giving small parts to young actresses he was seeing off the clock. But his leads were always of a type, dark, sultry, Madonnas. Cassie was no Madonna, but a slim blond with light blue eyes.

"Ann says Cassie's good," Griggs said. "Better than expected. Great chemistry with Ned."

"But she's not the type Rafe usually picks as his lead," I pointed out.

"No," Griggs admitted. "Not at all. But that's just another thing that's different about this movie."

I thought about traveling to Georgia. Headaches, chaos, complicated personalities. Rita's mailroom job started to look better.

"The trip will give you time to think," Griggs said. "Look at the rough cuts. Read Rafe's Bible. Decide for yourself. Two, maybe three days. Call me, tell me your decision, then catch your flight to France."

Outside, the rain stopped as quickly as it started.

"And you can read the book before you go," Griggs said.

"The book?"

"Yeah. Rafe left it in his office. I've got it for you. The book the script is based on is Murder in the Swamp."

"And you didn't read it?"

He shrugged. Of course, he hadn't. Nothing held his interest except numbers.

"One thing," Griggs said hesitantly. "There was an article recently about the area you're going to. A rash of alligators. More than usual. Be careful where you step."

"You're making a joke, right?"

Griggs didn't smile.

7.

I ended up in Georgia sooner than I'd planned. I had imagined a quiet weekend of sleeping, swimming, and letting the jet lag fade, but the neighbors decided to host their daughter's sweet sixteen at our shared pool. What began as a simple celebration quickly turned into a full-blown production. Music blared nonstop, laughter ricocheted off the walls, and at times it felt like the ground was shaking. Between the pounding bass and the endless stream of partygoers, packing my bags and heading south suddenly seemed like the most peaceful option.

Growing up with my mother and then with Griggs, I never belonged to that chaos. I lingered at the edge, watching everyone else.

I packed my bags and headed for the airport.

Griggs had given me the book Murder in the Swamp in a yellow mailing envelope, along with a bundle of faded newspaper clippings. The author's photo on the back showed Carol Treadway as a heavyset man with sagging jowls and a receding hairline.

I noticed that the book pocket had been ripped out of the back of the book, but there was still blue stamped lettering marking it as the property of the Charlton County Public Library.

I read the book on the flight from LAX to Atlanta. It was disappointing. Rather than feeling like a true crime book, it read as dry as somebody's grocery list. It offered a parade of statistics. People interviewed were reduced to stick figures, emotions and motivations stripped down to bare facts.

Carol Treadway did include a snippet from the actual coroner's report, which I found interesting.

Simone Bleu Laviolette was found dead at the historic Laviolette Homestead in the Okefenokee Swamp on April 7, 1968. The cause of death was determined to be a single gunshot wound to the back of the head. No firearm was recovered from the scene, but the recovered bullet was of an unusual caliber. There was no evidence of sexual assault.

Photographs showed Treadway at the crime scene, hat pushed back, jaw set, standing beside the inert shape beneath a tarp. He looked solemn, but there was something heavier in his posture than duty—grief, maybe? It made me wonder if he had known Simone personally.

There were also a couple of photographs of Simone herself. In one, she leaned against a fence, smiling at the camera as she ate an apple. In the other, she wore a cheerleader's uniform. Both were taken from a high school yearbook, as the caption underneath indicated: **Simone Bleu Laviolette, National Honor Society, Science Club, Environmental Club, Herpetology Club, Botany Club, Cheerleading Squad, Yearbook Staff.**

Her background looked fairly normal for a popular teenage girl in a small town, except I would have to look up the herpetology club. I had no idea what that was. Harvard-Westlake School in Culver City certainly didn't have one.

The photos made it clear why Rafe had chosen Cassie Rhodes. Her resemblance to Simone was uncanny.

Treadway's main suspect was a young man named Jace Whitfield, a local football jock supposedly in love with Simone. Simone, however, was devoted to someone else, a soldier serving in Vietnam at the time of her death. The classic love triangle.

I spent a few more minutes going through the collection of newspaper clippings.

THE CHARLTON COUNTY CHRONICLE
April 13, 1968

INVESTIGATION CONTINUES IN LAVIOLETTE HOMICIDE

By Staff Reporter

Authorities continue their investigation into the death of Miss Simone Bleu Laviolette. Officials confirmed the case remains an active homicide inquiry.

A descendant of a Huguenot family which settled the region in the early 1800s, Miss Laviolette was well known in the community.

She was active in the Girl Guides, sang in the choir at Camp Pinckney Baptist Church, and had hoped to attend the University of Georgia.

"Someone knows something," said Investigator Treadway. "We intend to learn what happened."

THE CHARLTON COUNTY CHRONICLE
April 18, 1968

COMMUNITY MOURNS "BLUE" AT CANDLELIGHT VIGIL

By Staff Reporter

"She had a presence one did not forget," said Ellis Dubois, a long-time friend.

Dozens gathered Sunday evening at Camp Pinckney Baptist Church for a candlelight vigil honoring the young woman known as "Blue."

Candles flickered against the darkening sky as hymns once sung by Miss Laviolette rose into the humid air.

Her slaying remains unsolved.

THE CHARLTON COUNTY CHRONICLE

April 23, 1968

STRANGE LIGHTS REPORTED NEAR LAVIOLETTE HOMESTEAD

By Staff Reporter

Residents are abuzz with reports of unusual lights near the Laviolette Homestead.

Several persons claim to have seen what one described as "a bluish glow" moving slowly near the rear porch.

Accounts vary. Some describe faint lights, others a steady shimmer in the fog.

Authorities declined comment, but curiosity seekers are said to be visiting the site after dark.

THE CHARLTON COUNTY CHRONICLE

April 28, 1968

PERSON OF INTEREST QUESTIONED IN CASE

By Staff Reporter

Local authorities confirmed that several individuals have been questioned in connection with the investigation.

Names have not been released, as some involved are minors.

Reports suggest interest in a local high school football player known to have been acquainted with Miss Laviolette.

"We urge the public not to draw conclusions," Investigator Treadway stated.

THE CHARLTON COUNTY CHRONICLE
April 8, 1969

SWAMP GHOST OR SMALL-TOWN LEGEND?

By Staff Reporter

One year after the unsolved slaying of Miss Simone "Blue" Laviolette, reports of strange sightings persist.

Several residents claim to have seen a figure in a white dress along the water's edge.

Others dismiss the accounts as mist and moonlight upon tired eyes.

Still, the tale has taken root.

The swamp grows quiet at night, some say—too quiet.

I put the clippings carefully back into the envelope. Unease settled over me, though I couldn't say exactly why. I'd been hoping for something more, something that would explain Rafe's sudden obsession with an unsolved murder of years past. What was so compelling that it caused him to change his work habits and possibly even climb into an airplane inebriated?

As a movie, it had potential. A murder mystery set in a small town, tangled with a ghost story, was undeniably compelling. But there were dozens of such stories and scripts galore. What made Rafe choose this one? It made no sense to me.

I was half asleep when we landed in Atlanta. On the tarmac, a Beechcraft Baron looked plucked from a museum. The pilot, tobacco-chewing ex-Air Force, joked about needing to take off before dark because his night vision "wasn't what it used to be." I hoped he was joking.

The flight was a blur of gauges, dials, and stories. C-130s in the Middle East. KC-135s in Germany. Modified Gulfstream still classified. Because of his comment about problems with his night vision, I stayed awake.

We landed just after midnight at a small rural strip. The narrow runway stretched into darkness, edges marked by flickering lights. A squat shack glowed weakly. Hangars huddled like silent sentinels. Beyond the tarmac, fields dissolved into black. Only the wind through tall grass whispered.

I slung my bag over my shoulder and climbed down.

"Watch out for the gators," the pilot called.

I scowled, looking back at him. "It was Walter Griggs who hired you?"

"I believe that was the name."

"And he told you to say that?"

"Nah. The paper said more this year. Mean ones, too. Watch your step."

The little plane bumped forward over the uneven strip, its tail wagging slightly as it picked up speed. Dust and bits of dry reeds spiraled up behind it, stinging my eyes. I stood there, squinting, while the sound grew thinner and higher, until the wheels lifted and the craft tilted toward the wide, dark sky.

Once again, I hoped he was joking about his poor night vision.

Near the office, a van waited. Sam "Sparks" Fisher leaned against it, broad-shouldered, sun-worn, steady. Cargo pants, faded green sleeveless shirt. Tattoo of a bee with a wrench and a machine gun on his forearm.

"Welcome to Georgia," he said. "It's not Culver City, but it makes up for it in heat, bugs, and gators."

"I'm getting a little tired of hearing about alligators," I said.

I tossed my bag into the back seat. The engine coughed, then caught. Headlights cut through the darkness. I saw a few jagged stumps like broken teeth along the end of the runway.

"Is this where it happened?" I asked.

"Yes," Sparks said. "Rafe was coming out here pretty much every other day. He said it cleared his head."

"He was a good pilot," I said.

Sparks shrugged. "The best I ever saw, but accidents happen. Even with good pilots."

The headlights flashed over the small sign: **Charley Snow Airport.**

"Charley Snow," I said. "He was mentioned in the book."

Sparks nodded. "One of Simone's sweethearts. A war hero, too. He jumped on a grenade in Vietnam and saved a lot of men. They named the airport after him. There's a school in Waycross with his name on it as well. Ned McDonald plays him in the movie."

"Why would Ned accept such a small part?" I asked. "Snow was barely mentioned in the book. He was overseas in Vietnam when Simone was murdered."

Sparks hesitated, then shrugged. "Flashbacks."

The word hit me almost as hard as when Walter told me Rafe had died.

"Rafe hated flashbacks," I said. "He used to say they were a crutch for weak writers and directors."

"Maybe so," Sparks replied. "But this whole film is a flashback. The story's told from Carol Treadway's point of view. He's sitting at the train viewing platform in Folkston, Georgia, looking back on it all. And at the center of those memories is the relationship between Jace Whitfield, Charley Snow, and Simone."

"A love triangle," I said.

"Exactly."

"And Rafe is writing this?"

Sparks hesitated. "He's been getting some help."

"From whom?"

He hesitated again. "Ann can explain later."

Something in his tone warned me there was a lot he wasn't saying.

I changed the subject. "Griggs told me Rafe has been drinking more, and it may have caused his accident."

"Rafe didn't drink when he was flying," Sparks said.

"Griggs said this movie was bothering Rafe more than usual," I said.

"You need to talk to Ann," Sparks said sharply. "I'm just the handyman."

He was far more than that, but I didn't push it.

"How is Ann handling his death?"

Low beams cut through mist, illuminating swamp grass like ghostly fingers. Sparks always kept his feelings subtle, but anyone could read him. He cared as much for Ann as she had for Rafe.

"She's holding up," Sparks said. "Rafe's gone. She has to keep moving. Stronger than most realize. Not the type to whine."

The van rolled on, tires crunching gravel. Fog drifted along the roadside. Sparks gripped the wheel tighter. Beneath his calm, tension coiled. Grief, worry, something unspoken for Ann.

"Rafe could have treated her better. Could have let her direct more. She's got talent."

"Rafe was Rafe," I said.

"Ann wants to direct the rest of this movie."

I couldn't give him the answer he wanted. Ann was capable, sharp, and patient, but lacked Rafe's spark. Most people didn't have it.

A darker thought slid in. Sparks knew engines, knew how things failed. If he wanted, he could make an aircraft drop from the sky. Make Rafe drop into the trees. But he had no reason to do such a thing unless he believed Ann would take over if Rafe were gone.

It was a crazy, unsettling thought. I liked Sparks.

"Rafe could have treated you better, too," Sparks said.

"Me?"

"Especially if it's true what everyone says."

"Which is?"

"Rafe was your father."

"Hollywood gossip," I said.

"You don't look much like him, except tall and thin. But he did have that accident and all that plastic surgery."

"I told you. Gossip."

Sparks grunted and tapped the wheel. "Brace yourself."

The van swung onto a narrow gravel road. Tires bit loose stone. A pothole rattled my teeth. I got the feeling Sparks was not just warning me about the road getting worse, but something else darker ahead.

8.

Driving up, I felt as though I had slipped straight back into the late fifties. A small weathered sign at the roadside read Swamp Lily Motor Court, its modest lettering easy to miss if you weren't looking for it. The motel itself stood in a tidy L-shape, its exterior washed in fading burnt-orange tones that must once have glowed beneath a brand-new neon sign. Time had softened the paint and muted the trim, yet the retro charm clung to every detail.

At one end, the office and small restaurant anchored the building, their wide front windows and simple, old-style signage hinting at decades of road-weary travelers who, despite misgivings, had stopped for the night.

"So," I said, "not the Holiday Inn?"

"Not even close."

"It looks…" I struggled for the right word.

"Uninviting," Sparks said.

"That's the word," I replied. "Why did Rafe pick this place?"

"No idea, but I have a theory."

"Would you like to share?"

"This place is owned by a couple named Dubois, Ellis, and his wife, Claire. They were part of the crowd that hung around with the murdered woman back in the sixties. I think Rafe believed they would have some answers about what happened or at least provide some background. If so, he was sadly mistaken."

"How do you mean?"

"Ellis Dubois is more than willing to talk about anything and everything—except the murder. Ask him about that, and he gets a faraway look in his eyes. Ellis is a semi-retired lawyer who still keeps a small office in Folkston and takes on a bit of scut work around town. His wife does the real work, running the motel and overseeing the restaurant staff. Ellis sticks to backslapping and handing out his business cards. I've already collected three."

"Sounds like a real winner."

"You'll meet him."

"I will?"

"You won't have a choice. He's a huge movie buff and thinks he knows this town's history better than anyone alive. The first thing he did was tell Rafe everything he was doing wrong with his movie."

"How'd that go?"

"Not well."

"I can imagine. What about Claire? You said she also knew Simone. Has she contributed anything?"

"Claire is an odd bird. She doesn't say much. She also doesn't seem to mind doing all the work while her husband struts around. She bothers me."

"Why?"

"Just a feeling."

"Yond Cassius has a lean and hungry look," I quoted. "He thinks too much; such men are dangerous."

"Exactly," Sparks said.

In front of the restaurant, a rusty ice machine hummed, begging to be left alone. Cracked, sun-bleached chairs sat outside a few doors, frozen mid-conversation from decades past. A Coke machine, faded to dusty pink, promised "Ice Cold" soda, but all the trays looked empty. A single porch light flickered over the main door. VACANCY blinked red behind a greasy screen.

"This isn't a place to get the creative juices flowing," I said, "unless you're filming Psycho. If we go ahead with the movie, we'll move somewhere else. There has to be someplace better."

"When we finish the movie," Sparks said defensively.

"It's not a done deal, Sparks," I replied. "That's why I'm here. I'm here to look at everything and make that determination."

I sensed his irritation with my answer, though I knew it wasn't really about Rafe's final movie. Sparks was good at his job, but he left the artistic sensitivities to others. His only concern was what would happen with Ann.

Three rented vans like the one I was riding in were parked in front of the motel. All were used to haul around people and equipment.

"We put you in Rafe's room. It's the only room left," Sparks said. "It's down at the end. Ann packed his clothes and personal stuff. She didn't figure you'd want to deal with that. She had it shipped back to California."

He said it casually, but the words lingered. I pictured boxes stacked somewhere in a back room in Culver City. Boxes and suitcases that would collect dust, and eventually, somebody would throw them out.

I imagined how hard it must have been for Ann to pack his things. I was quietly grateful she hadn't left that burden for me.

"Your room's the largest," Sparks said. "Rafe called it his editing suite. Two rooms with the partition torn out. Space to spread out gear."

He nodded toward the parking lot. "Rafe also rented the Nissan out front. Keys inside."

"After Rafe died, I'm surprised everyone didn't pack up and go home."

"Being in a Rafe Cardoc movie looks good on a résumé," Sparks said. "That credit's worth a few rough edges. But now, with Rafe gone…" He shrugged. "They may start leaving soon, and honestly, I can't blame them."

Sparks eased the van along the front of the motel. Headlights dragged long shadows across faded seafoam walls. Gravel crackled like dry bones. Nearly at the end of the row, someone stepped out of the darkness.

Sparks hit the brakes. The van jolted to a stop.

A tall, lean man lurched into the beams, barefoot and wearing only undershorts. He clutched a bottle of Jameson whiskey like a torch. In his other hand, he waved a pistol as he belted out a crude limerick, his voice roughened by years of dedicated whiskey abuse.

"There once was a girl from Saint Louie—"

I recognized both the man and the pistol. The gun was part of a matching set of .22 target pistols my mother had given her husband for his birthday.

"Roy Sterling is in this picture," I said.

Sparks glanced at me. "You didn't know."

"If I'd known, I wouldn't be here."

Sterling stopped singing and pointed the pistol at us. I tensed as he pulled the trigger. Nothing happened.

"He seems to be out of bullets," I said.

"Cartridges," Sparks corrected. "The bullet is the pointy thing that comes out of the end of the barrel. He doesn't have any because I snuck into his room and took them all."

"Smart," I said.

"It was Ann's idea."

Sterling pointed the pistol at us again and kept pulling the trigger. Frustration clouded his face. Then he turned the barrel toward himself and peered down it as if checking for a blockage. He shrugged, dropped the pistol on the ground, and took another sip of his whiskey. Staggering sideways, he took a few steps and then sat down on the dirt.

He took another swig from his bottle and continued his limerick.

"Whose dancing was terribly gooey—"

"I guess we can't leave him out here," I said.

"I guess not," Sparks agreed.

I opened the van door and stepped out.

"Keep a watch out for the alligators," Sparks said.

I gave him an ugly look. I walked over to Roy. I was pretty sure I was being conned about the alligators, but I stayed cautious, head on a swivel.

Roy looked up at me, confusion in his eyes.

"Do I know you?"

"We've met," I said.

He studied me, then nodded.

"You should be careful," he said. "There are ghosts around."

I caught the faint scent of stale smoke clinging to him, sweet and cloying. Grass and booze. Of course, he was seeing ghosts.

Roy had lost weight. Fragile, small, as if a strong gust could lift him and carry him away. I almost wished it would because he was trouble I didn't need.

Sparks scooped up the pistol from the ground, and then we each took one of Roy's arms and lifted him. He didn't resist, just sagged as if the world had finally caught up. We half-dragged, half-guided him to a room three doors down. Already, he had started his song again, loud, crude, off-key.

The door opened to a time capsule of bad taste: peeling wallpaper, twin beds with patchy floral spreads, carpet the color of dried blood. A cigarette-burned nightstand held a phone and a worn copy of a hunting and fishing magazine. A box TV sat on a dresser.

We guided Roy onto the nearest bed. Springs groaned beneath him like something alive.

He reached for the bottle again, but Sparks was faster.

"Uh-uh," he said. "You want to kill yourself, do it after we leave."

Roy swatted at Sparks half-heartedly, then slumped against the headboard with a sigh that deflated him. His body went limp like a rag doll. For a heartbeat, I thought he'd passed out. Then, suddenly, his hand shot out and yanked my collar, dragging my face close enough to taste the sharp tang of sour whiskey on his breath.

"You shouldn't have come here," he muttered, low and dangerous.

"On that, we agree," I said.

"She's waiting," he added.

I jerked back, wrenching free. "Who's waiting?"

"In the swamp... for you," he said, eyes glinting in the dim light. "Blue. She wants to take you in her arms. She wants to love you... to death."

A harsh, hollow laugh ripped from his throat, bouncing off the walls. I stumbled back, his words echoing in my skull like a dark promise. The air turned colder, heavier. I wasn't superstitious. I didn't believe in ghosts. But something about Roy's words felt too sharp, too real for whiskey and drugs alone.

9.

My room was bigger than Roy's, but no better.

The wallpaper had yellowed with age, curling at the corners like dead leaves. Long strips peeled back to reveal blotchy, water-stained drywall. The AC unit wheezed, sounding like a smoker on his last lung. It spat out air that wasn't cold, only clammy, carrying the damp stench of mildew mixed with something sour, festering beneath, like spoiled fruit left to rot in a crawlspace.

No drunks were playing loud music, and yet the place reminded me a lot of the room above the bar in Saint-Tropez.

All the moving around hadn't done my wrist any favors. It throbbed, and I no longer had painkillers to help me sleep.

The carpet might have once been red. Now it was a faded quilt of anonymous stains, some dark, some pale, nonidentifiable. I was glad I remembered my shower shoes. No way was I walking barefoot.

The bed didn't look inviting. The sheets appeared clean, but the bedspread was threadbare, its once-vibrant color now a dull, tired gray. Pressing my hand against the mattress, I felt rigid, unforgiving hardness. Maybe I'd be better off sleeping in the rented Nissan outside. But then there were supposedly alligators lurking outside.

I opened my bag, grabbed a bottle of aspirin, and went into the small bathroom. I clicked on the overhead light. It buzzed, flickered, and finally stayed on. A massive insect, part beetle, part nightmare, skittered across the cracked tile, trying to hide behind the rust-stained toilet. I stomped it under my boot. It crunched like a lobster shell, spiny legs, glassy eyes, a body the size of a kitten—just less adorable.

The bathroom came with little plastic cups. I filled one at the sink and took my aspirin. The water had a metallic taste.

The shower worked, technically. Tepid water dribbled from the head in uneven spurts, reeking of iron and something faintly rotten. Pressure barely qualified as running water. The mounted shampoo dispenser was cracked and empty, yellow with age. I didn't bother looking for soap. I didn't want to imagine who, or what, had last used it.

The towel felt like sandpaper that had given up pretending to be terry cloth. I dried off anyway. Afterward, I pulled on clean underwear and nothing else. Georgia humidity clung to my skin like regret.

I flopped onto the bed and stared at the ceiling. A gecko was doing slow push-ups on the exposed wooden beam above the fan. It paused mid-rep and stared at me with cool indifference. I envied it. At least it knew what it was doing.

No part of me wanted to spend another night in this place.

I scrolled through my contacts and found Griggs. Close to ten p.m. in Culver City, but I wasn't surprised when he answered immediately.

"Working late again, Walter?" I asked.

"I'm actually dining out this evening," he said. "What do you need?"

Griggs dining out meant he was probably sucking up to investors. Part of the job I hated, though I'd done it often. Griggs seemed to thrive on it.

"I just wanted to tell you I'm here," I said.

"And you thought you'd share that with me?"

"Misery loves company," I said. "Though honestly, I'm not even sure where here is. Doesn't feel like the U.S. More like that dump where we stayed in Cambodia. The one with giant rats and monsoon season."

"You've never been to Cambodia," he said flatly. "That was a film set in Oregon. It rained a lot, sure. But no rats. You've always had a flair for exaggeration."

"I just killed something prehistoric in the bathroom," I said. "And there's a lizard doing yoga on my ceiling. This place is a dump, Walter. If I decide the movie is worth finishing, we're not staying here. I will find something better."

A slight hesitation in his voice. "Okay, but watch the money. We're tight financially."

"Speaking of money, I need to get together with whoever is currently paying the bills and coordinating with the locals. In other words, doing the scut work that I usually do."

"Rafe."

"Rafe was handling finances?" I said incredulously. "He never handled money. He said it wasn't his thing. He said he was an artist."

"It was different this time. He opened a local account in Waycross. You should find his checkbook with the Bible, but you'll need to be added to the account. That shouldn't be a problem. Still, be careful. Rafe has already spent a lot on this project."

"On what? Certainly not accommodations or food."

A pause. Then his low, familiar chuckle.

"Have you looked at the footage yet?" Griggs asked, tone shifting to business. Always business.

"I haven't. And I won't. Not until tomorrow."

"Have you seen Ann?"

"Not yet. Sparks picked me up at the airport." I glanced out the window at the swampy dusk beyond. "And you're not the only one who's warned me about alligators."

"Then you should be careful where you step," Griggs said dryly.

"There are no alligators in Saint-Tropez," I reminded him.

"And your point is?"

"If I had stayed in Saint -Tropez, I wouldn't have been in danger of being eaten."

"If it happens, you'll be forever on my conscience."

"That makes me feel so much better."

Except I wasn't sure Griggs had a conscience.

I rubbed my eyes. They burned from jet lag, sleep deprivation, or both. My whole body still felt airborne, humming faintly from the flight, like I hadn't fully landed in Georgia, or anywhere, really.

I shifted the phone to my other ear. "And you didn't bother mentioning Roy Sterling was cast in this movie."

Griggs paused, just long enough for me to hear him swallow. "I didn't think about it."

"You're lying."

"Okay," he admitted. "I was afraid his being there might influence your decision."

"You were right."

"It's only a few days, Noah. Work around him. And don't let food, accommodations, or your rush to Saint-Tropez stop you from giving the movie a fair judgment. If it's as good as Ann says, we need to finish it. It's his last film. That should matter to you, too."

Griggs had never cared much for Rafe's work when Rafe was alive—too abstract, too moody, too unprofitable. And now here he was, talking like a convert at a revival meeting.

Something was going on with Griggs I didn't understand, but I wasn't going to figure it out in a room that smelled of dampness, with my head and wrist hurting, over two thousand miles away.

"We need this movie to be a hit, Noah," he said. Desperation laced his voice.

"All right," I said. "I'll look at it when I'm functional again."

"Good," he said. "And Noah?"

"Yeah?"

"Avoid the alligators. At least not until after you look at the movie."

I let out a short laugh that felt more like a sigh. "Sure. I wouldn't want to let you down."

10.

I slept badly.

I felt like I'd gone twelve rounds in a cement mixer. Every muscle was stiff, every joint protesting. My head throbbed with its own pulse. I dragged myself to the shower, bracing for disappointment. I got it: twenty seconds of lukewarm water, then a glacial downpour.

Walking back into the bedroom, I managed to crush another prehistoric-looking insect lurking near the doorway.

Great start.

I pulled on jeans, a black T-shirt, and beat-up tennis shoes. Breakfast became the singular thought keeping me upright. Maybe coffee would hit the reset button. Maybe.

Somewhere else, I might have gone for a short jog among the trees, just to loosen up and clear my head. Jogging usually helped with my headaches and jet lag. I might have done it anyway if I'd been braver, but I kept recalling all the warnings about stepping on alligators. I was fairly sure the pilot and Sparks were giving me a hard time, but not sure enough to risk my life.

Another reason for avoiding jogging was the heat. I felt it the moment I stepped outside. I waved away a few irritating bugs as I started toward the restaurant.

I hadn't seen much of the area the night before, but across the access road from the motel stretched a thickly wooded treeline, and a carved out picnic area with two wooden tables and a rusty-looking grill. I noticed that a volleyball net had been stretched between two trees.

A young woman sat in a folding camp chair, reading a book. I walked across to her. The heat didn't seem to bother her. She sipped from a chipped enamel mug, steam rising in delicate threads that caught the morning light, carrying the faint scent of coffee and something floral, like dried herbs or warm sun on grass.

Auburn hair tumbled over her shoulders in loose waves, kissed by sun and wind. Freckles scattered across her face, random, chaotic, perfect. Even in jeans, hiking boots, and a red University of Georgia t-shirt, she seemed impossible here, a fragment of another world dropped into the rough morning light. A café in Paris. A quiet terrace in Rome. The beach at Saint-Tropez. Anywhere but a picnic area of the Swamp Lily Motor Court.

When she looked up and smiled at me, something inside twisted. Her smile might not have launched a thousand ships, but for me, it sent a rowboat into murky water.

I wanted to tell myself it was absurd. Stupid. Love at first sight belonged in Casablanca, Romeo and Juliet, Breakfast at Tiffany's, and Roman Holiday. Not for me. Twenty-four, almost twenty-five, a cynical movie producer, someone who measured everything in schedules and budgets. And yet here I was, chest tight, pulse wild, completely lost.

"You must be Noah," she said.

"Must I?" I stammered.

"You're the only stranger around," she said, "but you don't look much like an ogre."

"An ogre?" I questioned.

"Some of the cast and crew think you're here to shut the movie down."

I shook my head. "It might be true. It might not."

"I'm Kate Thorne," she said.

"Kate Thorne," I repeated. "That's a great name."

"And you can see it on a movie marquee," she said. "That's not the first time I've heard that recently. I think you movie fellows follow the same script. I'm not an actress. The last part I played was a donkey in our youth church nativity scene. No, I'm Florence Nightingale."

I understood immediately. "You're the company nurse."

"Technically, I'm not a nurse," she admitted. "I'm a certified paramedic, but I'm the closest thing to a nurse Rafe could find around here. There are plenty of nurses, but they all have steady jobs. I'm sort of between jobs."

"Oh?"

"I'm in college," she said.

I glanced at her red T-shirt. "The University of Georgia?"

My eyes lingered a second too long, tracing the bold letters across the fabric before I realized what I was doing. She followed my gaze and caught me mid-stare. A slow smile tugged at the corner of her mouth.

Heat crept up the back of my neck, spreading to my ears. I cleared my throat, suddenly very aware of where I was looking and how obvious I must have been.

"Aren't you the observant one?" she asked, and I got the feeling she was laughing inwardly at me.

"You're studying to be a nurse," I said.

Open mouth, insert foot. My question was chauvinistic. She could have been studying anything: medicine, physics, law. And somehow I assumed nurse."

She shook her head. "Veterinary medicine. I have two years to go."

"And Rafe hired you as our nurse?"

"He did. Also, because I know my way around the swamp. I used to be a Girl Guide."

"Is that anything like a Girl Scout?"

"Kind of," she said, leaning back. "We sell cookies sometimes and earn badges, but Girl Guides know swamp lore. We can point out flora and fauna and identify snakes. There are about forty species in this park alone. We can tell which plants will make you sick if you touch them." She tapped her mug for emphasis. "We can even take you out on a boat and bring you back in one piece, alive and mostly sane."

I had to laugh, even though forty species of snake gave me pause. "So basically, you're a swamp sherpa."

"Exactly," she said.

She lifted her coffee mug to her lips, and the gold of a wedding band caught my eye. Disappointment slammed into me like a wave, sudden and merciless. It twisted my chest, hollowed my stomach, and stole the warmth her smile had just delivered. The pull I felt toward her didn't vanish but recoiled against the impossible, leaving only the bitter ache of something I couldn't have.

No redheaded girl for you, Charlie Brown.

Unlike Rafe and some others, I never saw a wedding band as a challenge. To Rafe, it was just another locked door, daring him to jimmy it open. A line in the sand, taunting him to cross. To me, it was an insurmountable barrier, solid granite topped with barbed wire. I didn't cross it, not even in my imagination.

"I think I'll go have breakfast," I said.

She gave me a wary glance, as if she'd felt the sudden chill in my voice.

"Hopefully I won't have to bring out the stomach pump," she quipped.

"The food isn't good?" I asked.

"I prefer eating at home," she said, "but the place has character."

I nodded, still hungry, but the edge of my appetite dulled. Over the years, I'd learned to trust my instincts about places with character. Too often, character meant terrible food and less-than-competent service.

"I guess I'll see you around," I said.

"Count on it. You'll be signing my paychecks."

I walked back across the access road to the fifties-style restaurant, its shape and form reminding me of a Howard Johnson's, except for a bulky addition jutting out at the back, awkward and unwieldy. I realized it wasn't part of the original building, but an apartment grafted onto the old structure, giving it a lopsided, off-kilter feel.

Ann waited at the restaurant's front door, petite, dark-haired, dark-eyed, olive-skinned, and mid-forties, yet moving like she hadn't aged a day. Her presence once ruled B-movie screens.

"Are you here to close us down?" she asked immediately.

"That's no way to greet me," I said. "Even Sparks said hello."

"Are you here to close us down?" she repeated.

"I'm here to look at things," I said. "Griggs wants to keep the movie going."

She seemed skeptical. I let her enter ahead of me. The place was half-full, lit with harsh fluorescent lights. Scattered among the tables were a few locals, truck drivers, construction workers, and a couple of cops in a corner booth.

Though conversation hummed and glasses clinked, there was an undercurrent of watchfulness. Heads turned subtly as we entered, then quickly returned to their own business. I was used to it. While actors might be stared at or approached for autographs, the crew remained mostly invisible. It sometimes caused resentment between cast and crew, but I preferred it that way. "Some of the food looks pretty good," I said.

"Ah," Ann said, "but the locals order from the menu. The contract Rafe signed calls for buffet-style dining twice a day."

The breakfast buffet was a culinary apocalypse. Cold scrambled eggs clung to the heat lamp like survivors of a disaster. Bacon resembled charred sticks from a campfire. Toast looked like it had survived a minor volcanic eruption, and the pancakes were so dry they could have been used as building material. The juice machine grudgingly produced something that might once have been orange juice, and the coffee was the only tolerable item.

I was introduced to Claire Dubois, a tall, angular woman of sharp edge with a jutting chin and hard, flinty eyes. Her long black hair was streaked with silver. She studied me with feline intelligence, alert, measuring, wary.

I could tell she had been hurt deeply at some point. Her narrow, watchful eyes spoke of someone who had learned long ago that trust was a luxury she couldn't afford.

Oddly, I thought I saw something else in her expression, almost a faint, wistful look that disappeared quickly.

She told me she charged by the week and expected payment on time. If we came up short or delayed, she would call the sheriff and have us tossed out. She said it politely, calmly, but there was steel behind every word, the kind that made me believe she'd done it before and would do it again without hesitation.

Picking up my tray to go through the buffet line, I spotted her by a back window, staring out at the parking lot. Hands folded in front, almost as if praying.

"She's an odd woman," I said.

"You'd be odd too if you were married to Ellis."

Getting through the buffet line took time, as cast and crew kept stopping by, asking if the movie would continue or if they should pack. Ann tried to shoo them away, and eventually we made it through and sat down at a table with Peggy Marsh.

"I'm all for packing," Peggy announced. "I miss my family.

Peggy was in her fifties, a brunette with a generous figure and a romantic history that included several marriages. Her home was now a tiny farm about seventy miles outside Los Angeles.

Peggy handled costume design, makeup, and hair, and occasionally stepped in as cinematographer. She could have worked the cameras full-time and was probably capable of directing better than anyone else on set. She possessed an almost uncanny, encyclopedic knowledge of the movie business.

"Your family is just a howling bunch of mongrels," Ann said snippily.

Peggy shot her a wounded look, pushed back from the table, and stomped away, leaving her half-finished breakfast. I couldn't blame her. It didn't look all that appetizing.

"You shouldn't tease her like that," I said. "She loves her dogs like family. And I'd like to point out that you have a big, scary-looking dog that sleeps in your bed, and you call it family."

Ann looked at me. "What's your point?"

It was an argument I'd made before that Ann ignored, and I wasn't ready to try again with so many other things to worry about. Ann and

Peggy simply didn't like each other. I thought they were too much alike, but I'd never tell them so. I preferred my face without scratches.

I ate half my breakfast, but the eggs tasted powdery, the bacon was nearly inedible, and even the few slices of toast were burnt and cold. Ann just picked at hers. I told her it might be a good idea to answer questions before I locked myself in my room and started tackling Rafe's Bible and the rough cuts.

"There's a picnic area by the trees," she said. "Some of our people put up a volleyball net. We play when it's not too hot, and the bugs aren't eating us alive. I'll gather everyone there."

Ann left me. I sipped my coffee and glanced toward the buffet, where a glass case at the end held a few doughnuts and what looked like a blueberry muffin. I started to move toward it, but a tall, leggy blond who looked barely eighteen beat me by a step,

She was already taking a bite when I reached her.

"Sorry, Mr. Sterling," she said. "Fast hands."

She didn't look all that sorry.

"And you are?"

"I'm Elly Wright. I'm your PA."

I nodded. Personal assistants were almost always young and were rarely paid much; they were usually college students majoring in theater, hoping to learn the business. This was a good way to do it. They did a little of everything. They ran interference, juggled schedules, fetched coffee, corralled the crew, and kept everyone, including me, from losing their minds. Part secretary, part traffic cop, part miracle worker. Everything ran through her, though no one noticed unless something went wrong, which on a set like this was practically guaranteed.

PAs were usually nervous around directors and producers, but Elly seemed perfectly at ease. Certainly, she had no problem stealing the food from my mouth.

"Enjoy it," I said.

She grinned and left me with the stale doughnuts.

11.

I took my coffee and two stale doughnuts outside. Some members of the cast and crew were playing volleyball. They had to be careful not to trip over the wooden picnic tables or the rusty-looking grill nearby. I noticed Kate on the same side as Dylan Welch. They laughed more than necessary, and it bothered me more than it should have.

I'd barely taken a few steps when the back door swung open, and a man came out, moving faster than his size suggested. Before he spoke, I knew who he was. He reached for my hand, his smile already wide, a flash of white teeth that didn't quite belong to the rest of him.

He wore an ill-fitting suit. He was three inches shorter than his wife and much plumper. His face was ruddy, his collar tight against a soft neck. He needed a haircut. There was eagerness in his grip, but it came on too strong, held a beat too long. Like he was trying too hard. I got the immediate sense of a man who had failed in life more than he had succeeded.

"You must be Noah," he said. "I'm Ellis Dubois. I was handling some of Rafe's legal work."

Sparks had warned me about him, but I would have known his type at first glance. I knew Rafe would never have trusted him with anything that mattered. Hollywood was full of men like Ellis, charming sycophants who fetched and carried, always smiling, always agreeable, but never contributing a single thing of real value.

So, Noah," he said, lowering his voice like we were sharing a dangerous secret, "I hear you're taking over the movie project now." His smile stretched a little too wide, the kind people wear when they hope for good news but secretly brace for disappointment. "Terrible business about Rafe. Truly unfortunate."

"Yes," I said. "It is."

Ellis nodded quickly, almost relieved by my acknowledgment. "But here's the thing... Before—well, you know, Rafe and I had been talking about my helping him with the script. I've always been a history buff. I know this area inside and out, and, of course, I knew Blue, so..."

I leaned forward. "What can you tell me about her murder?"

His eyes flickered, a shadow passing over them. Sparks was right. My question had hit a nerve.

"I told Rafe," he said, voice tight, "I don't know any more about Blue's murder than I did when Carol Treadway interviewed me back in the sixties. I was just a kid. I hadn't even started college yet. Claire and I were finally figuring things out. Blue's murder... it was a shock. Just like it was for everyone else."

"Then I guess you can't help me much," I said.

"Well, Rafe had me handling some legal matters," he said quickly, as if legal might lend him authority. "I thought maybe we could continue that arrangement."

"Could you get Orkin to spray our rooms or fix the water pressure?" I asked, innocently.

"I don't really handle the day-to-day running of the motel," he said.

"So you leave all the real work to your wife," I said.

I knew I was pushing him, and a part of me felt guilty. But I still had a headache, my wrist ached, and I'd spent a miserable night in a miserable room. He was just unlucky enough to be in the way.

"I was handling legal matters for Rafe," he repeated, awkwardly. "Permits, insurance forms. I know people here. I know the courthouse." He laughed, small and uneasy. "I want you to know I'm available."

I sipped my coffee, noticing Claire staring at us from the kitchen window.

"If I need anything like that, I know where to find you," I said.

"Yes, well..." He stammered. "We'll talk again."

I felt his eyes on my back as I walked across the access road to the picnic table.

The volleyball game stopped, and the cast and crew began to gather around. I felt the tension. Everyone waited expectantly. I knew a lot of the faces. Rafe always worked with a small cadre of professionals. But there were also a few newcomers, and not just the cast.

I sat on the wooden picnic table beside Ann. She was half-smiling.

"What?" I asked irritably.

"I see you met Ellis."

"Yeah. What a guy. When I get around to reading the script, I wouldn't be surprised if he turns out to be the killer."

Ann stopped smiling and looked uncomfortable. Before I could ask her what was wrong, Cassie Rhodes made her presence known. She approached with hands on her hips and a pouty look. I always thought the pouting was part of her performance on The Winthrop Saga, but I would soon learn it was her natural expression.

She introduced herself immediately, as if there were anyone in America who hadn't seen her face for the past twelve years. I heard tension in her voice, and braced myself for the coming storm.

"Are you the one in charge now?" she asked.

"I suppose so," I admitted.

She stood in front of me, arms crossed. "When are you going to make this better?"

Everyone looked at her, then at each other. No one spoke.

Cassie remained there, arms folded, the light filtering through the trees and casting pale bars across her face.

"Seriously," she said. Her voice rose and fell in the still air. "The food's garbage. The beds are worse. Half the time, the water doesn't even run hot. How are we supposed to make a movie out here if we can't sleep for worrying something's going to attack us in our beds?"

A young woman at the back of the group leaned toward the man beside her and whispered something. It carried just enough to be heard, something about how Cassie never worried about Rafe climbing into her bed. There was laughter, sharp and quick and mean.

At the sound of it, Cassie flinched, just enough to reveal a trace of vulnerability. It struck me then that this was her first away shoot, especially with a crew like Sweet Angel. Most of the company had worked together for years. They were professionals. I knew most of them believed Cassie had slept with Rafe to get the part. I half-believed it myself.

But she was barely nineteen. In The Winthrop Saga, she would have been treated like a child, constantly monitored, tucked safely behind a parent or chaperone. Here, there was no one to shield her. The seasoned crew handed out sharp remarks and practical jokes without pity. She needed to develop a tougher skin or find a new career.

I explained I would do what I could to find better living conditions if I decided to continue with the movie, and I watched her move over to sit on the grass, close enough to hear, but slightly apart from everyone else. I still didn't like her much, but it was hard not to feel sorry for her.

"I'm worried about the kind of meat we're being served," one of the junior cameramen said, breaking the tension. "I've heard the locals call this place the roadkill diner."

"I'm pretty sure last night was squirrel," Roy Sterling said.

"How would you know, cowboy?" someone shot back. "You haven't tasted anything but whiskey in years."

That drew more laughter, this time with a little mercy in it.

"It couldn't have been squirrel," someone near the edge of the group said. "None of them are missing. They were all on my roof last night, tapping out the Hallelujah Chorus."

The laughter eased and faded. I took a breath. I wasn't as worried about them anymore. The accommodations were poor, the food was passable, and they'd been away from home longer than expected, but they hadn't lost their sense of humor. Our crew was a tough bunch.

"I did think the bacon was almost edible this morning," Elly Wright said. "At least I didn't have to use my hacksaw."

"And what do they call that soupy stuff?" one of our grips asked.

"I think they call it grits," someone answered, "but I don't think it's supposed to be that soupy, and I'm not sure it's supposed to have those little chunks in it."

"Chunks of what is what I'm wondering," Roy said.

"Knock it off," Ann Giordana said sharply, her voice cutting through the group like a drill instructor from Parris Island. The shy, timid Ann, the one who had once played the helpless young woman chased and mauled by monstrous creatures, was long gone. She hadn't earned her position as second director by being nice.

"Let's hear what Noah has to say," she added, her tone shifting to something more measured but no less commanding.

I cleared my throat. "I don't have a lot to say yet," I admitted, rubbing my jaw. "I'm here to go over the script and the footage we've already shot. After that, I'll decide what comes next."

"You still might shut us down?" Dylan Welch asked.

I noted him sitting on the grass with Kate Thorne beside him. Too close, I thought. It didn't matter that the entire group was bunched together; she still seemed too close. I knew Dylan's reputation with women. His bad-boy persona worked well, and he had no scruples about wedding rings.

I had made an immediate assumption about Kate. She looked steady, dependable, the kind of woman who took her marriage vows seriously. Of course, I had been wrong before, and I had known too many women of the other type.

"Griggs said he'd trust my judgment," I answered.

The silence that followed was heavy, thick with skepticism. No one needed to voice it. I could see the doubt in their eyes. They saw me as Rafe's errand boy, useful at certain things. I could keep them dry, warm, and fed, but this movie required Rafe's vision, and none of them believed I had it.

"If we decide to continue," Peggy Marsh asked, "will you move us out of this place to somewhere with air conditioning that works?"

"I'm told we have very little of the movie yet to finish," I said, "but if we have to remain here for much longer, it will be my goal to find us better living conditions."

"And who will direct the rest of the movie?" Sparks asked.

It was the question I had been dreading, the one that tightened my stomach. I felt the faint nudge of Ann behind it, encouraging him, I was sure.

"I need to look at everything first," I said carefully, "study the footage, understand what we have, then decide."

"Griggs will decide the director," Ann interjected, calm but firm.

"Probably," I admitted, exhaling. "We'll talk about it, consider all the options."

"And will you try to convince him Ann is right for the project?" Sparks asked, curiosity edged with hope.

"I'm not certain what I'll do," I said honestly, fixing my gaze somewhere beyond him, "until I've seen everything, until I understand it all."

Dylan leaned back, a wry smile tugging at his mouth. "Things are going to get worse before they get better," he said. "You'd better hire a director who can handle us when we're cranky."

A ripple of laughter broke the tension, and slowly the meeting dissolved. People drifted away, some retreating to their rooms to kill time, others, the few hardy souls, ambling toward the flat stretch of land near the road for another spontaneous game of volleyball.

Ann didn't move. Instead, she settled onto the picnic bench beside me.

I pretended to watch the volleyball game, but I was watching Kate. She moved as if she belonged on that court, quick feet, sharp instincts, fearless at the net. What I didn't like was Dylan hovering around her every chance he got, brushing her arm, leaning in too close, making her laugh like he had earned the right.

"Something on your mind?" Ann asked.

"I've got a lot on my mind," I muttered, sharper than I intended.

"For when she enters," Ann said, "all his borrowed frost melts into air, and leaves his secret bare."

I stared at her. "Shakespeare? This early?"

"I do have legitimate acting credits," she said, "some stage work. Besides, it's appropriate. Kate is a very attractive woman."

"I noticed," I said. "I also know Dylan has zero boundaries. The last thing we need is some furious husband storming onto set, threatening to knock his teeth in. It's happened before."

"That's all you're worried about?" she asked, too casually.

"What else would I be worried about?" I shot back.

Ann sighed. "Then stop worrying. There's not going to be an irate husband showing up. Kate's a widow. Her husband was a local doctor named David Thorne. He was older than she was, but he was a really popular guy. They weren't married long. He found out he had cancer, a particularly savage kind, and he died not long after."

I said nothing. The game went on. Dylan kept laughing.

"Being married to a man like that," I said. "What could she see in Dylan?"

"He's a fun guy when he's not pretending to be James Dean," she said. "But if you're worried about Dylan taking advantage of Kate, don't be. Don't let her sugary southern accent fool you. She didn't get her paramedic license by being a pushover. She's one tough lady."

Ann folded her arms on the table and leaned forward slightly, her eyes boring into me. "Now the truth, Noah. What are you planning to do with Rafe's movie?"

"Just as I told everyone," I said evenly. "I think Griggs wants to continue. If there's a way to make that happen, we will."

"It's good, Noah," she said, quiet confidence in her voice.

"I believe you think it is," I replied, my eyes narrowing slightly. "But I need to make that determination for myself."

She held my gaze, then took a slow breath. "Okay. Will you and Griggs consider me as director?"

I shook my head, my expression soft but firm. "I'm sorry, Ann. I don't think Griggs will go along with that."

Her brow furrowed. She leaned in, her voice lower, sharper. "How about you? Would you go along?"

I considered my words carefully. "I think you're talented. I think directing is in your future. But I don't think you're ready for this one, not yet."

She didn't like my answer. I saw it in the tightness of her jaw, the way her hands clenched at her sides. For a moment, I thought she might say more, but she didn't. She stood and walked toward the volleyball game.

I hoped she'd get over her hurt feelings quickly. If we decided to continue with this movie, she'd be needed.

12.

The volleyball game was in full swing, and everyone seemed to be enjoying themselves, even as the day grew hotter. I noticed Cassie hadn't been asked to play. She was walking near the far end of the motel roadway, close to the thick woods behind the building. I hoped she was watching her step: she'd make less than a bite for a full-sized gator.

Ned McDonald fell in step beside me.

"Are you going to kill this movie?" he asked.

"I don't know. Honestly."

"Then I have a request. If you don't kill it, I need to leave for Vancouver on Thursday. I'll get back to you as soon as possible. I have a chance for a lead in *Redemption*. You've heard of *Redemption*?"

Of course, I had. Everyone had. *Redemption* was one of those sleek, big-budget, high-concept sci-fi flicks picked up before the first draft was even finished. Studios threw money at it like confetti. Critics prepped headlines in advance. And most importantly, it could launch a second-tier actor straight into headliner territory.

Ned had been chasing that kind of break for years. He always had steady work, sure, but always one rung below the top. *Redemption* wasn't just a job, but his golden ticket. And the timing couldn't be better.

Rafe was dead. Production was bleeding. Crew morale was circling the drain. And worst of all, I was in charge now, someone Ned had always seen as the assistant, the go-between. Not someone who could or would stand in his way.

He thought he saw a clean exit. Just slip out the back while the ship goes down.

"You see why I have to leave," Ned said, softer now, almost reasonable.

"I understand why you want to leave," I replied. "But that's not happening."

Ned's eyes narrowed. "Come on, Noah. You don't get it. This is my chance. My one shot. You can't—"

"I get it perfectly," I said, keeping my voice steady. "But you're not going anywhere until this movie is finished. That's in your contract."

He stared at me, jaw tight, fists clenched. "You're unbelievable," he muttered, low and furious. "I thought this was over when Rafe died. One day, you'll be sorry you ever came here."

Then he spun on his heel and stalked toward the volleyball game, shoulders stiff, muttering under his breath.

He was wrong about one thing. It wasn't going to be some vague "one day" in the future. I was already sorry.

Movies aren't all about glamour. The real work takes place behind the scenes, in dreary little offices where directors and producers spend long, grueling hours stitching scenes into a coherent motion picture. Editing is miserable work. I'd done enough of it.

Rafe's laptop and Bible still sat where he'd left them on the last day of his life, a small, silent altar in the corner. I sat down at the desk.

I began with the Bible. Inside was everything: notes, revisions, scene breakdowns, pages of scripts in his unmistakable hand. He rarely let anyone touch it, except Ann. Certainly not me. He believed someone might steal a fragment of his creative soul. And maybe he wasn't wrong.

Superstition ran deep among directors of his era, but Rafe took it further than most. I'd heard of Kubrick's obsessive research folders, Hitchcock's meticulously mapped storyboards, Scorsese's caffeine-stained notebooks. But Rafe's Bible wasn't just a planning tool; it was alive. He was always inside, refining, tearing out pages, taping in new ones, leaving the ghosts of abandoned ideas behind.

Even the cover told a story. Coffee rings marked where he'd set his mug. Tape residue clung stubbornly to edges where notes had once been pinned. A faint burn near the bottom hinted at a careless cigarette. Pages were warped, corners curled, edges dog-eared, all handled with equal parts reverence and frustration.

Clipped to the corner was a faded postcard. Its sepia-toned image showed two weathered cabins and a shed half-swallowed by swamp grass. Beneath, in looping, old-fashioned script:

The Laviolette Homestead — Established 1804. Family residence until 1917, before the creation of the Okefenokee National Wildlife Refuge.

The card was brittle and sun-faded, ink smudged in one corner as if handled too often. It looked like something you'd find in a dusty motel rack, wedged between souvenir magnets and packs of gum.

Typed across the center of the page was the movie's title:

The Weight of Blue

I already hated the title, but that was okay. Working titles changed all the time. What mattered was something more energetic, more likely to draw crowds.

On the first page was a list of the main characters:

- **Cassie Rhodes:** Blue (Simone Laviolette)

- **Ned McDonald:** Charley Snow

- **Dylan Welch:** Jace Whitfield

- **Roy Sterling:** Carol Treadway

I read the brief synopsis:

Carol Treadway sits at the train viewing platform in Folkston, Georgia. He's sipping from a bottle in a bag, his eyes blurry. He's remembering. Flashback. The meeting of the three young people, Charley, Jace, and Simone, who is called Blue. The story is told from Blue's perspective as Blue falls in love with Charley Snow and angers Jace. Eternal triangle. (There are many stories around about how Simone still haunts the swamp, and we'll add that to the script when we can.)

Underneath each character was summarized.

Carol Treadway: Once a disciplined and sharp police officer, now retired and haunted by past failures. Guilt over an unsolved case has pulled him into alcoholism, leaving him weary and reflective.

Charley Snow: Thin and blonde, a quiet dreamer who sees the world through books and imagination. Thoughtful and introspective, he drifts through life observing more than acting and lets his heart guide him.

Jace Whitfield: Local jock, squat and muscular, bold, charismatic, and ambitious. He craves wealth and status and often lands in trouble, but he pursues his dreams with relentless energy.

Simone Laviolette: Everyone called her Blue, partly for her middle name, Bleu, and partly for the extraordinary color of her eyes, almost violet. She makes the world feel fuller to those around her, offering encouragement unasked and turning ordinary afternoons into small adventures.

I sat back. Not bad. A murder mystery, a love story, a ghost—all loosely based on a novel about true events. But the unsolved murder troubled me. If the script wasn't done right, it would leave the audience unsatisfied.

I picked up the faded postcard again, edges curled and worn, turning it over like a detective hunting for fingerprints in a fog.

Someone had a sense of humor. I doubted the Laviolette Homestead even had a post office, yet the return address was scrawled in looping, almost elegant handwriting:

Laviolette Homestead, Okefenokee Swamp.

Beneath it, a sentence that was anything but funny:

"It's time you kept your promise."

Underlined in red. Three times.

13.

I looked at the address again. Rafe's name was on the front, along with our studio in Culver City. An odd postcard. Who had sent it, and what did it mean? What promise?

I pushed everything else aside and turned to the script.

I read for nearly an hour. The writing was tight and confident, layered with just the right measure of humor and ache. The dialogue did not merely sound real; it felt lived in. The characters did not just exist on the page. They breathed.

By the time I reached the last line, three things were certain.

First, Rafe had not written a single word of it. It was far too good. Second, there was something familiar about the scriptwriter's style. I had read countless scripts over the course of my career, and I was certain I had encountered this voice before. I just could not place it.

But it was the third thing I discovered that was most alarming. The script did not end. It simply stopped. The final scene showed Carol Treadway sitting once more on the bench at the train viewing platform. And that was it. No final turn. No unraveling. No catharsis.

People go to the movies because life is hard enough already. They sit in the dark hoping for relief, for meaning, for some thread that pulls the chaos into shape. They want resolution, however fragile.

This script offered none of those things.

I found two final scenes left to be filmed, but one was tucked away in the back of the Bible with the word "No" scrawled across the top. I didn't bother reading it; if Rafe didn't think it was worth filming, well, he was the genius.

The other scene was good, but it didn't solve my problem with the ending. The scene was set at Stephen Foster State Park. Jace and Blue were trying to coax Charley into a boat ride. The dialogue snapped and sparkled, light on its feet. Simone and Charley practically glowed on the page.

Charley was shy and bookish, still haunted by the swamp—not a passing fear, but a slow, gnawing, almost irrational dread that seemed to live under his skin.

Jace was his opposite in every way: bold, reckless, sharp-tongued, carrying a swagger that dared the world to challenge him. Sometimes too much. Sometimes a bully. But magnetic.

And Simone, smart, steady, gentle, balanced them both. She held the fragile peace while their rivalry simmered just beneath the surface.

Every element worked.

But it still wasn't an ending.

And after reading through the script, I also had another question. What was Roy Sterling still doing here? His small part had been filmed. There was nothing else for him to do. He should have already been released.

What was Ann thinking? Unless she had a good answer, I was done. I was already at the airport, booking my tickets to France. Sliding my chair back, I set off to find her. I took deep breaths to keep my temper in check, but after a miserable night and a breakfast that sat like a rock in my stomach, I knew this confrontation with Ann wasn't going to end well.

I thought I might find her at the volleyball game, and I was crossing the access road when I heard Cassie Rhodes screaming. My first uncharitable thought was that she was practicing her craft badly, until she came running from the thick woods near the rear of the motel. Her long legs pumped like pistons, and her eyes were wide with terror that no actor could fake.

Alligator, I thought stupidly, and wondered how fast an alligator could move because I had run track at Harvard-Westlake High School, and I was pretty sure I could keep up with Cassie.

The underbrush cracked and groaned behind her. A massive, shaggy shape burst through the trees, snapping branches like matchsticks.

Relief hit me for half a second. Not an alligator. Just a bear.

Just a bear.

Then it stepped fully into view.

No cute storybook bear. This was a prehistoric slab of muscle and mud, its thick coat clotted and wild, shoulders rolling under its fur like tectonic plates. Its head was the size of a cooler. Its paws looked capable of ripping open a car door out of curiosity.

All that track practice suddenly felt useless because I was pretty sure I wasn't fast enough to outrun a bear.

The bear was only a few feet behind Cassie, and I knew it would catch her in moments. Then I did something I couldn't believe. I've never called myself brave, but I ran toward her anyway, arms flailing, shouting like a lunatic. Maybe some deep, caveman protective instinct kicks in for the male of the species and overrides common sense. Maybe females have it too, but if so, it had skipped Cassie. She barely registered me, just a wide-eyed glance as she vanished up the gravel trail toward the motel.

Too late, I remembered I was a selfish, pampered Beverly Hills type, and that I wasn't exactly cut out for self-sacrifice.

I stopped, bracing to become bear chow. The bear stopped too, just a foot away. I could almost smell its fishy breath, or maybe I was imagining it. Imagination isn't always a friend. Along with the smell, I imagined the feel of those enormous teeth and claws tearing into me.

"Go away, bear," I said. "Please."

I figured politeness couldn't hurt.

I stepped back slowly. The bear stepped forward. I took another step, and it mirrored me. Its dark eyes were impossible to read, and its bright pink tongue slipped between yellowed, sharp teeth. I could have sworn it was laughing at me as it advanced while I retreated, step by step.

We continued moving in that weird kind of waltz. I thought about singing, then remembered my mother's friend once said my singing sounded like a cat being strangled in a dryer. I suspected my voice would only irritate, not soothe the savage beast.

Pinecones crunched beneath us. My heart hammered, my mouth felt impossibly dry.

Then came the sharp, precise crack of a firearm. Twenty-two caliber. Twice.

Don't shoot the bear, I thought. Maybe prayed.

The bear stood up on its hind legs. Suddenly, it was towering, massive, every muscle coiled and powerful, its sheer size overwhelming. I felt like curling into a ball. Maybe if I played dead. The bear regarded me as if the sound of the .22 firing was my fault, or maybe it was judging whether I would taste better than berries or fish.

I've heard that near death, a person's entire life flashes before their eyes. Nothing flashed before mine. My mind felt numb. My body felt fragile. I was still imagining the pain to come.

Finally, with a snort, the bear dropped down on all fours and lumbered off into the woods.

At least, it wasn't an alligator, I thought.

I was pretty proud of myself. I didn't pass out, and I managed to stay upright as I walked to the picnic area where the crowd had gathered. But my heart was hammering, and my knees felt like mush. I noticed Ann looking at me as if I'd returned from the dead.

Cassie was at the center of the group, sobbing uncontrollably. I couldn't blame her; I felt like crying too. Then, without warning, she broke free and ran straight toward me. Her arms, slick with sweat, wrapped around my neck, and she pressed wet, trembling kisses to my lips. I tasted the salt of her tears.

"You saved me," she whispered, her voice shaky. "You saved my life. You were so brave."

True, I thought, but it had been more an instinct than a conscious act of heroism. If I had had time to think, I might have run the other way. Even now, I was paying a price: clammy skin, a queasy stomach, and a pounding headache. Relief washed over me when hands finally pulled Cassie away.

I remembered I had started to find Ann because I was angry at her, but now I only wanted to go someplace and lie down. I started back to the room and heard a muffled shout and turned to find Ellis Dubois hurrying across the yard, followed by Claire.

"The bear wasn't our fault," Ellis said. "We haven't had a bear in years. There are animals in the woods. If you go walking out that way, you've got to expect to see them. You can't sue us for that."

"Relax," I said. "Nobody was hurt, and nobody is going to sue."

"And it wouldn't do you any good to sue us," Claire said. "You wouldn't get a dime."

"Please go away. I just want to rest."

Halfway back to my room, I saw Roy Sterling sitting in a plastic chair in front of his door, sipping from a glass, one of his twenty-two pistols resting on the metal table beside him.

"I see you found some bullets," I said.

"Cartridges," he corrected me.

"Yeah, Sparks enlightened me already. The bullet is the little piece that comes out of the barrel when you fire. I'm very glad you didn't shoot the bear."

"A twenty-two would have bounced off him like a raindrop," Roy said. "It would have only irritated him. Still, I was tempted."

"Why didn't you?"

"I never liked you much," he said. "Just another spoiled Beverly Hills kid. But I guess it's not your fault who your daddy was."

"Thanks, I guess."

"And besides, if the bear had eaten you, this movie would have shut down, and right now I'm getting paid for just sitting on my rear."

"You're a sweetheart of a guy, Roy," I said, sarcasm dripping.

"That's what everybody says."

14.

My head hurt so badly I thought I was going to pass out. I was suddenly unbearably thirsty. My skin felt clammy. I drank from the bathroom sink. Mistake. Swamp water would have been better, and it didn't help my thirst.

I thought about walking up to the restaurant and getting something cool, and I made it as far as the bed before I collapsed. The air-conditioner did nothing but circulate hot air, and I was having a little trouble getting my breath.

A knock at the door pulled me from my misery. "It's not locked," I called.

Kate Thorne stepped in, balancing a small cooler.

"The Girl Guide," I said weakly, managing a faint smile.

She set the cooler on the bedside table and popped it open. "Gatorade. I think you've got a touch of heat stroke."

"No chance," I said, waving my hands as if the world were listening. "California. It's in my bones, my eyeballs, maybe even my brain. Heat? Ha. 'The sun doth shine too hotly for my temper,' or something like that. Tickles a little, that's all."

"And you sound a bit dizzy," she said.

"I think I got dizzy when I first saw you," I said.

She shook her head slightly and put a cool hand against my forehead. Then she twisted the lid off a bottle of Gatorade. She sat on the edge of the bed and held the bottle to my lips.

"Drink this," she said.

I started desperately gulping it down, but she gently pulled it away. "Easy," she said. "Just small sips now."

I took a few small sips, and she finally let me hold the bottle. My mind was clearing a little. My insides felt slightly better.

"I don't understand," I said.

"Where have you been lately?" she asked.

"Saint-Tropez," I said.

She hesitated. "Saint-Tropez? In France?"

"That's the place."

"That explains it," she replied. "By the coast, your body cools easily. Here, the humidity traps the heat. Drink plenty of fluids, and you'll adjust."

I nodded reluctantly and took a cold sip. Relief slid down my throat, but my legs still felt like lead.

"You're looking a little better," she said. "Keep the cooler. Two more bottles. Rest. Hydrate. And do try to stay away from our bears."

"Alligators, I was worried about alligators," I muttered.

She blinked. "We're not all that near the swamp, and our gators don't normally wander in town. The only one you'll see is the nineteen-foot sculpture on Main Street in Folkston."

I raised an eyebrow. "Someone's definitely messing with me."

She stood, ready to leave.

"Thanks," I said.

"It's what you pay me for," she replied. She smiled. "You know, yelling at that bear was a very brave thing. I would have run the other way."

It felt a little dishonest, but I didn't tell her I hadn't been brave at all, that it had mostly been instinct, that I hadn't had time to think. Maybe someday I'd admit the truth. But not now. Not while she was smiling at me like I was a combination of Clint Eastwood and Alvin York.

"You have a little more color in your face," she said. "I think you'll be okay now."

"You should stay and keep an eye on me," I protested.

She shook her head. "Movie people."

She went out and closed the door.

I leaned back, shut my eyes, and ended up napping for an hour. I felt a little better when I opened them. I also woke with the idea of calling Griggs and telling him the movie was a bust. It would be the easiest thing. I could avoid alligators and bears, and ghosts who waited in the swamp.

I was reaching for my phone when I made a mistake. I decided to look at the scenes already shot.

I knew Rafe's password, and I knew he stored every single scene somewhere in the cloud, but I easily found his app. Ann had been right about one thing. Rafe's powerful computer already contained a lot of complete scenes, everything except editing. I wasn't sure if it was eighty percent done, but there was certainly plenty to work with.

Movies aren't shot in script order. The ending might be shot first. Scenes are filmed based on sets, actors, or the director's whim. The first scene I opened was a love scene. Charley and Blue. An awkward scene. Two young people stumbling through their feelings. It ended in a hug and a brief kiss.

I thought the scene was good. I thought it worked. Rafe did not, because the second scene I watched was the same one, and it went the same way. Not a single change. Except for a few different camera angles, I would have thought it was a duplicate. And I found a third scene, the same. I wondered what Rafe was looking for.

But in the third take, everything shifted.

Cassie didn't look like herself. She didn't sound like herself. This wasn't Cassie from The Winthrop Saga. She wasn't playing Blue. She was Blue. Blue's eyes were described as a startling color, and I was seeing that color pop out from the screen. Cassie's voice deepened. The camera seemed drawn to her.

Rafe did a close-up. The frame wobbled before settling on her face. She didn't speak. She stared just past the camera, her expression unreadable. Then slowly it changed: pain, longing, rage, exhaustion. Each emotion surfaced, lived there for a breath, then vanished.

This wasn't a performance. It was possession.

I leaned back, hand frozen on the mouse. I had only meant to skim, just enough to say I'd looked. Instead, I sat, transfixed, watching something too real to be fiction. Rafe had captured something rare. And Cassie. Cassie had become someone else entirely.

I went through more scenes and found the same thing half a dozen times. The rest of the players were professional, but Cassie was the soul of the movie. Somehow, even without an ending, I knew we had to finish it.

It also left me another question. Nowhere did I find where Rafe had copied any of these scenes. All of his work seemed to have been left on his laptop, and things weren't done that way. There were usually at least three copies of the completed scenes. One was a working copy where everyone involved could study them, especially Ann, who helped with the editing, and one was a copy put on safe disks to be transported back to Culver City. It didn't appear as if Rafe had taken any precautions except for his password.

I turned off the computer just as a soft knock sounded at the door. I had a momentary hope Kate had returned, but Ann stepped in, carrying a tray of sandwiches and a tall glass of iced tea. I straightened up. My spine popped, my neck ached, and my eyes burned from hours over Rafe's chaotic notes.

"I brought you something," she said, balancing the cup and tray. "Honestly, I'm not sure what it is. It might be tuna salad. Chips, too. Careful with the tea. It's basically liquid sugar."

"You don't have to fetch and carry for me," I said, though the smell of the sandwich made my mouth water.

"I wasn't sure you'd remember to eat, especially if you started watching the footage."

I took the cup and sipped. She was right. The tea could probably dissolve teeth, but I kept drinking. The sandwich didn't look promising, but I took a bite anyway.

"You said this was tuna?" I asked, trying to identify the taste.

"I said it might be tuna. Didn't say it was good."

"I was hoping you were exaggerating."

She shook her head, amused. "Worse than prison food. And I actually know what that's like."

"Yeah. Women in Chains. Women Caged," I said with a grin.

She gave me a crooked smile. "Two of my finest movies."

The tuna was terrible, but I ate it anyway, tearing into the chips as I'd just washed up from the sea, onion-flavored, if that mattered.

"What have you decided?" Ann asked.

I took a breath. "I decided I was mad at you. You told Griggs the movie was good."

"It is."

"But it's not finished."

Ann's face flushed, and she looked down at her hands.

"I know," she said quietly, but her voice lacked conviction.

"You know?" I snapped, irritation sharpening every word. "You told Griggs it was almost done. That is why I am here. Even if I want to continue, we do not have an ending. We cannot just leave it with Charley at the train station. Not even direct-to-DVD. Audiences would burn the theater down."

Ann swallowed hard and nodded, her lips pressed tight.

"We have no murderer, and no motivation for Charley to just walk away. What were you thinking?" I pushed, my voice rising. "I know Rafe was not writing this script himself. All the words are spelled correctly. Someone was helping him, right?"

"Yes," she admitted, her voice small.

"And is there more? Another scene or two? Something that answers at least a few of the movie's questions?"

"I'm not sure," she said, her tone flat, almost hopeless.

"You're not sure?" I questioned disbelievingly.

"I don't know who it is," she confessed.

I stared at her. "You're telling me we have no clue who is writing this, and no way to reach them?"

"Rafe never told me," she said, voice low. "I was hoping the person would contact me, or maybe you. I was hoping we would get the ending scenes."

"But that hasn't happened?"

"No," Ann said miserably, her posture slumping as if she were carrying the weight of my anger.

"At least it answers one of my questions."

"What's that?" she asked.

"The reason Roy Sterling is still here. You can't release him because you're not sure if he will show up in later scenes."

Ann nodded.

"What are you going to do?" she asked.

"I don't know," I admitted. "The script is good. And the footage. It's incredible. How did you get Cassie's eyes like that? Contacts."

"No."

"Then she's better at her craft than I ever gave her credit for."

Ann leaned over and put a hand on my knee. "I know you're upset. I don't blame you. But I want a favor. If you decide to shut the movie down, give me one last opportunity."

"I don't know what you mean."

"I know, going forward, that neither you nor Griggs would want me as director, but we still have one last scene ready. Let me do it. Let me direct it. For old time's sake. Please."

I hesitated, then finally said, "I still might decide we can't finish it. Your work might be wasted."

"I know that, but it's experience. Please."

I gave in reluctantly. "Okay, but only because your poster gave me so much enjoyment as a teenager."

"Pervert," she said.

15.

Early the next morning, I watched the vans leave. I didn't want to ride with the group and spend more time answering questions.

I had found the keys for the Nissan and planned to follow them, but when I opened the door, I had to step back to take a breath. The inside smelled of cigarette smoke and a little like the tuna sandwich I'd had for lunch the day before, not a great combination.

I stood with the back door open, letting a slight breeze drift through the interior as I sorted the mess: fast-food wrappers, crushed coffee cups, wadded napkins, and a truly impressive stack of Mitchell Stop and Go receipts, all from the same location on Kingsland Drive. I kept the receipts, thinking Griggs might want them for taxes. Everything else went into a dented trash can by the curb.

"Is it less of a biohazard yet?" a voice asked.

I looked up to see Kate standing nearby.

"Aren't you supposed to be with the group?" I asked.

"I was sent to find you," she said.

"Oh?"

"I'm your guide to the park."

"I thought it was easy to find."

"For most people," she said, eyes teasing, "but I hear you once followed your GPS into a lake."

"It was an artificial pond," I said defensively. "For a set. It wasn't on the GPS."

I couldn't get angry at her. I liked her smile, and I knew her riding next to me to the park would be nice. I could get to know her better and keep her away from Dylan.

Driving to the park took over two hours, a winding route along rural roads skirting the swamp's southern edge. Along the way, we passed dozens of signs advertising the upcoming Fourth of July celebration, only a short time away.

It struck me that I was going to be twenty-five in a few days, and my life didn't feel much different than when I was twenty-three, twenty-two, or ten. I did have a nice, new watch, thanks to Griggs, although I still wasn't sure of his motivation for giving it to me.

We also passed signs for Mossy Creek Campground, advertising spacious cabins, horseback riding, and catered meals. I asked Kate about it.

"Oh, it's an amazing spot. You've got towering pines and maples, the kind that make everything feel tiny, like the forest itself is showing off. Mossy Creek winds through the property like it's in a painting. And the cabins are wood and stone, with huge porches, and real fireplaces. Most of them have kitchens."

"It sounds a lot better than where we are."

"There are five cabins with multiple bedrooms, but there's also a main lodge that has another ten bedrooms. I live there. It has an enormous front room. The actor Walter Brennan once stayed there. There's a signed photograph on the wall behind the registry desk in the front room."

"Walter Brennan. Really?"

"He made a couple of movies around the swamp."

"Interesting. I know a lot about movie history. I didn't know that."

"It also has an industrial-sized kitchen and a dining area. So, to answer your question, yes, it's big enough for everyone."

"You sound like a brochure for the place."

"I do, don't I? But I do like living there. It's owned by a retired Air Force guy and his wife. They do a lot of business retreats and family reunions, that sort of thing. They get catering from the Okefenokee Restaurant in Folkston, and it's good food. Honestly, there's nothing else like it in the state, and it's right across the street from the place where they hold local fairs and the Fourth of July celebration."

It sounded interesting. Big enough to house our entire cast and crew, with a conference room and catered meals that tasted like food. I imagined it would also be expensive, but we wouldn't stay for long.

Just long enough to complete the movie.

Except I was afraid down deep that we wouldn't finish it. We couldn't unless I decided to write an ending myself, and I had no clue how. All I knew from the script was that Jace Whitfield might have murdered Blue, but it couldn't be proved.

And what of Charley Snow? What had happened with him? From the script, he had been terribly in love with Simone. And then suddenly, he was joining the Army, heading off to Vietnam.

Had Rafe somehow discovered something about the murder, or about Blue, or even Charley Snow that had solved all the parts of the mystery? Had he discovered the identity of the murderer? If so, the name had died with him.

And so had the name of the mysterious scriptwriter who had become our only hope for salvaging our movie.

When we finally drove into the park, the air was already thick with heat, even in the shade of the towering trees surrounding the lot. Through the foliage, I caught glimpses of the crew setting up by a narrow channel.

The park was beautiful in a wild, untamed way, with ancient trees draped in Spanish moss forming a natural cathedral, their branches filtering sunlight into shifting patterns. The water lay dark and still, mirroring the canopy above like black glass. It felt primordial. Exactly as the script demanded.

The crew moved with efficient ease, unloading cables, lights, and gear. Voices carried through the woods, Sparks barking about generator placement, Ann calling after makeup, Cassie swearing at the mosquitoes with a flair that would make a longshoreman blush. The scene Ann was preparing to shoot would come early in the film: Blue coaxing a nervous Charley onto a boat.

Kate stepped out of the car and went to join the group. I got out and started after her, but almost immediately a strange tightness gripped my chest, like a band squeezing harder with each heartbeat. A faint, nagging pressure pressed behind my eyes, and I wondered if it was a lingering effect of the minor heat stroke from the day before. I stood there a long time before I could make myself move.

Finally, I took a hesitant step toward the swamp, and my chest tightened even more, my feet suddenly heavy, as if the ground itself resisted me. The air was thick and rank, carrying a damp, unfamiliar smell, and shadows pooled between gnarled trees.

I'd never felt anything like this. I half-feared I might be having a heart attack. All I knew was that every part of me wanted to run away.

Blue is waiting for you, Roy said.

Drunken nonsense, I thought.

I sensed there were people in the cast and crew already looking at me strangely, and I forced myself to take another step. And another. Suddenly, it seemed a little easier as if I'd broken through some kind of barrier. I found myself breathing again.

I made it all the way down to the water's edge, but it felt wrong.

I walked closer to where the crew was setting up. In California, we would have had a fancy truck with an enormous generator and several monitors for Ann to watch as the cameras filmed.

Here, though, all we had was a piece of canvas stretched over the uneven ground, a small generator purring softly like a contented cat, and only two flickering monitors. It would be enough. We had worked under worse conditions.

Ann moved with a focused efficiency I envied, adjusting lights and camera angles. I walked a little closer and froze. Only a few feet away, stretched across a flat rock, lay an alligator.

Big. Greenish gray. Mouth half-open, eyes closed, soaking up the sun. Easily eight feet long, its hide scarred and weathered. I immediately thought of several other places I'd rather be and made a wide circle back up to where the crew was standing.

"Anyone notice the beast?" I asked.

Peggy Marsh barely glanced at me. "Him? He's a big doll. He's always around. Just don't step on his tail. He hates that."

Her matter-of-fact tone suggested alligator encounters were routine, just another hazard alongside mosquitoes, humidity, and temperamental equipment.

Sure. Just routine.

16.

Down at the water, the big alligator slipped in with a loud splash, and I moved again, closer to the taped-off area where the spectators had gathered.

The script had mentioned over and over that Charley was scared of the swamp. I was beginning to relate. I didn't care for it much myself. Staying far away from it seemed a good idea.

I found myself standing near a tall, lanky man who made me uneasy. He had a military bearing and reminded me of a terrible mistake I'd made in my sophomore year in high school.

"The girls go for guys in uniform," I'd been told, and I'd gone into the ROTC with the idea of strutting around campus in my neatly pressed Class A uniform with a long string of broken-hearted girlfriends trailing along behind.

Nobody had mentioned the extra classes to learn the military way of doing things, the hours of drill in the hot sun, and the Cadet Colonel who found fault in everything I did.

I hadn't lasted a year.

The man standing nearby had the same military bearing as my Cadet Colonel, but he looked a bit like a skid row bum. His jeans were threadbare at the knees, sneakers scuffed and sagging, a black T-shirt hanging loose over a frame that had once been solid but now looked hollowed. The Atlanta Braves cap on his head was sun-bleached and fraying at the edges.

But it was his eyes that held me. Eyes that had seen too much of life, and none of it good.

"There's never been a case of an alligator attacking a man in the Okefenokee Swamp," he said. No greeting, no preamble, just the statement, as if he'd overheard my earlier worry about our toothy neighbor, or he somehow recognized my concern.

"Oh?" I said, raising an eyebrow.

"I read it on the internet," he added, expression neutral, almost unreadable. "And, as you know, everything on the internet is true."

"I've heard that," I replied. "I guess since you had to check the internet, that means you're not a local."

"I've never lived here," he admitted. "But I was around a few times because of my work."

"What kind of work?"

"Nothing anymore," he said, leaning back slightly. "I'm retired."

A pause hung in the air, heavy as the humid swamp mist. Then, unexpectedly, he asked, "What's wrong with your wrist?"

I glanced down, confused. I had thought my wrist was healed. I hadn't been holding it any differently, and nobody had said anything.

"I broke it a while ago," I said cautiously. "How did you know?"

He shrugged. "I notice things." He smiled faintly. "It's a blessing and a curse."

I recognized the line from Monk, the old detective show about a brilliant but broken detective. It felt like he was telling me something about himself. Was he saying he was crazy?

I hoped not. I already had enough to handle with moody actors, an unpredictable crew, and a film that might never be finished. I didn't need an outsider adding his own brand of instability to the mix.

I turned back to Ann, who had just finished setting up the scene. I got a little closer. I nodded at her, and she called for a roll. She didn't have Rafe's chaotic genius or volcanic passion, but she was competent, methodical, efficient, and capable of managing the moving parts of a shoot without unnecessary drama.

I was letting her do this despite my misgivings. It was probably a waste of time.

The scene itself was deceptively simple. Charley, played by Ned McDonald, was crippled by fear of the swamp. Blue was coaxing him out while Jace, Dylan's character, hovered around making smart re-marks.

On paper, there were a handful of lines and glances. In story terms, it was a turning point: intimacy, vulnerability, contrast. Everything that made their connection feel real.

They ran it flawlessly. No missed lines. No fumbled cues. Cassie delivered with polish, Dylan hit his marks, and Ned embodied fear perfectly. The camera caught everything.

By most standards, it was a solid take. Ned thought so; he was already heading back to the van. But I knew it was wrong. I couldn't say how, but the spark was missing. The soul of the movie wasn't there, just actors saying lines.

Ann looked at me. I shrugged.

"Okay, that's a take," she said.

I'd been hoping she would see what I was seeing and somehow understand what was wrong.

I shook my head. "I think we should do it again."

Ann's brow furrowed, a flicker of annoyance crossing her face, but she called for a reset. Nobody complained, though they'd believed the first take was fine. They hit their marks, running through the scene a second time, almost exactly like the first, but I knew it still wasn't right.

"Okay," Ann said, looking at me.

"I want another," I said.

Groans rippled through the crew. Even the seasoned pros, usually quiet, were giving me ugly looks. In my head, I knew it was probably stupid. The movie was effectively canceled, and yet I was forcing them to redo a scene that might never appear on screen.

Sweat ran down my back as we reset and shot again. Still not right.

"What don't you like?" Ann asked, frustration creeping into her voice.

I was looking for what I had seen in the rough footage, and it wasn't there yet. I couldn't explain it.

"Just run it again," I said.

I heard Sparks mutter something about the alligator getting hungry.

Another take. Then another. Each one closer, but never quite there. Dylan remained steady, professional. I watched Cassie, waiting for the moment when the polish would crack and something real would surface.

Finally, it happened.

Cassie became Blue. Her posture shifted subtly. Her voice found a natural rhythm, less rehearsed, more lived-in. Her eyes held something new: wonder, vulnerability.

"That's it," I said.

Nobody looked at me. Pretty much everyone was mad at me, especially Ann. I knew what she was thinking. I had ruined her chance at directing. It hadn't been my intention. I only knew what I had seen in Rafe's footage.

I looked for Kate as the vans rolled out, but it looked as if she had gone with the rest of the cast and crew.

I guess even she was mad at me, or maybe she just wasn't worried about me driving into a lake on the way back.

Maybe she wished I would.

17.

I wasn't ready to face the group again. Instead, I drove to the small town of Folkston. I needed distance from the people who'd spent the last hour looking at me like I'd kicked their dog.

Folkston wasn't far. The town was quiet, with broad streets, faded storefronts, and a few locals chatting in the heavy June air. A railroad cut through the center, the tracks polished from constant use. I passed a gas station, a bait-and-tackle shop, and a Dollar General. Then a sign on the front of a red-brick building made me stop.

Sun-faded window decals promised burgers, steaks, and real vegetables. A couple of old pickups sat out front, their doors dented, plates local. That was all the invitation I needed.

I stepped inside. My eyes adjusted to the light. I heard laughter and silverware clinking against plates. A waitress greeted me who looked as if she had just stepped out of another decade. Her blonde hair was pinned up retro style, and she had a genuine smile.

Her uniform was black with white trim, the skirt flaring out with neat white polka dots and a band of red along the hem. A red scarf was tied loosely at her throat, and a small black apron held a row of order pads and pens like tools in a carpenter's belt.

She balanced a plate lightly on one hand and tilted her head when she saw me standing there.

"Sit anywhere you like, hon," she said, her voice bright enough to cut through the hum of the room. "You want sweet tea, soda?"

"Sweet tea is fine," I said.

"Grab a tray and hit the buffet."

The buffet line started just past the register, near a faded Coca-Cola cooler stuffed with bottled water and sweet tea. I grabbed a plate and stepped behind a man in overalls, already reaching for the cornbread.

When I got back to my table, the lanky guy in the Braves cap from the park was sitting there. My plate was piled high with a couple of pork chops and every kind of vegetable I could find, and two chunks of jalapeno cornbread.

"That looks appetizing," he said.

"Should I be worried that you're stalking me?" I asked.

"I'm harmless," he said. "Well, mostly. Depends on who you ask."

I set my tray down and slid into the seat across from him. "If you're here angling for a movie role, you're out of luck; the cast is full. And if you're looking for a job, I'm sorry, but you don't look healthy enough to haul around our heavy equipment. Maybe Sparks could find work for you as a driver."

I took a bite of cornbread that burned my mouth and sipped my water. I cut one of my pork chops into a bite-sized piece and found it delicious.

"I'm afraid I couldn't even do that," he said. "I don't have a driver's license."

"You seem to be getting around pretty well."

"Right now, I have a friend who's chauffeuring me. He's a nice guy for a lawyer."

I glanced out the window. A mud-caked Dodge Ram sat near the entrance, roof stacked with fishing gear, thick tires sunk in gravel, looking ready to crawl through swamps or over rocks.

"I had an accident a couple of years ago," he said, touching a faint scar on his left temple. "Still recovering. The DDS isn't eager to give me my license back, and honestly, that's probably for the best. My reflexes aren't what they used to be."

He took a sip from the water he'd poured from the pitcher. "Luckily, my friend would do almost anything to avoid practicing law. His real passion is fishing. When I'm done here, we're heading to Brunswick. He's determined to catch some king mackerel."

"When you're done here," I said. "That sounds vaguely ominous."

"By the pricking of my thumbs, something wicked this way comes," he intoned dramatically.

"And now you're quoting Macbeth. Fantastic. You've gone full ominous. Are you sure you're not secretly auditioning for our movie?"

"Not me," he said. "But I have a friend who'd be great in your movie. Or any movie. Her name is Michaela Magliano. I call her Micki."

"I remember an actress named Magliano."

"That's Micki's mother. Micki's acted in a few films too, but her real passion is flying. She's done stunt work and a lot of air shows. That's where she met Rafe Cardoc."

A knot of unease tightened in my stomach.

"And Rafe is why you're here?" I asked.

"Yes. Right now, I'm supposed to be overseeing the construction of a lakeside house in North Georgia. If we don't finish before the end of summer, it'll just sit there all winter. But then Micki called. She's in

Europe, trying to untangle a mess the lawyers handling her mother's estate made. If you'd ever met Micki, you'd probably be feeling sorry for the lawyers. Anyway, she saw the news about Rafe Cardoc's crash. It made international headlines."

I leaned back. I was liking this conversation less and less.

"I read the FAA findings," he said. "Pilot error. Micki isn't okay with that. She says Rafe was the most careful flight jockey she ever met."

"He was," I said. "But Rafe had been drinking more lately. Everyone on set knew it."

He shook his head. "Maybe so, but he had no alcohol in his system at the time of the crash. I've seen the coroner's report. Had a friend at the medical examiner's office pull it. Clean as a whistle. Not even trace amounts."

I straightened. "You've seen the official report? Wait... are you some kind of cop, Mr...?"

"Atkins," he said. "Tobias Atkins. I'm a retired detective for a little community in North Georgia you've probably never heard of."

"And you're here simply because this woman called you and told you she didn't believe it was pilot error?" I shook my head. "Even the best pilots make mistakes."

It was something I wanted to believe, but wasn't sure I did.

Atkins pulled a weathered notebook from his jacket and opened it with practiced hands. "I've spent some time talking to people, your crew, the NTSB investigator who did the preliminary pass, the deputies who responded to the crash site, even the mechanic who worked on the plane the week before."

"And?"

"The investigator's sharp but green when it comes to general aviation," Atkins said. "His report is solid and by the book. But once he heard about Rafe's reputation for drinking, it framed the entire narrative. That's human nature. You find one explanation that fits, and you stop looking for others. I'm bringing in someone I trust. Used to work for Cessna. Twenty years on the line. He's retired now, but he knows how to spot subtle signs of tampering, sabotage, anything that could slip past standard forensics."

It sounded like a good idea, but I wasn't sure I wanted to know what that expert might uncover.

"I still think it's an accident. But if there's any doubt, any chance of wrongdoing, I'd want it investigated. Rafe deserved that. And I'd like to know what you find."

Atkins looked at me, expression unreadable. "Would you?"

"Of course," I said, though the words felt less certain than I wanted.

He flipped to another page. "I was surprised to discover Mr. Cardoc was quite the ladies' man."

"Why were you surprised, and what does that have to do with anything?"

"I understand he was severely injured as a child, his face shattered in an auto accident."

"True."

"Most women are not all that attracted to men who are so badly scarred. Especially in your world?"

"My world?" I asked.

"Where beauty is everything?"

"Rafe was scarred," I said, "but he was also a survivor. He was smart and witty, and he had a forceful personality. I guess women were attracted to his strength and not his looks."

"That makes sense, I suppose," Atkins said. "Is that why his assistant was attracted to him. The woman who used to be in so many horror movies. Quite attractive. I've heard they were having an affair."

"Not true," I said. "They worked well together, that's all."

"I wonder if her boyfriend felt that way," he said. "I've heard he's the jealous type."

"Sparks is not her boyfriend," I protested.

"I hear differently. Former Seabee. Good with his hands. Could fix an airplane to crash." Atkins lowered his voice. "I hear he once stuffed a guy in a trash can for making an offhand remark about Ann."

"Somebody on set said something crude," I said. "It didn't have to be about Ann. Sparks would have reacted the same if the remark had been made about any woman."

"And then there's Roy Sterling," Atkins continued.

"What about him?"

"He hated Rafe. Threatened to kill him several times, or so I'm told."

"He talks a lot when he's drunk," I said.

"Same last name as yours."

"What a coincidence," I said, though I was pretty sure he already knew the truth.

"Roy might know enough to tamper with an airplane."

"I doubt it. His brain's fried from all the alcohol he drinks."

Atkins studied me for a moment longer. "And then there's you."

"Me?" I asked.

"I'm told Rafe was your father."

The words hung between us. My jaw tightened. Anger stirred.

"You've learned a lot awfully fast," I said, "but Rafe never claimed me as his son. There was no DNA test. No certainty."

"And your mother never told you the truth. That must have hurt."

"It stopped bothering me a long time ago," I said, though the lie sat heavy.

"I'm also told you had a serious argument with him and he fired you. Now, suddenly, you're here. Quite a promotion."

I saw where he was heading and didn't like it.

"I don't think I like you much, Detective Atkins."

"Retired detective," he reminded me. "And I get that a lot."

"I was in France when Rafe died," I said. "Nearly five thousand miles away."

"Nobody's saying otherwise."

"Even if I knew how to sabotage a plane, I wouldn't have. I don't think anybody in our production would have."

Yet even as I spoke, I thought of the people he hadn't mentioned. Like Ned McDonald, who had begged to be released from his contract for a role he believed would make him a star.

But I couldn't believe it of Ned. Or anyone.

Atkins watched me a moment longer, unreadable. Then he stood.

"I intend to find out what happened to Rafe."

"You must care a lot about Micki to go to all this trouble," I said.

"I do," he replied. Then he paused, as if remembering something. "By the way, do you know a lawyer named Dubois? Ellis Dubois. Local guy."

"I've met him."

"He and your father argued not long before your father died, right here in this restaurant. Voices got loud. No punches thrown. I thought you might have some idea what it was about."

"Not a clue," I said.

"Okay," he said, though his face said he didn't believe me. He stepped out of the booth and walked outside. I watched through the window as he got into the dark sedan beside his lawyer friend.

I sat there a little longer, finishing the last of my meal and letting the conversation settle. Then I paid the bill and went outside.

I opened my car door and stopped cold. I hadn't bothered to lock it, figuring nobody was going to steal anything in a place like this. On the passenger seat was a blue folder with gold lettering embossed on the front.

18.

I slid into the car and shut the door with a soft thud. I started the engine, absurdly ready for a fast getaway.

The parking lot was empty. No one had left a sign saying I put the script in your car. A few cars passed in the distance.

I reached for the script as if it might explode. Flipping through the first pages, I skimmed. The voice was unmistakable. The cadence, the rhythm, the structure, every line belonged to our mysterious scriptwriter.

This was no coincidence. Someone had been watching, waiting for the right moment to slip the script into the car, just as they had with Rafe.

But who?

Someone from the cast or crew? Unlikely. There were no private vehicles on set except Rafe's rental, parked in plain sight. Could someone have taken one of the vans? Too risky. Sparks kept a close eye on those.

And if it had been someone from our cast and crew, they could have found a dozen easier ways to leave me a script, without risk to themselves.

A local person made more sense. Someone who knew the story, who had talent and a feel for dialogue. Whoever they were, they were not ready to be known.

I read through the new scene—disappointing. It had its strengths, but it wasn't what I'd hoped for. Still, it meant the scriptwriter was around, still working. And that meant I'd get an ending eventually, even if this wasn't it.

The new scene was set at the Folkston train-viewing platform, where Jace confesses his love to Blue. Blue tries to let him down gently. When she says she loves Charley and plans to wait for his return, Jace's temper flares. His face darkens for a moment. Something dangerous flickers beneath the hurt. Could this anger turn into something worse? Was this moment foreshadowing Jace as Blue's killer?

I drove back to the motel and slipped into my room unseen. I sat on the edge of the bed, lost in thought.

No matter what Rafe Cardoc was like in real life: difficult, charming, enigmatic, flawed, often hurtful, his last movie was undeniable art. Raw, unfiltered vulnerability that felt almost autobiographical. I could not let it die.

I called Griggs. He picked up on the second ring.

"Noah," he said.

"I have read everything," I said. "The script, the show bible, the footage. Ann was right. I have looked at the footage. I think it's the best Rafe has ever done. We should move forward."

I did not mention we had no ending yet. No point in confusing him.

Music and voices hummed in the background.

"Dinner with clients," he said too quickly. My gut told me he was lying, though I had no idea why.

"Are you sure it is good?"

"You sent me out here because you said you trusted my judgment. I judge it is good."

"Can Ann finish it?"

"We already discussed this. She's a competent director, but I don't think she's ready for this movie. You need someone more experienced, someone more like Rafe."

"Could she finish it with your oversight?" he asked.

I wasn't sure I liked the sound of his question.

"You worked with Rafe for years," he continued, "and you're probably one of the best editors I know."

"That wasn't the deal, Griggs," I protested. "I agreed to come out here and give you a yay or nay on the movie. I've done that. I'm going back to France."

"We can't afford to hire anyone new. I told you before. Money's tight."

"I'm not doing it, Griggs," I argued.

"You and Ann together will finish our movie," Griggs said. "It's the only option. Otherwise, we close it down."

The words hit me like a punch. I saw the setup for what it was. Griggs had played me from the start, dangling the film, knowing I would get pulled in, knowing he could corner me like this.

And he was right. No matter how Rafe treated me, no matter how bitter things got, I could not let the movie die. Griggs knew it. He counted on it. I hated him for being right.

"This was your plan all along," I accused him.

He didn't answer.

"If I agree to do this, we'll still need money. I'm not staying here. I'm moving the company somewhere else."

"You'll get what money is available," he promised. "Just finish the movie. Quickly."

I heard a woman laughing in the background. Then Griggs hung up.

In my entire life, I've been in two fights.

My first was in the fifth grade when a seventh grader said something foul about my mother, and I went after him without thinking of the consequences. He was twice as tall and twice as wide, and his father worked as a stuntman for Paramount. I ended up with a missing tooth and several bumps and bruises.

My second fight was standing in line for Batman v. Superman, and someone broke into the front. I told him he couldn't do that, and he responded with violence. I ended up missing the movie for a trip to the hospital.

I had no idea my third fight was going to be the next morning.

I told Ann I wished to meet with everyone early. Like any group, we had our malingerers, and I was surprised to find everyone waiting out by the picnic table.

"Listen up," I said. "A decision's been made. We're going ahead with the movie."

Ned's disappointment was obvious. I was killing his shot at stardom, at least in his mind.

"Who's directing?" Ann asked.

Of course, she had to ask.

"I am," I said.

Judging by the looks I received, no one liked that answer.

"Are we moving somewhere with air-conditioning?" Elly Wright asked.

"And fewer bugs," someone added.

"I have a few ideas about that," I said.

"And I've got a suggestion," Ned commented.

"Yes?"

"Why don't you work on that and let someone who knows how direct? Like Ann. Just because your mother might have slept with the great Rafe Cardoc doesn't make you a director."

Ann gasped. Everyone went silent. It wasn't just the insult. It was hearing gentle, steady Ned lash out. They didn't know he was desperate, watching his last chance at a new career shrink because I wasn't canceling the film.

"I guess we'll find out," I said, keeping my voice even.

"At the cost of what?" he shot back. "Reputations? Careers? We're all treading water. Sweet Angel Productions died with Rafe. Everyone knows it."

His voice had slipped into a nasal whine, not great for someone trying to sound reasonable.

"You're upset," I said. "You think you're missing out on the sci-fi project. Maybe you are. But you signed a contract, like the rest of us. And you're going to honor it."

He rolled his eyes. "This isn't about that. Let Ann take over. She has actual talent. In the first scene you directed, we stood in the heat for nine hours getting eaten alive, and the final take looked exactly like the first. Flat, dead, pointless. We could spend the rest of the summer watching you fail."

There was enough truth in what he said to hurt.

"Any more suggestions?" I asked, scanning their faces

A few heads shook. Others pretended to study their clipboards.

Ned's face flushed. His jaw worked like he was chewing something foul. For a moment, I thought he'd let it go.

Then his eyes narrowed.

"Maybe you'll get finished first," he said.

The words hit hard. Final.

"Just like Rafe?" I asked quietly. "Is that what you mean? The problem is, I don't fly planes, and I don't drink. It'll be a lot harder for an 'accident' to happen to me."

I knew I spoke recklessly, yet I still couldn't accept the idea that Rafe had climbed into an airplane while he was drunk. And then there was Ned, another person who believed we would stop filming if Rafe ended up dead. I didn't truly think Ned could hurt anyone, but the old saying is true: the tongue can be an evil master. And in that moment, mine was out of control.

I was sorry immediately, but I couldn't take the words back. I never expected Ned to go crazy.

One moment, he was slouched on the ground, wearing that smug little grin, the one that had charmed audiences in a dozen romantic comedies, and the next, he exploded upward like a coiled spring finally released.

The top of his head slammed into me like a charging ram, and we both stumbled backward. My coffee cup flew into the air, the lid popping off, and hot coffee spilled down my right arm and soaked the front of my shirt. I yelped, hopping on one foot as if I could somehow escape the scalding liquid.

People started shouting, a chorus of voices blurred and far away. Ann screamed Ned's name. Kate called out something I couldn't catch. None of it mattered. Ned's momentum carried him forward, his expression no longer petulant but predatory. This wasn't a set piece or a stunt. He was furious, unhinged, and trying to seriously hurt me.

The only thing that saved me was the fact that Ned was about as useless in a fight as I was. We collided again, elbows and shoulders flailing wildly, arms swinging like windmills in a storm, each hit mostly missing or bouncing off awkwardly. My fist grazed his shoulder, and his hand barely tapped my chest.

A wild, swinging roundhouse grazed my temple, and judging by his wince, it hurt his hand more than my head. But he got lucky with the next one. His fist landed flush against my sternum. For a second, I thought something had cracked, and pain bloomed sharp and deep.

I threw a desperate counter, a lucky shot that split his lip. Blood glistened on his teeth.

"Not in the face!" someone shouted. Probably the makeup artist was worrying about what the camera would catch.

My punch didn't slow him. He barreled into me, driving me back against the picnic table. His next hit landed above my eye, a hot burst of pain like a camera flash detonating behind my forehead. Instinct took over. I wrapped my arms around him, and we toppled over one of the picnic tables.

We hit the ground hard. I scrambled up faster than he did and kept swinging. I caught him under the chin with another punch, a solid, satisfying crunch that staggered him and sent a bolt of agony up my wrist.

I froze mid-motion, tasting bile and realizing with a sinking familiarity that I'd broken it again. The sharp, insistent, familiar ache radiated up my arm.

I stepped back, a mistake. Ned blinked once, his mouth curling into a snarl that belonged on something feral, and then he lunged. I lost my footing and went down hard, Ned crashing on top of me. My right arm was useless; I could only hold him off with my left. Everything dissolved into a blur of motion and noise, Ann's voice cutting through it— "Stop!"

I would have, but Ned just kept swinging.

And then he did something worse. He knocked my good arm aside and closed both his hands around my throat. I frantically punched at him with my left hand, but he was a lot stronger than he seemed.

His grip was iron. My vision tunneled, the world shrinking to a pinpoint of light as my heart thundered in my ears. This wasn't acting; it wasn't a choreographed stunt. This was real. And deadly.

I clawed at his hands, but my broken wrist made leverage impossible. Panic roared up as the edges of my vision turned gray. The noise vanished, leaving only a hollow rush. Absurdly, I thought how humiliating it would be to die here, on the hard ground by a picnic table, strangled by a second-tier romantic lead with anger issues.

"Hey, he's choking him," I heard Elly Wright shout. "Cut it out."

Cut, I thought hazily. The director was calling for the scene to end. They'd better end it soon because I was running out of time.

Sparks and Dylan finally stepped in, each grabbing an arm and hauling Ned off me. They probably could have done it sooner, should have done it sooner, but the look on their faces told me they'd been as taken by surprise by Ned's sudden violence as I had been.

Ned thrashed once before giving in, breath sawing in and out of him, blood running from the split in his lip. Sparks pinned him with a knee while Dylan held his shoulders down, both of them acting like this was just another part of the day's schedule.

I rolled onto my side, trying to get air back into my lungs. My chest felt like it had been struck with a sledgehammer. Ann was kneeling beside me, one hand hovering near my shoulder like she wasn't sure what would hurt worse, touching me or leaving me alone.

"Are you done?" Sparks asked Ned, his voice low, almost bored.

Ned spat to the side, breathing hard. "He shouldn't have said—"

"Doesn't matter," Dylan said. "You're done."

19.

I hadn't done much damage to Ned, nothing a camera couldn't hide. But by the time they hauled me off the ground, my wrist throbbed like fire, and my arm and chest were turning bright red from spilled coffee.

Kate was unusually silent as she drove me to a nearby emergency clinic. Her quiet felt heavy.

"I didn't start the fight," I complained.

"It wasn't much of a fight," she replied after a moment. "More like a clown act. Why was Ned so angry?"

"He sees time running out."

"I don't follow."

"He's always played the boy next door. The good kid everybody likes. Hollywood doesn't pay for that anymore. The big money goes to bad boys like Dylan. Ned thinks this film is his chance to change his image. He's desperate. He thinks I'm holding him back."

"And are you?"

"Not really. I don't think he'll get the part he wants. He's got skills, but they're narrow. His fans won't buy him as anything else. I think he knows that."

"And he took it out on you."

I shrugged. "I was available."

She glanced at me. "And that thing you said about not drinking or flying. It sounded like an accusation."

"It was a stupid thing to say."

"Then why say it? I thought Rafe's accident was pilot error. He flew into trees because he'd been drinking."

"That's what the report said."

"But you don't believe it?"

"There's a guy, a retired detective, Atkins, asking questions around town. I'm surprised he hasn't talked to you. He's convinced it wasn't an accident. Says he's seen the reports. Claims Rafe wasn't drinking."

I leaned back and closed my eyes as the pain crept higher up my arm. "From the beginning, I never believed Rafe would get into a plane drunk. But he had a lot of weight on him. The movie. Money. Reputation. He struggled with depression. Maybe he missed something in the preflight check. Or..." I hesitated. "Maybe he didn't."

"Suicide?"

"Rafe was always a troubled soul."

The Walls Clinic sat between a pharmacy and a convenience store along Highway 301. A small wooden sign by the door read *Walls Clinic – Family Practice*, the paint chipped at the edges. Inside, the air carried antiseptic and old paper. Numerous certificates lined the wall above the desk.

The receptionist took one look at the coffee stains on my shirt, the blood at my temple, and the way I cradled my wrist, then addressed Kate instead.

"Back at the firehouse? I thought you were off to veterinary school."

"I was. I'm working with the movie group for the summer."

"Oh." Her eyes flicked back to me. "Are you an actor?"

"No. Just hired help."

She returned her attention to Kate. "Dr. Walls will be right out."

I lowered myself into a chair, studying the photographs on the opposite wall. Dozens of them, a tall man with various aircraft, in uniform, beside runways, smiling into the wind.

A small metal plaque beneath the photograph bore his name.

Dr. David Thorne.

The name landed a second later. Kate's husband.

In one photo, he wore a Naval flight uniform, jaw set, eyes steady. In another, he stood in a white coat with two children leaning against him, grinning. Pilot. Doctor. Hero.

I glanced at Kate, animated now, laughing softly at something the receptionist said. A pang worked its way through me. Compared to the man in those frames, I felt a little shallow.

An elderly man in a lab coat emerged from the hallway and pulled Kate into a quick hug before listening to her rapid account. Then he waved me back.

"Shirt off."

I obeyed.

"The burns aren't too bad," he said. "Salve will take care of it."

He lifted my wrist gently. I winced.

"Ah."

"Is that your diagnosis?"

"It is. Your wrist is a mess."

"I was hoping for something more clinical."

"Fine. Your wrist is a complete and total mess. Better?"

"Much."

"I'll wrap it. It'll hurt. I can give you something for the pain."

"Please."

"And when you're my age, you'll feel it every time it rains."

Encouraging.

An x-ray confirmed what we both knew. He wrapped the wrist efficiently and gave brisk instructions. Keep it elevated, don't bang it on anything, break it again, and risk permanent damage.

It was a speech I'd already heard from a woman who might or might not have been a doctor in the clinic in Saint Tropez.

I was exhausted, but there were stops to make. Kate agreed to keep driving.

At First National Bank in Waycross, I added my name to the account and confirmed Griggs's deposit. The balance made my throat tighten. Moving the crew would carve a deep chunk out of it. Griggs would not be pleased.

Then we headed toward Mossy Creek.

"You're really moving everyone out of Swamp Lily Motor Court?" Kate asked. "Ellis and Claire won't like it."

"That's a burden I'll have to carry," I said. "Look, do you know the owners in Mossy Creek well? I mean, do they like you?"

She shrugged. "I guess. At least they've never hinted otherwise."

"The issue is we're kind of tight with money right now, and the locals usually assume movie people have deep pockets. I thought you might help me negotiate with them. We desperately need to get out of Swamp Lily, or our group may decide to just head home without completing the movie."

"Yes. I see your problem. I'll put in a good word if you promise to be on your best behavior and no more fights."

"No more fights," I promised.

"Good. Frankly, you're not very adept at it. You could use a few boxing lessons."

"I'll keep that in mind," I said.

The trip took twenty minutes, and Kate asked about my mother as she drove. It was not a question I was comfortable with, and I gave her my standard answer. Patricia Alden was a competent actress and a terrific businesswoman. She had originally founded Sweet Angel Productions. She made a lot of money, and she spent a lot of money, and I was her only child.

"But what was she like?" Kate asked.

I tried to find some way of explaining the woman I called mother, and couldn't. The truth was I had known her only superficially, except for those times when, in an alcoholic stupor, she talked to me about her feelings, her dreams, and her disappointments.

Even then, she was acting. I sometimes felt she had lost her real self in the characters she played.

I had wanted her desperately to love me, to behave like a mother, but it was the one acting job she could never manage.

I stumbled over a few words, trying to describe her, but I couldn't find the words. Not even for Kate. Kate seemed to sense it and changed the subject.

"And Rafe Cardoc was your father?" Kate asked.

"That's the rumor," I said.

"You certainly don't take after him much," she said.

"I think that's a compliment," I said.

"He was bigger than life," she said. "He was amusing, charming, and could be quite nasty. He was like watching a snake from a distance. Fascinating, but you didn't dare get within striking distance."

I couldn't help but ask another stupid question. "Did you ever?"

"What?"

"Get closer."

"Five minutes after Rafe hired me, he tried to feel me up." She gave a short laugh. "I grew up a tomboy. I know how to punch. He didn't mind me breaking his nose."

"You broke his nose?"

"Didn't mean to hit him that hard. It bled. We had a hands-off agreement after that."

We reached Mossy Creek as the sun slipped behind the trees. Spanish moss hung like tattered lace. A row of tidy cabins faced the woods, rocking chairs waiting on each porch. Horses dozed in a small corral nearby.

Across the road, a Fourth of July carnival was taking shape, canvas tents rising, strings of red, white, and blue lights glowing against the dusk.

"Isn't it a little early to start celebrating?" I asked.

"We have our traditions," Kate said. "On Friday night, they'll start roasting the meat in the fire pit. They'll chop the ingredients for the Brunswick stew and get it going in a big cast-iron pot. People gather around in camp chairs and tell stories while someone stirs the stew. You have to keep stirring it, or it'll burn. Years ago, it was mostly men doing it. Now, a lot of the local women come too. It's really a lot of fun. David and I used to love the Fourth of July."

Her voice choked up a little as she mentioned David, and I was glad when she pulled up in front of the main building. It was shaped like the rest of the cabins, but much larger, and had an enormous wrap-around porch with rocking chairs. It had a comfortable, pleasant vibe, unlike my feelings when I arrived at the Swamp Lily Motor Court, and I feared that I was walking into Hitchcock's Psycho, and Tony Perkins living somewhere nearby with his dead mother.

"I like it," I said.

"I thought you might," Kate said.

A man came out of the door and walked down the steps. He was big, brawny, and reminded me a little of Sparks. He had the same self-confident manner. I got out of the car. He eyed my cast and sling, then stuck out his hand. I used my left hand to shake.

"I'm Paul Deerfield," he said.

"Noah Sterling."

A woman followed him out the door and down the steps. Taller than he was, her hair was iron-gray and cut short, and she had the same self-confident look as the man. I liked them both, and I doubted they were the type to put up with much nonsense.

Kate came up hurriedly and introduced the woman. "And this is Beth Deerfield. They're my landlords, and they've been pretty good to me."

Beth Deerfield gave Kate an odd look.

"Noah is in charge of the movie people I've been working with," Kate continued, " and he wants to move out of Swamp Lily."

"Who wouldn't?" Beth said.

"I've told him that maybe I could negotiate with you all and get a good rate for him. He says he's a little tight with money right now."

"I thought movie folk always had lots of money," Paul said.

"That's not always the case," I explained. "And you know, this movie could help your business."

"How so?"

"Books and movies always bring tourists out to look at the places they mention or talk about."

Paul grunted. I wasn't sure if that meant he believed me or not.

We toured the cabins, clean, comfortable, blissfully free of insects. The main building, which Deerfield called the lodge, was spacious, its interior dominated by a sweeping staircase with additional rooms upstairs.

The front room had a television mounted above the fireplace and a cluster of worn, comfortable furniture. Behind the reception desk hung a framed poster for Swamp Water. Beneath it was a black-and-white photo of Walter Brennan, smiling above a neat signature: Keep your feet dry.

"I'm going to have to watch that movie," I said. "I'd never heard of it until Kate mentioned it. And Brennan actually stayed here when he was filming?"

Paul chuckled. "Not exactly. This place wasn't built when he made those swamp movies. All his scenes were shot on soundstages in California."

"And the autograph?"

"I suspect the former owners got it through the mail. Or maybe it's a forgery. If people ask, I tell them the truth. Most don't ask."

Illusion sells better than fact. I understood that.

The dining room would not seat everyone at once, but the kitchen was industrial, more than capable of handling the load.

He led me down a hallway with a large conference room on the right and two more rooms on the left. At the very back were two much larger rooms. The one he showed me had a balcony overlooking Mossy Creek, a writing desk, and wide glass doors that spilled light across polished wood floors.

"Nice," I said.

Outside, Mossy Creek slid through cypress and pine, dark and slow.

"If you sit out in the early mornings," Paul said, "you can see a lot of animal life. Deer, beaver, foxes, birds of all kinds."

"And alligators?" I asked.

"Occasionally. They don't bother us."

"I'm sure."

"And I won't charge you for the mosquitoes," he added.

"One of these is yours?" I asked Kate.

"The next one over."

She smiled. I couldn't read it.

I found myself thinking about her more often than I liked. She felt solid in a way I wasn't. A woman who had loved, married, and lost. I had lived in scripts and second takes, in endings that could be rewritten. Kate was not fiction. Any life with her would demand permanence.

I wasn't sure I was built for permanence.

And maybe I was wrong about her. Maybe she would knock on my door in the middle of the night.

Sure. And pigs fly.

Kate checked her watch. "I'm going to talk to Mom before we head back."

"Mom?"

The resemblance between her and Beth snapped into focus, same posture, same eyes. I felt slow for not seeing it sooner.

"Mom," she repeated, and left us.

Paul was smiling. "I guess she played a little joke on you."

"I guess." I looked back at the creek. "This will work. If we can agree on a price."

Paul named a number. I swallowed. It was steep—but doable.

"I'll take this room," I said. "The conference room can serve as an editing space. Ann can use one down the hall."

"Whatever you like," Paul said. "You're the paying customer."

If he'd known I chose this room for reasons that had nothing to do with editing and everything to do with Kate being right next door, he might have reconsidered.

20.

I t took us all day to move from Swamp Lily Motor Court to the Mossy Creek Campground, and I had never seen a group of people work so hard and so enthusiastically. Paul sent a few of the locals in pick-up trucks to help, and soon it turned into a round-the-clock caravan of vans and trucks hauling equipment, luggage, cables, props, and half-built set pieces.

Despite the confusion, there was a rhythm to the madness, a kind of unspoken camaraderie that kept everyone going. People laughed through the exhaustion, even when their hands were blistered or their backs sore.

I still needed to settle with Ellis and Claire. I stopped at the restaurant and was told Ellis was away on business, and Claire was in her apartment. I walked around, and she opened the door before I knocked.

Inside, the apartment was clean, spotless even, but crowded with furniture that looked as though it had collected one comfortable piece at a time over several decades. A corduroy recliner sat beside a floral-print loveseat. A polished walnut side table stood next to a sagging plaid armchair. Nothing matched.

A row of family photographs hung on the wall. Babies, school portraits, and a wedding picture. Snapshots from different years in mismatched frames.

One photo caught my eye.

A tall man in an Army Air Forces uniform stood beside a wartime bomber. He held his cap under one arm and looked straight at the camera, serious and composed. The aircraft loomed behind him on the runway, its broad wings stretching wide.

Someone had placed the photograph in the center of the wall, as if he mattered more than the others.

Claire noticed me looking and said, "My father."

Something about Claire felt different from the first time I'd met her, a softness that hadn't been there in the restaurant. Her movements were looser now, unguarded. Her eyes held a lazy shine, lids dipping just slightly as though the room were warmer than it was.

When she stepped closer, I caught the scent of whiskey on her breath.

"I just wanted to pay you what I owe you," I said. "I couldn't find Ellis."

"Who cares about Ellis?" she said.

"If you'll just give me the amount, I'll write a check," I said.

"You're moving to Mossy Creek," she said.

"For a short time. We're nearly done."

"That's good," she said. "You need to get finished. You need to get out of this place." She leaned into me, her hand casually stroking my arm. "You need to leave before she gets you. You know, she's waiting."

"I think you might be a bit tipsy," I said.

"If you go out there, she'll keep you."

She sounded like Roy, and I was tired of drunken warnings. I asked impatiently for the amount again, and she gave it to me. It sounded a little high, but all I wanted was to get away. I wrote the check quickly and handed it to her. She looked at it as if it were tainted, and then folded it up and stuffed it into the pocket of her dress.

I felt her eyes on me when I left and walked down to my car.

Discounting Ellis and Claire, Ned McDonald was the only one who was unhappy about the move. I knew it was because he saw his chance at stardom slipping away for what he considered was going to be a movie flop. If it was even released.

I wasn't much help. Lifting things was impossible with my wrist. I tried to pitch in at first, but people warned me to stay out of the way. I ended up on the back deck of my new room, working on the train script.

I edited the pages, marking some of the dialogue for trimming and jotting notes in the margins about camera placement and lighting, but there wasn't much else to change. It was a short, powerful scene, one day's work.

Then we were out of scenes again. I hated working this way, at the mercy of whoever was writing the script. I started reading it through again when my phone rang. Walter Griggs.

"I was just going to call you," I said. "I've spent some money, but we've moved. I've paid for a week. If we can't finish this by then, I'll need another deposit."

For a moment, there was silence, and then Walter said flatly, "There'll be no more deposits."

"Are we that broke?"

"I'm shutting the movie down."

I held the phone away from my ear for a moment in stunned disbelief. Surely, I had misheard."

"That's not funny, Walter.'

"It's not meant as a joke. Close everything down. Someone will come around to pick up everything you've got, including Rafe's Bible. Pack it up for them. Send everyone home."

"I don't understand."

"I'm making it clear enough. The movie is finished."

"But you told me we needed this film. It's why you sent me out here. And I'm telling you it's a good film. It will be profitable."

"Things have changed," he announced.

I stood and walked to the railing and looked out over the creek. Suddenly, my wrist was hurting a lot worse. "What could have changed in just a few days?"

On the other end, I heard him exhale, the kind of theatrical sigh he used when he was about to lie. "Just... things," he said. Something clattered in the background, maybe a pen or a coffee mug. "Look, David Parker sent me a script. A good one."

"Oh, please." I pinched the bridge of my nose. "David Parker has never written a good script in his life. His idea of dialogue is just a series of clichés stapled together. The man has the sensitivity of a sponge."

"Well, he writes good action films," Griggs said defensively. "And they make a profit. A big one."

"He makes soft porn with fast cars and gunfights," I said. I went back to my chair and sat. "And I'm not producing a David Parker film."

There was a pause, a quiet clink, perhaps his ice settled in a glass. "I'm sorry to hear that," he said, though he sounded exactly as sorry as someone reading a weather report.

I said bitterly. "I doubt you could get Ann to direct it either."

Although I wasn't sure of that.

"I can get other directors," he replied casually.

I stopped pacing. "Do you think my mother wanted her name associated with those kinds of movies? "

My hand tightened around the phone. I could practically feel him shrug through the line.

"I didn't know you were such a prude," Griggs said. I heard him shifting, maybe leaning back in that leather chair he loved. "Even Disney does adult themes now."

"And I doubt he would be happy with the direction his studio has taken," I said. "Profit isn't the same as integrity, no matter how many explosions and nude girls you slap into a third act."

For a moment, there was nothing but static and Griggs's faint breathing.

The silence had edges, sharp ones.

Finally, he spoke, voice lower, colder. "Integrity doesn't keep the lights on, Noah."

"And selling garbage won't fix the fact that you've forgotten what this studio was built on," I said quietly.

"I hoped you'd be more mature about this," Griggs said. "You won't change your mind."

"No."

I'm sorry because that—" Griggs paused, letting the words stretch, the rustle of papers sharp in my ear "—that is the future of Sweet Angel Productions. No more art stuff. Just movies that make money."

His certainty made something cold settle under my ribs. He was talking about profits; I was talking about purpose.

I tried again, slower this time. "Rafe's movie will make money. His movies always did."

"Rafe's movie is dead," he said, flat as granite. "And I'll hear no more discussion."

I swallowed. I had one more chance to save the movie, even if it was a small one.

"Then why don't you sell the movie to me?"

A beat of silence. I could almost hear him blink. "What?"

"Let me have the rights," I said. "I'll finish the film. I can get independent distribution. I know how this works."

"You don't have that kind of money," he said, with a faint air of amusement.

"I have my mother's trust fund," I reminded him.

That made him laugh. A short, sharp bark that hit my ear like an insult. "Of course you do. And of course you'd spend it on something like this. After all I've taught you about money, you'd throw it away on sentiment. And for Rafe Cardoc, of all people. He didn't care about you. Why should you waste time worrying about his movie?"

"Sell me the rights," I repeated. "I'm not asking for favors."

"No," he said, instantly. "That won't happen."

I opened my mouth to argue, but he barreled on, voice shifting into something smoother, more calculating.

"I'll tell you what I will do," he said. "If you're so disappointed in Sweet Angel Productions, I'll buy out your shares. I'll give you an excellent price."

And then he named the number.

Far more than I thought my twenty percent was worth, almost an obscene number.

I felt as if my focus had tunneled down to just the sound of his breathing on the line.

But the money wasn't what made me hesitate.

Selling the shares didn't just mean leaving the company. It meant cutting the last thread tying me to my mother's vision, to the work she fought for, to the part of her that still lived in those studios and scripts and half-finished dreams. Selling would be a clean break, a final separation.

Yet, I knew down deep I'd already made my decision. I couldn't work with Griggs.

"Send me the papers," I said.

"I think it's the best thing for both of us," Griggs said and hung up.

I sat for a long time just thinking about nothing.

Just let the tide go out, I thought. Sell Griggs the shares, find something else to do with my life. Call Rita or just live on my mother's trust. Drift along as usual.

Thinking about Rita gave me an idea.

Deep down, I felt anger and hurt, and for once, I didn't want to just give up. I knew I was right about Rafe's movie. Despite all the issues, I knew it would work.

I wanted to finish it. I didn't know how I could do it, but I did know someone who might care as much about Rafe's movie and was smart enough to give me direction.

I reached into my wallet and pulled out a business card I'd nearly forgotten was there. I had wedged it behind an old parking stub and a faded photo of my mother, one I rarely let myself look at anymore. The card felt stiff, new, out of place among the relics.

Rita Boucher — Legal Consultant

Entertainment. Intellectual Property. Production Disputes.

A name I hadn't expected to need. Maybe a lifeline.

I turned the card over twice, running my thumb along the embossed lettering. My pulse drummed beneath the paper. Calling her meant admitting I needed help. But if I didn't do something, I knew I'd regret it.

I drew in a steady breath and dialed.

The line rang once. Twice. Three times. By the fourth ring, I nearly hung up.

Then: "Noah?" Her voice was low, even, unbothered, as if she'd been expecting me to call all along.

"Yeah," I said, trying for casual and missing by a mile. "Is that job in the mailroom still available?"

A soft laugh warmed the line. Not mocking, just knowing. "Is that really why you're calling?"

"No." I shifted the phone to my other hand, staring again at the card. "I have a legal question."

"You know I charge for those," she said, her voice tightening just enough to become professional.

"I figured."

A pause. I could almost hear her sitting in her chair, shifting into work mode. "Go ahead."

"It's about the company," I said.

"Sweet Angel?" she asked. Skepticism laced her tone. "I thought you were quitting."

"So did I."

"What's the question, Noah?"

I swallowed. "I own twenty percent of Sweet Angel Productions, or I will in a few days. Does that... give me any actual power in the company? I mean legally, not morally, not historically. Legally?"

"It depends," she said.

"Is that lawyer speak for I'm out of luck?"

"Twenty percent?" she repeated. I heard the faint click of keys or papers shifting, her mind switching gears. "It's a substantial stake."

"But does it mean anything?" I pressed. "Can I stop Griggs from killing a project? Can I override him? Slow him down? Anything?"

Rita exhaled, thoughtful, measured. "A lot depends on how the company is structured. But in most cases? Twenty percent would be large enough to make you impossible to ignore, but that's based on the group of shareholders. Do you know who they are in Sweet Angel?"

"All I know is that my mother set it up so Rafe and Walter were equal partners."

"And this movie. How is it financed?"

"The same way as usual. Walter seldom spends his own money. He usually has a half-dozen investors."

"Mostly the same people?" Rita asked.

"I would say so, yes."

"As a shareholder, do you get dividend statements?"

"I'm not a shareholder until my birthday," I reminded her. "I've never collected a dividend."

"That's right, I remember," she said. "Well, let me see if I can find some information online. I've got an investigator who's good at this stuff. I'll put him on it just as soon as we hang up. Information is power."

"Thank you, Rita," I said.

"I'm charging you a hefty sum," she said.

"I figured."

"And there may be something else we can do, if you're willing."

"What's that?"

"With your twenty percent, under California law, you can demand financial transparency. And if there's a dispute about fiduciary responsibility..." She paused. "Well, a twenty-percent shareholder filing a complaint is a headache Griggs wouldn't want. It would make investors in this movie nervous."

A thin sliver of hope slid in, cautious but present.

"You're talking about an audit?"

"Yes."

My throat tightened. "I don't think that would make Griggs happy."

"I imagine it would make him uneasy. Outside audits tend to complicate matters. I mean, Griggs might be perfectly legit in his bookkeeping, but many accountants develop certain methods or workarounds they'd prefer not to have examined too closely—especially by the financiers backing the films. Nearly everyone in that profession has a few gray areas they'd rather keep private."

"Let's hold off on that for now."

"Okay. But keep it in mind."

"Griggs did make an offer for my shares," I said.

Rita was quiet for a moment. "Did he now? That's interesting."

"He offered more than the shares are worth," I said.

"Then you definitely need to think about going ahead with an outside audit. Everybody knows Griggs is cheap. If he's offering you more than market value, it could mean he wants you out of the way."

"I told him I might be willing to sell," I said.

"Are you? Honestly?"

I pressed my fingers against my eyes. "Selling would be... it would be the last piece of my mother gone. The last thing she built. No, I don't want to sell."

Rita's voice softened, not pitying, just human. "Then don't. At least not yet. Not until we can find out what kind of leverage you have."

I let out a slow breath, the first steady one since the call began.

"Okay," I said.

"Good," she replied. "Now tell me about the movie."

"It's why Griggs sent me out here in the first place. To look at the movie. He told me he wanted an honest opinion, no politics, no studio pressure. Just whether the movie was good."

"And?" she prompted.

"And it's good," I said. "Really good. Maybe the best thing Rafe's ever done. Sharp, tight, emotional."

"So, you told Griggs it was good."

"I told him it was great," I said. "And that we needed to finish it right, promote it right, actually give it the support it deserves."

Rita made a thoughtful sound. "And his reaction?"

"That's the part I can't figure out. At first, he was happy about it. Counting dollar signs. Then he calls me back and tells me he's changed his mind. He's killing the movie. No explanation, no reasoning. He wouldn't tell me why."

"That's... sudden," Rita said carefully. "And suspicious."

"Exactly. There's no reason for it, none that makes sense. Rafe delivered something incredible. A career high. And Griggs wants to bury it." I shook my head, stomach tightening. "I don't understand why."

"Has he done this before?" she asked.

"No," I said. "Not like this. Griggs loves money, and this film would make money. He should be celebrating it, not shoving it in a drawer."

Rita was quiet for a moment, absorbing that. When she finally spoke, her voice lowered, more serious.

"Noah... this isn't just creative interference. It sounds as if he's intentionally killing a profitable film? That may be a breach of fiduciary duty to the shareholders. I think you might consider that audit again."

"Just the threat for now," I said.

"And since he's acting desperate to buy you out, your twenty percent might be a lot more powerful than you know. At least we can hold him up for a while. In the meantime, you ignore Griggs and go ahead with finishing the film. I'll be making phone calls. I'm sure once I make the threat of an outside audit, you'll be hearing from Griggs."

"I think we can count on that," I said.

"But whatever happens, don't stop the movie, and don't sign anything Griggs sends you."

"I can do that."

"And what of Rafe's will?" she asked.

"I wasn't aware he had one."

"You have no idea to whom he left his shares?"

"No. I just figured he and Griggs had some sort of partnership agreement."

"Rafe disliked Griggs intensely," Rita said.

"True."

"I doubt he would have agreed to leave him anything. I believe he would have left his shares to someone else. Maybe you?"

I laughed sourly. "No, not me. Never."

"Still, it would be nice to know what he did with his shares. I'm putting that on my list. I'm going to find out about Rafe's will. Under California law, you have thirty days to probate. Griggs might be having Daws and Mays hold onto the will until the very last minute."

"Why would he do that?" I asked.

"Let me ask you something. You said Griggs wanted to buy your shares. If he sent you a document to sign, a hundred pages of small print, with the actual number of shares buried somewhere in the middle, would you read it thoroughly?"

I shook my head. I knew I wouldn't. I didn't have the patience.

"Noah," Rita said, and I realized she couldn't see me shaking my head over the phone.

"No," I admitted.

"I didn't think so," she said. "Like I said before, if he sends you anything, anything at all, don't sign it. And don't stop making the movie. If you stop, it's finished. Give me a chance to find out exactly what Griggs is doing."

"Okay," I said, "but there's one other issue."

"Finances," she said immediately.

"I've paid for a week where we are," I said. "I can't stay any longer without financing, and I'm sure Griggs won't be making any deposits."

"How much do you believe in Rafe's movie?" she asked.

"A great deal," I said.

"We could get a loan from your trust fund to continue?"

I swallowed nervously. "If it's necessary."

"It may become so," she said. "Let's just worry about finishing the movie for now. If we can find a way to keep going, we'll find financing. My hope is we'll make Griggs pay for it." She laughed softly. "And Noah? If all this doesn't work out, we can still find you that job in the mailroom."

"It'll be a lot less stress," I said.

21.

We went to Folkston the next morning, and everything went wrong.

The heat was suffocating, worse than usual. It clung to your skin like a second layer, heavy and oppressive. I stood at the edge of the weathered wooden platform at the Folkston train viewing area, watching Cassie and Dylan grind through yet another take.

Kate was everywhere, making sure people were hydrated. We had water bottles stashed all over the area, and we had temporarily rented a former garage just to the south of the viewing platform that had water stations and bathrooms.

The cops had taped off the area, excluding the weathered building at the end of the parking lot that was also a bathroom for the many tourists who gathered to watch.

It should have been simple. A straightforward scene. Jace Whitfield, the brooding protagonist, confesses his love to Blue, his unrequited crush. Blue, in turn, tries to let him down gently, explaining that she doesn't feel the same way. Naturally, Jace gets angry, accusing her of being in love with Charley, and when Blue doesn't deny it, the tension thickens.

The scene was meant to be raw, electric, and full of emotion. But instead, it felt flat. Flat and lifeless.

Cassie stumbled on her lines for the second time. Her face was flushed, not from the heat but from pressure. Frustration was pulling her mouth into a tight, tense line, and I could see the thin thread of her patience snapping.

"I'm sorry," she said before I could even open my mouth.

"It's all right," I lied. But it wasn't. Not at all.

A small crowd had gathered, several people holding their phones out to film. Technology had certainly changed things; gone were the days when film cameras weighed hundreds of pounds, and film itself cost a fortune.

And yet there was no question in my mind that before the special effects, the camera illusions, the Hollywood pixie dust, movies were better. For one thing, writers had to actually write. The scripts had to be tight to hold an audience's attention. Scripts had to be laced with just the right amount of humor and pathos. And very few of the actors, except maybe Hope and Crosby, went off script. Improvising costs money, and the studio system was notoriously cheap.

Today, the old classics are shown on television or in arthouse movie theaters, and the argument is that the audience for them is dying away. The younger generations want movies that are fast-paced and exciting, and without a lot of dialogue.

Perhaps it's true, but when all those movies are forgotten and when all the directors like Rafe, considered arty, are gone, something valuable will be lost.

New directors needed to come along to take the place of men like Rafe, but I was beginning to fear I wasn't one of them.

I had envisioned this scene as quiet and intimate, low-key. Natural, even. Just two characters in a moment of painful honesty. Instead, it was unraveling before my eyes, and I had no idea how to stitch it back together.

Behind Cassie, I heard Dylan muttering, just loud enough for her to hear, "Why didn't they find me a professional to work with?" His tone was thick with annoyance, and though he wasn't looking at her, the words still stung. Cassie froze, her shoulders tense, her expression darkening. She was trying, and there was no reason for Dylan to be cruel.

I sighed, trying to keep my face neutral, but the tension in the air was suffocating.

I called a water break and returned to the car, my shirt drenched in sweat. The heat hit like a wall when I opened the door. It was just as stifling inside as it was under the sun. I slid into the driver's seat, the vinyl scorching against my legs, and grabbed the half-empty bottle from the passenger side. The first swallow burned cold down my throat, a brief mercy in the heat.

The passenger door creaked open.

Someone got in.

I jumped, nearly spilling the bottle.

"You're letting them intimidate you," Atkins said.

"You know something about movies?" I asked.

"Not a thing except what Micki has told me, but I know something about people. You're letting that bunch walk all over you. You need to stand up for yourself. You need to stop worrying about hurting their feelings. You're the guy in charge. You're responsible. If it goes well, you'll take the credit. If it goes badly, you'll get the blame. None of them will."

"You're giving me a lecture on leadership," I said.

"Somebody better, or your movie is going to crash and burn."

I took a sip of my water and wished he would go away. The truth is, I knew he was right. Rita had told me Rafe said I lacked self-confidence, but confidence isn't easy to find if you've spent most of your life avoiding responsibility.

"So, what do I do?" I asked.

Atkins shrugged. "Why ask me? I don't know anything about movies."

"Right. You're a big help."

"Just take charge," he said. "Use your experience. In the meantime, I've been talking to people."

"How nice for you."

"I no longer think you killed your father."

I laughed once, humorless. "That's comforting."

"But someone did tamper with his plane," Atkins said. "My Cessna guy says there's a little part on the tail... well, never mind the technical details, but it caused the plane to drop at the wrong time. My Cessna guy is good. He said it had to be somebody experienced with aircraft."

I sucked in a breath. I'd half suspected it, but hearing it out loud made my stomach churn.

"I checked you out. You've never been a pilot, and there's no other pilot in your company. At least, no one on record. Of course, your guy Sparks probably knows enough to fly a plane or to sabotage one. But I doubt he did."

"Why not?"

"He just doesn't strike me as the type of guy who'd mess with an airplane. I think he's more the type to go after somebody with a wrench."

"I agree."

"My friend's impatient to go fishing," he said. "I wondered if you had any ideas."

"No," I said. "You're the cop. Why don't you stop bothering me and go arrest somebody?"

"I'd like to arrest Dylan Welch," Atkins said. "He irritates me for some reason."

"He irritates a lot of people," I agreed.

"But Welch didn't kill your father either," he said sadly.

"How can you know that?"

"He was with a girl from Waycross when Rafe got killed. Spent the entire weekend with her in a motel room. Had takeout. I talked to the person who cleaned the room and the Uber driver who took him to Waycross."

"I wasn't even aware they had Uber drivers around here," I said.

"Well, technically, it's just a guy with an SUV who gives rides."

"Figures," I said. "So, you have no more suspects."

"Oh, all of you are still suspects," he said, with a grin that didn't quite reach his eyes. "I've been wrong before." He shook his head. "But I get the feeling there's something else going on. I'm thinking his murder had something to do with the movie you're making."

"I don't see how."

"Does your last scene name the murderer, by any chance?"

I didn't want to admit there wasn't a last scene. Yet.

"The movie is based on the book," I said. "The book didn't name a murderer."

"But maybe your father knew something the rest of us don't."

"Rafe found a book he liked that had a murder, a ghost, and a good love story. That's all. He's not a detective. He didn't come up with some Sherlock Holmes reveal."

"But maybe somebody thinks he did," Atkins pointed out. "I found a copy of the book, Murder in the Swamp. It was a poorly written book, and a bad investigation, but you came away thinking it was Whitfield."

"I agree."

"If your last scene names Whitfield as the murderer, Whitfield might be just a little upset. It could start a new investigation. There's no time limit for murder."

I shook my head. "If Whitfield is still around, which I doubt, he'd have made his presence known by now. No, I think he probably died a long time ago. He certainly wouldn't be coming around sabotaging my father's airplane."

I could see the actors and crew getting restless, and it was time to go again. I started to get out of the car, and Atkins tugged at my elbow.

"What now?" I said irritably.

"How was your father injured?" he asked.

"What has that to do with anything?" I asked.

"My mother made quilts," he said, which I thought had nothing to do with what I'd asked. "A couple of them were so good, they're in the Smithsonian as examples of Appalachian art."

"That's impressive," I said.

"But some quilts she made, she didn't like. She saw flaws in them that nobody else could see. I tried. It took me a long time to see what she was seeing. You just had to study every square until you saw the crooked one, the piece that didn't fit."

"I'm still not quite sure I understand what point you're trying to make."

"It's simple. Something doesn't fit. I'm not sure what it is yet, the pattern isn't right."

"And Rafe's injury has something to do with your pattern not fitting?"

"Maybe? Maybe not."

"I don't see how it could have any connection. He was injured in a car wreck when he was a toddler. One side of his face was badly burned. The nerves in his left eye were damaged. It didn't hurt his directing abilities."

Atkins nodded. He opened the car door and stepped out.

"I'm going to be around," he said.

"That gives me great comfort," I said.

22.

One miserable hour later, I called for another break, knowing the scene was failing and unsure how to fix it. The sweat on my back stuck to my shirt, the late afternoon sun burning down through the high, cloudless sky. I had watched Rafe handle problems on set, his calm command like a magnet, but I did not have his temperament or instinct. I did not have the way he could make everyone move without a word, or the authority that felt like a weapon in his hands.

The air smelled of sweat, dust, sawdust, and a faint tang of engine oil from the tracks out front. A breeze rustled through the nearby trees, carrying the metallic whiff of the rails and the fragrant, sweet smell of honeysuckle vines.

I noticed somebody had pulled up a food truck near the taped-off area and was selling tacos, burritos, and soft drinks. I walked out to the truck and purchased three loaded fish tacos and two Diet Cokes. I sank into one of the chairs on the Folkston train-viewing platform and ate my tacos and drank one of the Cokes.

Ann approached me, her tenseness still showing her disapproval of my taking over.

"This isn't working," she said.

I sensed a smug, "I told you so," in her voice.

"I'm aware."

"There are a few more changes in the script we could make," she suggested. "Heighten the tension."

She knew as well as I that it wasn't the script giving us problems, but the actors, and I hated the changes we had already made.

Part of the problem was that Atkins was right, and I was allowing everyone to intimidate me. I was trying to please everyone, honor every suggestion. Maybe the scene at the swamp had been a fluke when I insisted on the retakes. Maybe I was the failure Rafe had always accused me of being.

I drank my second Coke and thought about what I had seen so far. Dylan was delivering his lines perfectly, mechanically, but I felt very little anger in him. I knew Rafe had cast Dylan for his intensity, his rebellion, and he wasn't showing it. I didn't believe for a second that he was desperately in love with Blue or furious that she had chosen another over him. If I didn't believe it, the audience never would.

And Cassie had not yet fallen into character the way I had seen her in the raw footage, or on the day at the park. Enough. I could not keep waiting for inspiration. No one else was going to step in.

When I stood, I felt every eye on me. The sun bounced off the plywood floor, casting my shadow long and distorted across the set.

"Alright," I said, voice sharp and steady. "Everyone, listen up. We are going back to the original script. No changes to marks. No changes to dialogue."

A few eyebrows rose. Even Sparks looked surprised. The crew murmured, but they moved. They always did when someone made it clear they were serious.

We started the scene again. For the first time in hours, I felt a spark I had not felt in a long time, control. Not full confidence yet, but enough. Enough to call the shots and believe we could finally make this scene work.

I suddenly knew how to make it happen. It would take more than I had ever given before, but I could feel it deep inside. I could make it work.

I had to find whatever was in Cassie that made her Blue. And I had to make Dylan deliver the scene as it needed to be. A scene that was supposed to crackle with emotion had limped along like a bad elementary school play.

We went through it, and halfway through, I knew it wasn't working. Again.

"Cut," I said quietly.

No one moved.

"Cut!" I shouted again, louder. My voice cracked like a wire snapping. The crew shifted uneasily. One of the grips coughed. The actors froze mid-scene, eyes flicking toward me for guidance. From behind the camera, the sound guy sighed and adjusted his boom mic with tired resignation, shoulders sagging, as if he had seen too many days like this.

Ann approached from behind the monitor, clipboard clutched like a lifeline. Her brow was tight, shoulders stiff. Sweat dampened the collar of her shirt. The sun reflected off the monitor, making her squint.

"I think we go ahead and use what we already have on digital," she said. "It's not going to get better."

"It will," I said, more to myself than to her.

I stepped onto the platform. The vibration echoed faintly up my legs. Dylan was slouched in one of the folding chairs, legs sprawled, arms limp, as if the whole thing bored him. He did not even glance at me until I stood directly in front of him.

"The woman you love has just told you no," I said. "Not maybe. Not later. No. You are supposed to be upset. Angry. Hurt. Something. Anything. But right now? You're giving me nothing. And you're intentionally stealing the scene from Cassie."

He gave me a mocking look. "Moi?"

"Stand up," I said.

"Oh," he said, with that same mocking tone. "Are we going to fight now?"

"I'm going to show you how it should be done," I said, turning to face Cassie.

The crew adjusted, cameras rolling, lights glaring in the midday sun. I could feel their eyes on me, and for the first time, I did not care. This scene was mine.

Cassie stood a few feet away, fists clenched at her sides. Her voice, usually strong, was barely above a whisper. She delivered her lines perfectly, and I could see her chest rising and falling unevenly, the tension in her neck and shoulders raw and visible.

But she wasn't Blue yet. Not yet.

I delivered the lines. I became Jace Whitfield for a moment, and I poured out all his frustration, anger, and hurt at being turned down by the woman he loved. I knew a part of my speech was directed more toward Rafe himself, for his lifelong denial of me, and perhaps something from my own failed relationships.

Cassie's eyes seemed to change, almost glowing with something I had never seen before. Her voice shook, quivering, and she spoke her lines, not in English, but in French. Each word trembled with uncontained emotion, echoing against the metal and wood of the platform.

"Cut," Ann said from behind the monitor.

Cassie was shaking. So was I. My knees felt weak, and the sun beat down on my back, hot and relentless.

Ann approached. "What just happened?"

"I'm not sure," I admitted.

"Was she speaking in French?"

"Do it again," I said.

We did it again, and I once again let all the anger, resentment, and hurt of my entire life come to the surface. I spit it out at Cassie, as Blue. I saw her face change, saw her eyes get that light, saw her speak the words.

"Cut," Ann said again.

Then came the applause.

It started with a few scattered claps, then grew louder. Real applause. A few whistles. Someone shouted, "Yes!"

I blinked in the sudden sunlight, stepping out of the frame. One of the grips slapped me on the back, warm and firm. Cassie looked at me like she was seeing me for the first time, really seeing me.

Even Dylan seemed stunned. I stepped in close. "You say you are a better actor than I am. Show me."

We did it again. And Dylan delivered this time. He delivered the emotion needed, no shortcuts. His way was different, but it would move an audience.

"Cut," Ann said again. "That is our take."

Ann approached, arms crossed, expression unreadable. "You did it."

"We did it," I replied.

For the first time on this set, I did not feel like I was holding everything together with duct tape and grit. I felt part of it, alive in chaos. I was part of something that mattered.

I felt lightheaded, my wrist throbbed, but I ignored it. The heat radiated off the platform. The crowd behind the tape murmured in excitement, energy buzzing through the air. The faint smell of sweat and engine oil mixed in a strange cocktail of anticipation.

And then I saw Atkins, standing with arms folded, watching, his face unreadable. He nodded once and stepped back into the crowd. Deep down, I wished he'd go away. I now knew I could finish this movie, but I wanted to finish it without him looking over my shoulder for a killer.

23.

F ish tacos should not be eaten in the heat.

It was a lesson I would remember for the rest of my life because I spent the next day bedridden or in the bathroom. Fortunately, it only lasted one horrible day and only part of the night, and I felt almost human the next morning.

I didn't sing in the shower. I wasn't ready for that. But the hot water felt good, and there was no mildew in the bathroom, and no bugs. There was real soap in the dispenser. Tiny shampoo bottles stood in a neat row like hotel room soldiers. It made me smile. Someone cared.

I stayed in the shower longer than I meant to. Let the steam and hot water strip away the sick, the travel, the stress. I scrubbed until I felt like myself again.

When I finally stepped out, toweling off, I felt lighter. Cleaner. Clear-headed.

And starving.

Out in the hallway, freshly showered and halfway to functional, I saw the meeting room door open just a few steps away. Sunlight poured through the tall windows, illuminating what had become a full-blown editing bay: laptops, monitors, cables, hard drives. Organized chaos. Functional, bright, alive.

Ann sat at one of the tables, headphones draped around her neck, eyes locked on a monitor. Probably reviewing the last shoot before we bailed on Swamp Lily Motor Court. She looked up when she saw me, her face breaking into a grin equal parts relief and sarcasm.

"Well, look who's back from the dead."

"You didn't get the stuff?"

"I never eat food off a truck," she said. "Sparks did, and it didn't bother him, but then he's got a cast-iron stomach. Nobody else got sick.

"Lucky me."

"Kate was concerned. She looked in on you a few times yesterday, but you were sleeping. She said it was the best thing for you."

I stepped into the room, still blinking at the brightness. "What have you been doing?"

"Looking through the rough cuts. Some good stuff." She looked at me. "The stuff I directed at the park was good."

"I never said it wasn't," I said.

"But you implied it when you kept asking to do another. I didn't understand. I'm still upset with you, but then I saw the last take, and I figured it out. Cassie was acting in all the other takes, but she was Blue at the end."

"Yes."

"I think you might have Rafe's vision, after all."

I had a feeling it wasn't about talent or vision at all, but about whatever was going on out in the swamp. The idea that Cassie was being possessed by the spirit of Simone Laviolette? I couldn't quite buy it. Maybe I didn't have a better explanation, but possession felt more like something out of a Hammer film. Still, for the moment, at least until I found some new way to mess things up, Ann was on my side.

I left Ann and walked down the hallway and past the deserted reception desk. The scent of frying eggs, fresh-brewed coffee, and something sweet, cinnamon rolls, maybe, floated in the air like a promise. My stomach growled despite the weight in my chest.

I pushed through the swinging doors into the large dining room and was immediately hit by the brightness, fluorescent lights humming overhead, harsh and unflattering. I blinked, adjusting, and almost bumped into Paul, who was standing just inside the doorway.

"Feeling better?" he asked.

"I'm getting there."

"Good. We got strong coffee and eggs, bacon, and pancakes. The guy will make you an omelet if you ask, and there's fruit and cereal. Better than bad fish tacos."

"Please don't mention fish tacos ever again."

Paul laughed. Behind the counter, I noticed Beth orchestrating the action like a general on the front line.

The kitchen buzzed with the kind of organized chaos that comes from feeding a crowd. At the far end, an older man stood behind an enormous griddle, his white apron dusted with flour and the faint shadow of a coffee stain near the hem. His hair was more silver than gray, curling slightly where the steam hung thick in the air. With the practiced flick of a wrist, he turned pancakes—each one a perfect, golden circle—stacking them high on a nearby tray before ladling more batter onto the sizzling surface.

Two teenage girls—sixteen, maybe—darted between tables laden with trays of eggs, fruit, and pastries, their faces glowing with a mix of enthusiasm and mild panic. They whispered quick updates to each other as they worked, juggling tongs and trays, trying to keep up with the steady demand from the buffet line. Every so often, they glanced toward Beth, who stood at the center of it all like a general surveying her troops.

Beth didn't need to raise her voice. Her authority was quieter, sharper, a calm command wrapped in steel. One arched brow from her was all it took to send the bacon guy scrambling to refill the tray as if the fate of breakfast itself depended on him.

I wondered if Beth would be willing to take a job as a PA on set.

Forks clinked against plates, and laughter floated across the room. Warm light spilled over smiling faces, the air alive with easy chatter and the scent of good food. Everyone seemed caught up in the cheer of the moment, everyone except Ned. He sat a little apart, shoulders hunched, a faint frown tugging at his mouth as he looked at me with accusing eyes.

The way he glowered, I could almost believe he could murder someone.

I didn't see Dylan until I started through the line. I heard him first. His voice was loud, theatrical, and unmistakable. I knew right away he was doing his Hamlet routine again, the one he dusted off for every wrap party, cast dinner, or bored intern with a pulse.

"Alas, poor Yorick," he boomed, holding up a ladle like it was the famous skull. His tone was a pitch-perfect blend of parody and skill, just enough thespian flair to make the joke work. "I knew him, Horatio... mostly because he owed me five bucks and kept promising to pay me back next Tuesday."

A wave of laughter rippled across the room.

I never thought Dylan lacked talent. Far from it. He had that maddening combination of timing, presence, and self-awareness that could make you forget, at least for a minute, that you wanted to punch him in the face. But I'd seen this particular act more times than I could count, and I wasn't sure who he was trying to impress.

He pressed on, wielding the ladle like a sword now. "To be or not to be—that is the question. Whether 'tis nobler in the mind to suffer the slings and arrows of craft services running out of bagels, or to take arms against a sea of hunger and, by opposing, grab some bacon?"

More laughter. Even I had to bite down a smirk. The crew, once restless and bitter, now looked almost content, eating, smiling, not actively planning a mutiny. Credit where it was due: Dylan knew how to work a room.

I noticed Kate sitting nearby, her eyes fixed on him like a kid at a circus. There was a softness to her expression I hadn't seen before, and I felt a jolt in my stomach that had nothing to do with hunger. I suddenly understood who Dylan was trying to impress.

He wrapped up with a grand bow and disappeared behind the counter. I moved through the buffet line, piling a little of every-thing onto my plate, trying to ignore the sound of Kate's laugh—a full-bodied, throw-your-head-back kind of laugh—echoing through the room.

I headed toward her table, but Dylan got there first. He leaned in, said something I couldn't hear, and she touched his arm as she laughed again.

Wonderful. Just wonderful.

I sat across from Peggy Marsh, who smiled at me as if she knew exactly what I was thinking.

"What?" I snapped.

"She's getting under your skin. I don't think I've ever seen you get jealous before.'

"I'm not jealous," I protested.

"Then you must be getting ill again, because your face is all red.

"Nonsense," I muttered.

She saw the tension rising in my jaw and, to her credit, backed off. "The food really is great," she said instead. "At least you've solved that particular problem. Yesterday, people were complaining about everything—the accommodations, the schedule, the catering. Today they're actually smiling."

I nodded absently, forcing my eyes away from the table where Kate was still talking with Dylan. "One problem down, about seventeen more to go."

I couldn't stop myself from looking at Kate again. She was leaning in now, her shoulder brushing his as he spoke. His hand ran along her arm—not casually, not incidentally, but with intent. It was intimate, deliberate.

And she let him.

Dylan wasn't improvising. This was another performance, one he'd practiced many times. Polished. Efficient. Effective.

And Kate, whom I'd thought of as thoughtful, measured, even a little guarded... she was falling for it, perfectly on cue.

Like an actress hitting her mark.

I'd much rather have watched her break his nose.

24.

I took coffee back to the editing room, where Ann was still working at one of the monitors. At least someone was doing work. I could see she had started numbering the scenes, building a kind of list to bring order to the chaotic mess Rafe had left us.

She took one look at my face and asked, "Was breakfast bad?"

"Breakfast was great," I said sourly.

"Oh," she said, and left it at that.

I took a deep breath. There was no sense in taking my pangs of jealousy over Dylan's obvious flirtation with Kate, or my frustration at not being able to continue filming, out on Ann. I just wanted to get this movie over and done with, and I hated being at the mercy of an unknown scriptwriter.

At least I could keep busy. I sat down and pulled the Bible toward me. I took out the script and began making notes of things that needed doing for the final edit. I couldn't seem to concentrate.

At the back of the Bible, I came across the scene Rafe had discarded. With nothing else to occupy my mind, I pulled it out and skimmed it. It caught my interest, and I read it through again, this time more carefully.

"This is good," I said. "It's a strong scene. Why did Rafe dislike it?"

She shook her head. "No idea. When Rafe looked at the scene, he went out to the Laviolette Homestead by himself and looked it over. When he came back, he said it wouldn't work."

Rafe must have had some reason.

"Maybe because of the location," I said.

Ann shrugged.

"Have you been out there?"

"Not me."

"And he never told you why he discarded it?"

"Nope."

"It's a good scene," I said. "A love scene. Charley and Blue. It moves the movie along. We should do this scene."

"Even if Rafe didn't want it?"

"I know I'm going against genius, but it's good."

"Or you're desperate," she suggested.

"Maybe a little of both," I admitted.

"If you think it's that good, then we should give it a try. But here's my suggestion. Why don't you go out there and take a look around? Maybe you'll see a problem, maybe not. You make the determination."

I started to tell her that it was the dumbest idea I had heard so far. I was not about to go traipsing around the Laviolette Homestead, deep in the swamp. I had not been crazy about the idea of going near the water at Stephen Foster State Park.

"Maybe somebody else could go," I suggested.

Ann shook her head. "I think it has to be you. You're in charge. The decision has to be yours." She sat up straight in her chair. "I've got an idea. We could ask Kate to take you out there."

I hated her idea, and I loved it. A day alone with Kate, and even more importantly, a day without Dylan hanging around. Ann had found the only thing that would have tempted me to go near that swamp again.

She grinned, infuriatingly, like she had known all along exactly which string to pull.

"People do go out there all the time, you know," Ann said innocently. "They camp, fish, and enjoy the beautiful scenery."

"Whoopie for them," I said.

"I could ask her," Ann said.

"You do that," I said, before I could stop myself.

A little after five in the afternoon, I was making notes on a yellow legal pad, outlining the new scene. If Kate and I actually made it to the homestead, I wanted some idea of how the scene would unfold. I had filled half the pad when my phone rang.

"Noah, darling," came Rita's unmistakable rasp. "How you ever put up with Griggs all these years is beyond me."

"He's giving you trouble?"

"Trying," she corrected. "Did you know he had a girlfriend?"

"A girlfriend?" I repeated. "Griggs?"

"A sweet, hot young thing. He's put her in the office Rafe never used, and apparently her new official title is 'Producer.'" Rita managed to turn the word into an insult.

"You're not serious."

"Oh, I am. And Griggs has been taking her to Vegas. Designer clothes. Jewelry. He's spending serious money."

The recent changes in Griggs were starting to make sense.

"He can afford it," I said. "He's never spent a dime he didn't have to spend. He's got a lot saved up."

"Then it's slipping through his hands like quicksilver. He recently took a second mortgage on his home."

I sat up straighter. "A second mortgage doesn't make sense. Griggs has always been careful with money. Pathologically careful."

"Maybe so," Rita said, her voice sharpening, "but sometimes a woman can make a man do foolish things. Remember, it was a woman who started the Trojan War."

I rubbed my eyes. "Griggs is not Paris."

"No, but he did go a little crazy when I mentioned an audit. I'm now convinced he's dipping into company funds. Maybe even the money set aside to finance your movie."

"I just find it hard to believe that he would steal." Even to my own ears, I sounded naïve. "He might have a girlfriend, but I don't think he would steal."

"Then you have a problem," Rita said. "There are only three share-holders in Sweet Angel: you, Griggs, and Rafe. And I was right about Rafe's will; it still hasn't been probated. If he left you nothing, you don't have a prayer of stopping Griggs. Not unless you call for an audit. It's your only leverage."

"I still hate the thought of doing that."

"Then kiss your father's movie goodbye. Griggs won't stop until he's bled the company dry."

"You really think the audit is the only way?"

"I do."

I stared at the half-finished notes on my desk. "Then call for the audit, Rita."

"Good. Now let me tell you what's going to happen if I'm right, and I'm sure I am. Griggs will call, all friendly. He'll say he's changed his mind and is ready to finance the movie after all, if you call off the audit. When he does, you'll know exactly where his hands have been."

"This is unpleasant."

"It's the way of the world, Noah. Meanwhile, I'll keep digging into Rafe's will. I think you might be wrong. You may have more shares than you think, and that could be why Griggs is delaying probate." She paused. "And I'm going to start calling some of the investors in Rafe's latest film. I don't want you surprised if you start getting phone calls."

I was beginning to understand why they called Rita "the Butcher."

When she hung up, the door opened, and Kate stepped in.

"You missed lunch," she said. "And you're close to missing supper. Come eat."

"Sounds good." I stood and stretched.

"And Ann says you want a tour of the Laviolette Homestead. Is tomorrow soon enough?"

Tomorrow.

No. Not tomorrow. Not the next day. Not ever. Not that swamp. Not with Simone waiting.

But I had to finish this movie, and Kate was offering to take me. I told myself it would simply be time alone with her. A quick look at a few abandoned buildings. Nothing more.

So why did I keep hearing Roy's whiskey-soaked voice warning me that Simone was out there?

"Tomorrow," Kate said again.

"Tomorrow is fine," I said, the words coming out thin.

"Good. We'll leave early. You might want to leave that watch behind. It looks expensive. Water sometimes gets into the boat."

"Boat?"

"Sure. How else do you expect to get to the homestead?"

How else indeed.

25.

I learned two things the next day.

First, anyone raised in Beverly Hills had no business in the Okefenokee Swamp, even with a very attractive guide.

It wasn't just the swamp itself. It was the way it breathed—heavy, slow, ancient. The kind of place that didn't care if you drove a Range Rover or wore limited-edition loafers, which I did, foolishly. There was no one to impress. Just cypress trees, gators, and the vague suspicion that everything around me wanted me gone or eaten, or both.

And I get it. If anyone's offended because it's supposedly a beloved national preserve, I apologize in advance. I didn't love it. Truthfully, I wouldn't have come at all if not for my desperate need for another scene.

And Kate, of course.

That was the other thing I learned. Kind of foolish, maybe, but something slid into place inside me with a quiet, undeniable click. Not the itch of infatuation I used to mistake for something deeper, but a sudden realization that I had never known anyone like her before.

I was going to tell her as much if I lived.

The boat waiting for us wasn't much to look at, but it was built for the swamp. Broad, shallow, stubborn. A flat-bottomed aluminum skiff, about sixteen feet long, with a dent in the bow that looked like it had stories of its own. The hull was scuffed from years of bumping against hidden logs, its dull gray metal patched in a few places with riveted plates.

A small mud motor sat on the stern, one of those long-tail rigs with a propeller that could churn through water, weeds, or mud. It sounded like a chainsaw with a busted chain. A tangle of nets, gas cans, and a coiled rope lay in the bow.

"I thought something a little bigger," I said.

Kate laughed. "This is what you need on the black water. Light enough to slide over lilies, low enough to duck under branches, tough enough to hit a submerged stump without coming apart. We don't want your feet wet."

Or chewed off, I thought.

Simone is waiting, I thought. Maybe she'd take the day off.

I found a place to sit. The floor flexed a little under my shoes.

"Here we go," Kate called over the engine's growl, grinning at me from the bow like she was born for this place. Hair tied up in a red bandana, sunglasses catching the sun.

A couple of alligators lounged on the nearby shore.

"Are you alright?" she asked. "You look like you're about to pass out or puke or both."

I gripped the side of the boat. "No. I miss the sound of motors and the smell of exhaust fumes of Culver City."

She laughed. "You'll live."

The water around us was slick and black, like glass poured over secrets. Bald cypress trees rose from the shallows, their flared bases anchoring them deep in mud.

"Those are cypress knees," Kate said, pointing to a patch sticking up like crooked fingers. "Breathing roots. Swamp science. But they make the place look like goblins clawing their way out."

I laughed, uneasy. She wasn't wrong.

She nodded to the right. "See that big guy?"

I followed her gaze to a towering tree, wider than a truck. Its bark curled and knotted with age, branches clawing at the sky. The base twisted into thick folds, and I could swear it had a face—a drooping eye, a bulbous nose, a mouth that might yawn.

"Locals say that's the oldest tree in the swamp. It survived the big fire. Some folks call it the Watcher."

"Looks like something out of Babes in Toyland," I said. "One of those creepy Disney trees that talk when nobody is looking."

Kate grinned. "Exactly. This swamp is full of old magic if you are willing to squint at it."

I nodded, though every instinct screamed I didn't belong here. The air was thick enough to chew, heavy with wet bark and slow decay. Somewhere in the trees, a heron gave a harsh cry and took to the air with a fluttering of wings.

"How much farther?"

"About ten minutes. You're doing fine. Color's coming back to your face."

"Glad I'm entertaining."

"You're adorable when you're uncomfortable."

I leaned back against the bench seat and let the engine's drone take over, scanning the dark water for anything that might rise from it. Hard to believe people used to live here, not just visit or camp, but live—raise kids, cook meals, bury their dead. We passed a wooden platform along the bank.

"What's that?"

"Camping platform."

"People camp on those?"

"All the time."

"But can't the creatures climb up?"

She laughed. "You're not much of a nature person, are you?"

"I admit I'm no Daniel Boone," I agreed.

Ten minutes later, Kate pointed ahead.

"There."

The trees opened into a small cove, the shoreline curling around weathered wooden structures. We eased up to a rough dock, sun-bleached and crooked. I stepped out with relief, knees wobbly.

The Laviolette Homestead looked like a ghost town that had politely decided not to collapse. A wide-planked main house, gray and silvered by time, stood near the center with a low roof and deep porch. A moss-covered smokehouse and a leaning barn waited nearby.

A tourist family wandered around the grounds. Kids darted up and down the porch steps, laughter light and sharp. Parents pointed out the hand pump and rusted mule-drawn plow.

Something occurred to me. "How did they get here, Kate? There's no boat."

She chuckled. "There's a road on the far side, part of a heritage tour out of Waycross. The shuttle van stops a few times a week. Sometimes even a bus."

I looked accusingly at her. "There's a road? We could have come on a road."

"Where's the romance in that? You wouldn't have gotten the real experience."

"I think I've been the victim of a cruel hoax. I'm beginning to regret not inviting Dylan."

Kate grinned. "You don't mean that."

"No," I admitted.

She hopped off the boat and shouldered a canvas bag. "Come on. They preserved most of the house as they found it. No AC, no insulation. Just good wood and hard living."

We stepped onto the porch. The boards creaked under our shoes. Inside, the house was dim and cool. Narrow planks underfoot, a cast-iron stove in the corner, shelves lined with dusty mason jars, a rope bed beneath the single window. No screens, just the open air and hope that mosquitoes might be merciful.

"This wasn't a vacation home," I said softly.

Kate traced her fingers along a worn table edge. "Nope. People like the Laviolettes lived off what they could grow or hunt. Cane syrup, cooter stew, swamp cabbage. They made their own soap and clothes. No help, just your people and your know-how."

I heard admiration in her voice.

A glass box stood against the wall, holding old photographs from past events at the Laviolette Homestead. Faces had faded, corners curled, moments once ordinary carefully preserved. Several young girls in uniform, expressions proud but tentative. Beneath it, a hurried caption read, "Girl Guides of," the rest lost to time.

I picked Kate out immediately.

"You look pretty good in uniform," I said.

"I'd forgotten about that picture." She folded her arms. "You do know I was twelve when it was taken."

"And now you're not."

She gave me a sharp look. "I'm beginning to think you're a bit of a lecher."

We explored the rest: the chicken coop, old garden plots, and the one-room school shed. I still couldn't think of a reason why we couldn't film here, especially now that I knew about the road.

Around noon, we found a shaded patch near the woods. We spread a checkered blanket on the sun-warmed grass. A crusty baguette, creamy brie, crisp apple slices, and juicy grapes were laid out in a small wooden basket. We tore bread, shared cheese, drank water from plastic bottles, and nibbled fruit, laughing as the afternoon sun warmed our shoulders.

"You think you could've lived like this?" I asked, chewing.

"If I'd grown up here? Probably. Dropped in now?" She laughed. "No. I love AC and Netflix. But I like remembering people who didn't need any of that. People who could gut a fish, build a house, keep bees, and bury a snakebite victim all in the same day."

"Comforting," I said.

"That was the way they lived."

"Did you ever bring David out here?" I asked.

For a heartbeat, something cold flickered in her eyes, maybe regret—and I braced myself. Then she nodded.

"I did. But he was always busy. There never seemed to be enough time."

"Tell me about him," I pressed.

"Why?"

"Because I want to know you. And I think I'll understand you better if I know who David was."

She drew in a slow breath. "He was a man who believed in things," she said finally. "He believed he could make the world better. He charged into everything like a wild elephant, and somehow... somehow he really did leave things better than he found them. I met him when I was working as a paramedic, and we brought a few accident victims to his clinic."

"And you fell in love?" I asked.

"I did. But we had such a short time together." Her voice thinned, like she was speaking through a memory she still hadn't figured out.

"Could you ever love someone else like him?" I asked.

She studied my face, and her expression was unreadable. Curious, maybe amused.

"You mean, like Dylan?" she said, teasing.

"I mean anyone," I said, hoping my face wasn't turning red.

"I don't know," she admitted quietly. "But you know what David told me when his cancer got really bad? He told me I wasn't allowed to stop living. That I needed to keep going, find my direction." She looked toward the horizon. "I guess I'm still trying to do that."

We sat in silence, just the buzz of cicadas and the fading voices of tourists drifting through the trees. Sunlight poured through branches in golden shafts, catching dust and pollen like tiny stars in honey.

"You think you can film here?" Kate asked.

"You said there's a road. It'll take our van with equipment?"

"Easily," she said.

"Then I don't know why Rafe didn't want this scene. I think it'll be good."

We gathered up our trash, folded up our quilt, and walked down the slight incline to the dock. Despite my misgivings, I'd had a pretty good time. I wasn't looking forward to getting back into the boat, but at least the enormous pressure in my chest I'd felt before had eased.

As we stepped onto the dock, I turned back for one last look at the house.

Then, just beyond the tree line, I saw something move.

A flicker. Quick. Deliberate. Not big, but not the wind. A flash of tan against deep green.

Kate noticed me pause. "What is it?"

"Something in the trees."

"Don't tell me you're seeing ghosts."

"No. Maybe a deer?"

She followed my gaze. "Could be. Or a feral hog. Maybe a bear."

"No more bears," I muttered, shuddering.

She smirked, nudging me toward the boat. "Come on, swamp warrior. Let's get you back to dry land."

The engine roared to life. We peeled away from the Laviolette place, water parting in slow ripples behind us. I glanced back. Whatever I saw was gone. Probably nothing. But the feeling lingered, like we hadn't been entirely alone.

26.

We didn't waste any time. We headed out to the Laviolette Homestead early the next morning.

The sky stretched wide and pale above us, bleached and translucent, thin as breath. A morning that felt like it could vanish if you looked too hard at it. Too still. Too perfect. As if even the light was holding its breath.

We brought only a skeleton crew: camera, sound, grips, and a couple of hands for props. No extras. Peggy came along to handle makeup and costume fixes. Elly came along for everything else that might be needed. The scene I planned did not require much, at least on the surface.

And this time, of course, we went by road. No more little boats for me. No more dirty water curling around the dock. No more pretending I wasn't terrified.

I felt a little desperate. This was the last scene I had. My ghostwriter had gone silent, no pages slid under my door, no typed monologues tucked into glove compartments. And to make it worse, this was the scene Rafe had not wanted to do.

And I still wasn't sure. My every instinct said it was a good scene.

Walking the homestead with Kate, listening to the wind through brittle grass, imagining their voices, I knew it worked. The love story between Blue and Charley held the movie together. Leaving it out made no sense.

The movie was not about danger, betrayal, or even murder. It was about Charley and Blue, what they had meant to each other, what they could have had if the world had not gotten in the way. Without this moment, I felt we would miss the point entirely.

Still, Rafe had not wanted it, and it bothered me more than I wanted to admit. What was I not seeing?

He was the guy who could cut something essential and somehow make the film better. I had watched him do it more than once. Scenes I loved, gone. I only understood why later, when everything clicked into place.

The old house cast long shadows on the dry grass. Birds flitted between fence posts, cautious, as if waiting to see how this day would turn out.

We scouted a spot down the hill from the house, above the bend in the river, and waited while Kate and another crew member brought her boat around from the state park. At least I had given the job to a crew member. Instead, it was Dylan who came with her, smiling and acting as if he had grown up around the swamp.

He had no part in the scene and no business being here. I started to tell him so, but realized I would end up looking like a jealous idiot. I would embarrass Kate, and Dylan would only be amused.

We pulled the boat close to shore and then had Ned and Cassie climb in. We then filmed them getting out with Ned as Charley, looking visibly shaken. Ned was acting, but he captured the way I had felt climbing out of the boat the day before.

The first take was good, but I needed something more. I wanted the kind of fear a man shows when he's forcing himself to be brave for someone else. It took several takes but I finally got what I wanted.

I felt a hand on my shoulder. Kate stood beside me.

"He looks like you did on your trip out here," she said. "A little peakish."

"I was more than just a little," I admitted.

She laughed. Someone yelped about a splinter down at the boat. Kate walked to take care of it.

I watched her go, then turned back to the monitor.

I do love you, Kate, I thought.

We laid the blanket near the house, exactly where Kate and I had put ours. If she noticed the parallel, she said nothing.

The camera rolled. Ned spread the blanket, weighing corners with river stones. Every motion mattered. Cassie stood a few feet away, holding the picnic basket loosely in one hand, brushing the hem of her dress with the other, grounding herself. Her expression was unreadable, but not blank. Almost frightening.

I felt a chill and looked toward the tree line. Nothing. Kate caught my eye, amused.

I turned back to the monitor.

The sun filtered through trees in thin ribbons. Dust swirled in the golden light. One of those moments you do not plan—it just arrives.

Sparks murmured about easing the camera in. I watched for the scripted lines. We had rehearsed this scene a dozen times, but what came next was not in the script.

Cassie turned to her scene partner, eyes distant yet focused.

"I've always loved you, you know. Ever since you knocked me down that day in the hallway in school."

I flipped the script, confused. That line was nowhere to be found.

Ned faltered for a moment, then replied not as an actor, but as someone remembering.

"I didn't mean to knock you down. You just... walked right into me. But I remember thinking you were the prettiest thing I'd ever seen."

It was not Ned. The accent was different, closer to the locals. I felt cold air. Others on set shivered.

Sparks mouthed, Did they change the lines?

I shook my head.

They were not acting. Cassie's voice had softened, a sadder timbre, her eyes glistening, the uncanny shade of blue we had seen on monitors. Almost violet. She was Blue. I had already seen it happen, but never before had I seen Ned change. Maybe I was a better director than I was giving myself credit for.

"You used to leave me those notes," she said. "Folded so small. I kept them in a box under my bed. Mama never knew."

"I remember the box," he replied, voice tight. "Green, broken clasp."

The monitor flickered. The air felt colder. Heavier.

"And then you went away," Blue said. "Why did you leave me?"

"This isn't in the script," Ann said weakly. "Cut."

"No, let it go," I said.

Blue stepped forward, bare feet sinking into the soft earth.

"You went away," she said. "You went away."

"I'm here now," he said.

They embraced. It was supposed to be a short, tentative moment. This was no mere embrace. It was passionate, urgent, like Lancaster and Kerr on a beach with waves crashing over them.

"Cut!" I snapped.

The spell broke.

Both actors blinked, confused.

I stared at the monitor, pulse hammering. This was not method acting. It was a haunting, a memory etched so deep into the land it had found voices again.

Sparks whispered, "You want to tell me what that was?"

"I would," I said, "if I knew."

We took a break. Cassie and Ned seemed oblivious, like it had never happened.

Twenty minutes later, we rolled again.

"Sound speed.""Rolling."The clapper snapped shut."Action."

This time, they followed the script exactly. Love scenes are awkward, but the spell was gone.

"Cut," I said.

Wardrobe straightened Cassie's ribbon. Makeup dabbed Ned's forehead. A grip shifted the reflector to follow the sinking sun.

I stood beyond the monitors, arms crossed, trying to hide my relief. No more odd happenings. The scene worked, but I already knew the first take—the passionate one—would be the one I used.

Across the way, Kate caught my eye. Arms folded, faint smile, amusement flickering in her gaze. She knew exactly what I had done.

She did not need to call me on it. Her look was enough.

"Reset!" Ann called.

Everyone hurried back. Cassie lifted the jar. Roy leaned in. The ghost story began anew, the unspoken sorrow between them tightening.

We did it twice more. We did not need to. I knew I was wasting time.

No blown lines. No malfunctions. No arguments. Maybe everyone sensed the end was near.

Either way, it flowed.

By late afternoon, we wrapped. The sun glinted off black windows as we packed the last of the gear.

"Okay, we're done," I said.

The crew exhaled. Props gathered the blanket, jars, and basket. Equipment clattered into cases.

A tour bus rolled up just as we left.

The spell dissolved.

Movie magic, done.

27.

One of the crew volunteered to take Kate's boat back to the park, and Dylan went along. He wasn't happy about it. I think he expected to ride back with Kate, but she announced she was riding with me.

I probably shouldn't have been so pleased with Dylan's unhappiness, but I'm no saint, and sometimes joy comes from the little things in life.

The van carrying the cast and crew pulled away, disappearing down the winding road. Kate and I stayed behind to help Sparks finish loading the last of the gear onto his truck. Once everything was strapped down, he climbed into the cab, waved tiredly, and we watched his taillights vanish through the thinning trees.

Everything felt suddenly silent. I felt one of those chills again and looked back at the homestead. Did I see a glint of light in the far trees?

"Looking for ghosts?" Kate asked teasingly.

"Maybe I am," I admitted. "All I know is something weird just happened that I can't explain."

"I saw it too," she said. "When they went off script?"

"Yes."

We followed Sparks's van down the narrow frontage road, the late afternoon sun casting long shadows. The trees thinned as we approached the highway, the sounds of the forest giving way to distant traffic hum.

Somewhere along the way, I pulled off onto a shaded stretch of road about a mile from Mossy Creek Campground. Pine trees crowded close, their scent sharp in the warm air. We sat in silence.

"And we're stopping here because...?" Kate asked.

I kissed her.

She didn't stop me.

I kissed her again.

"I haven't been parking since I was seventeen," she protested.

"It's good to stay in practice."

Another kiss. This time, she leaned in. The hesitation slipped away. Warm, certain, the kind of kiss that makes the world tilt. Her hand found the back of my neck, her lips pressing firmly against mine, and for a moment, I felt like I could stay there forever.

She pulled back, breath quick. "This is getting more complicated by the second."

"Yes," I said, and kissed her again.

Ten minutes later, she pressed her hands gently to my chest, letting me up for air.

"This is not a good idea," she said.

"It's a great idea," I replied.

"Let's get back to the campground."

She was serious, so I drove slowly, keeping one eye on the road, the other on her.

"I'm thinking I should be at least mildly insulted," Kate said, breaking the silence.

I blinked, caught off guard. "Why? Did you hate kissing me that badly?"

She smiled, eyes sharp, teasing. "You used our day in your script. That walk, that conversation—the entire afternoon. Word for word. I should get a percentage of the movie."

"If there ever is a percentage," I said with a shrug, "you're welcome to it."

She raised an eyebrow. "Do I hear a note of self-doubt?"

"More than a note," I admitted with a grin. "It's practically a symphony."

"I know nothing about making a movie," she said, "but I think it's good."

"I hope it is," I said. "A lot of people are counting on it."

"But what happened this afternoon?" she asked.

"I'm not sure," I said. "Maybe Cassie and Ned forgot their lines. Anyway, we got it straightened out."

I didn't tell her part of me half-thought Cassie and Ned had been possessed by Blue and Charley. Out loud, it would sound insane.

We drove into the campground and spotted a dark blue BMW near the front door. Faded paint, worn tires, the body covered in dings and scratches. Ellis Dubois stood on the steps, facing Ann, who was rigid, her face red with emotion. Few things brought Ann to tears.

"What does our neighborhood ambulance chaser want?" Kate asked.

Kate followed me up the stairs. Ann looked near tears. "He's here for Rafe's movie," she said, voice cracking. "He claims he owns it. Wants everything."

Ellis tried to smile and failed as I walked up the steps, Kate behind me.

"Noah," he said. "Noah, this is a misunderstanding, I'm sure."

"Then you're not here to steal the movie?" I asked.

"Not steal. Of course not. Your bosses back in California sold the rights to the movie, and my client expects everything in his custody. The Bible, rough cuts, notes, every scrap. He's purchased it outright." He tapped his fingers together like a magician about to pull a rabbit from a hat.

"You're not getting anything," I said, teeth tight.

He blinked rapidly, as if the world were more complicated than his morning crossword. "It's not my idea," he said, voice trembling slightly, "but... my client owns the rights." He added emphasis like it was sacred, leaning forward eagerly, as if my agreement could make it true.

"Who is your client?"

"I'm not at liberty to say."

"You're not getting the movie, and neither is your client. I suspect you are involved somehow in Simone Laviolette's death. Perhaps you don't have a client at all. Maybe you're trying to buy the movie for yourself."

He blinked and stepped back.

"I don't have that kind of money," he said.

"But it's starting to make sense. Both Jace and Charley are dead. You and Claire are the last of your group. I saw the photo at the Laviolette Homestead. Charley, Jace, Blue, and even Claire were in front. You were tucked in the shadows. Always in the background. A third wheel?"

Dubois's shoulders stiffened. I saw anger flare in his eyes. I almost felt sorry for him. I knew insecurity.

"I... I was told we could get a court order," he said, fiddling with his pen as if it might summon authority.

"But you don't currently have one?"

He forced a smile that barely masked panic. "I don't want to get nasty with a court order."

Other members of the cast and crew were gathering on the porch.

"But that's what you're going to have to do," I said, stepping closer.

Kate stepped past me. "Go ahead, Ellis. Talk to the sheriff. He doesn't think much of you. I seem to remember him saying he'd kick you into the street next time you showed up in his office. I'd like to see that."

"Look," I said, keeping calm, "you're not taking Rafe's work, so take a hike before someone helps you leave."

He stepped back, nearly losing balance. "Are you threatening me?"

"It wasn't a threat," Sparks said, stepping forward. Ellis's eyes widened. He hurried to his car and drove away.

Ann let out a shaky breath, relief washing over her face. I put a hand on her shoulder. "He's not taking anything today," I said firmly.

I wasn't as brave as I looked. We returned to our rooms. I showered, then called Rita.

"I've just had a lawyer show up claiming his client owns the movie."

"Who's his client?"

"I haven't a clue."

"Then the lawyer hasn't got word yet," she said, relief in her voice. "Griggs just had his lawyer reach out. He's capitulating. He'll continue financing the movie and handle distribution as well."

"But why did Dubois think his client owned it?"

"Probably a communication breakdown. You did the right thing. Griggs can't sell it, not with the audit hanging over him like a dark cloud."

"You think that's why he called you? The audit?"

"For sure. He's worried about my questions regarding Rafe's will. He's running scared."

"But he'll still finance the movie?"

"Only if you stop the audit."

I sighed. "And your advice?"

"You could get what you've wanted all along—the movie finished—and work out arrangements with Griggs to cover what you've already spent."

"But your advice?"

"I think Griggs is a crook. Wait until Rafe's will is read. Continue with the audit."

"What's the worst that could happen?"

"I could be wrong. Griggs isn't cheating. Rafe left you nothing. The movie succeeds, he takes all the credit, and fires you."

"But you'll still give me a job?"

"Of course."

"Go ahead with the audit," I said.

"You know," Rita said, laughing, "I was hoping you'd say that. I just hope, when it's over, you end up with enough money to pay my fee."

She was laughing when she hung up.

28.

Just before dark, I left the campground and walked across the highway to where a fire was burning. The low thump of country music reached me, mingling with the unmistakable scent of burning coals and slow-cooked meat. Smoke drifted lazily into the evening sky from the fire. String lights were draped between trees like fireflies frozen in midair.

Long folding tables sprawled across the grass, littered with paper plates, half-empty bowls of chips, plastic cups, and a cooler overflowing with soda, ice melting fast in the southern heat. A Bluetooth speaker near the food table pumped out Charley Pride.

Kate sat in a camp chair near the fire, her face flushed from the warmth and activity.

"Burgers are already cooked under the pan," she said.

I grabbed a paper plate, adding sliced tomato, lettuce, and charbroiled burgers from the table. I grabbed some potato chips from a nearby bag, a Coke, and made my way back to her, claiming an empty chair beside hers.

I noticed Paul Deerfield nearby, deep in conversation with a stranger about politics and the economy.

"This is Dad's favorite time," Kate said. "He'll argue all night, taking all sides of everything. He just likes to argue."

I ate my burger and listened. Politics usually bored me, but tonight the stories kept shifting, weaving in local history and personal tales. I found myself drawn in, partly because the stories were interesting, and partly because this was Kate's heritage—and I wanted to know as much about her as I could.

I hadn't realized how much time had passed until Kate touched my hand.

"It's getting late, and I'm tired. Walk me back. Unless you want to stir the Brunswick stew."

"I'll pass. Maybe some other time."

We said goodnight to Paul and started down the gravel path, just as Dylan stumbled into the firelight—drunk, sloppy, and angry.

"Let's dance, Kate," he slurred, holding a half-empty beer like a bouquet.

"I don't think so," she said firmly.

"Come on, baby. Don't make me beg."

"Leave it alone, Dylan," I said.

His bloodshot eyes darted to me, lips curling. "Well, well. Noah, you think you're ready to go a couple of rounds with me?"

"I'm ready," Paul said, his voice low and dangerous. "You need to leave."

Dylan laughed, sharp and bitter. "Whatever. You all take yourselves too seriously." He turned, muttering, and staggered toward the cooler.

"And he promised to take me to Hollywood," Kate said, shaking her head.

I laughed.

"Do you think he'll be okay?" she asked.

"Dylan's an actor," I said with a shrug. "Always on stage. Appearing drunk or out of control is part of the act. The play's the thing. He'll convince himself you were his one unrequited love and use it for emotional leverage."

"You sound cynical about actors."

"Some of my best friends are actors," I said.

Kate laughed.

We left the firelight behind, walking side by side. The woods hummed with cicadas. Pine and swamp water thickened the air. Moonlight glinted off the road, and somewhere, a bullfrog croaked like a distant drumbeat.

"I wanted to tell you," she said softly. "The day we spent at the homestead... it was very nice. The nicest time I've had since David died."

"But...?" I prompted gently.

"We're just so different."

Moonlight caught the line of her jaw and the soft curve of her mouth. I wasn't expecting it when she kissed me.

It wasn't like the tentative, exploratory kiss the day I parked. It wasn't fireworks or swelling music. It was quiet, warm, real. Her lips brushed mine, light and certain. Her hand found mine in the dark, fingers curling between mine like a secret.

She pulled back slowly, breath mingling with mine.

"Wow," I whispered.

Kate grinned. "Yeah. Wow."

We held that quiet for a long second. Back at the fire, music rose again—laughter, clinking bottles, smoke drifting into the trees. But here in the dark, it was just us. And maybe Simone Laviolette, if she was watching.

29.

I woke to the sound of shouting and a car horn blaring somewhere outside. It was still early, but the day had already begun without me. After a quick shower, I grabbed coffee and a muffin and stepped outside, squinting into the sunlight.

Kate was already up, sitting on the porch rail. She wore shorts, a black T-shirt advertising a band I'd never heard of, and tennis shoes.

Without asking, she took my coffee cup and sipped from it. The gesture felt oddly intimate. I found that I liked it.

The narrow road through camp was packed with cars, every make and model wedged into whatever space could be found. The newly cleared parking area beyond the tree line was already full, and sometime during the night, even more tents had appeared across the grounds. Bright domes and sagging canopies stretched out like a patchwork quilt.

The Fourth of July celebration had started.

People from Folkston and the smaller towns scattered along the edge of the swamp had arrived in force. Lawn chairs formed loose circles beneath pop-up tents. Coolers sat open in the shade. American flags hung from pickup trucks, porch rails, and stroller handles.

Children tore through the crowd with popsicles and watermelon, their laughter rising above the steady thump of an upright bass from the makeshift stage in the center of the grounds. A bluegrass band played there, the fiddle leading while a banjo cut sharply through the rhythm.

From the loudspeaker near the stage came a burst of static and an announcement.

"Three-legged races in twenty minutes!"

Kate slipped her hand around my arm. "C'mon. It'll be fun."

"I'm not convinced."

"Don't be stuffy," she said, already pulling me toward the signup table.

Ten minutes later, we were standing at the starting line with a faded red bandana tied tightly around our ankles. The summer sun pressed down, and the grass beneath our feet was patchy and uneven.

"This is a bad idea," I muttered.

Kate grinned at me. "A faint heart never won fair lady. Or a three-legged race."

The whistle blew, and the field lurched into motion.

Pairs stumbled forward in tangled rhythm while spectators shouted encouragement. Someone fell almost immediately, bringing their partner down with them. Another pair spun in a slow circle before collapsing into the grass.

Kate counted softly under her breath, guiding our steps. "One, two. One, two."

We lurched forward together, barely coordinated but somehow upright. By the time we crossed the finish line, we were both laughing and out of breath.

"We didn't win," Kate said, pushing her hair out of her face.

"But we didn't eat dirt," I replied. "I'm calling that a victory."

She laughed and slapped my hand in a high five while the bandana hung loose around our ankles like a surrendered flag.

Afterward, we wandered through the maze of vendor tents while our legs recovered. Families crowded the walkways, and the smell of deep-fried food hung heavy in the warm air—ribs, hamburgers, hot dogs, fish, and something sugary that might have been funnel cake. We stopped at a booth selling candy apples and walked away with sticky fingers and lips, the sun warm against our backs.

For a while, the day felt easy. Whatever tension had been building around the film and the script seemed distant.

We were passing the softball field when Sparks called out from the fence.

"Hey, Noah! We're short a hitter."

I hesitated, but Kate nudged me with her elbow. "You play, don't you?"

"Not much."

"That's not what I asked."

I borrowed a glove and jogged out to center field for a few innings. Kate joined the batting lineup and came up third. When the pitch arrived, she swung hard and sent the ball sailing over left field, nearly into the parking lot. She rounded the bases with both arms raised while the crowd along the fence cheered.

In the field, she played just as fiercely, snagging two fly balls and making a scrambling throw to third that caught a runner by a step. I couldn't have made that throw.

When my turn came to bat, I expected a quick out. I planted my feet at the plate while Kate stood on second base, grinning at me.

"Hit it over the trees!" she called.

The first pitch came straight down the middle. I swung, and the crack of the bat surprised me almost as much as the ball sailing high over left field.

By the time I finished circling the bases, the team was cheering and slapping my back. Kate jogged beside me, laughing.

"See?" she said. "You're full of surprises."

After the game, we wandered through another row of booths selling homemade crafts. Crocheted dishcloths in loud oranges and greens hung beside jars of preserves. Wooden bowls and chairs were stacked beside a table of thick fudge squares.

Halfway down the row, I stopped so abruptly that Kate nearly walked into me.

"What is it?"

I wasn't looking at her.

My attention had locked onto a folding table covered with paperbacks. A cardboard sign read:

USED BOOKS — PROCEEDS TO LOCAL GIRL GUIDES

Behind the table sat a woman in her seventies with gray-blonde hair pinned into a loose bun and wire-rim glasses balanced on her nose. She was signing a book for a young boy.

A banner beside her read:

MEET THE AUTHOR — AUGUSTA BLOOM

The name landed heavily in my chest.

Spread across the table were the *Moonbeam Meadows Mysteries*—*The Lantern in the Marsh*, *The Clocktower Cipher*, and *The Secret of Briar Hollow*. I had read those books until the spines cracked and the pages loosened from their glue. I used to hide beneath the covers with a flashlight long after I was supposed to be asleep.

Kate touched my arm. "Noah?"

But my mind was somewhere else.

The rhythm of the dialogue in the anonymous script pages. The quiet humor. The way information slipped naturally into conversation.

Suddenly, the familiarity made sense.

I knew that voice. I had grown up reading it.

"Augusta Bloom," I said quietly.

Kate followed my gaze to the banner. "Oh. Have you heard of her? She lives somewhere around here. Camp Pinckney, I think."

The woman looked up and met my eyes.

Something in her expression told me she already knew who I was.

I stepped closer to the table. She handed the signed book to the boy and patted his shoulder before he hurried away.

"I'm a big fan," I said.

"Really?" she replied with a small smile.

"And it's quite a coincidence finding you here."

"Oh?"

"I'm not a big fan of coincidence."

She studied my face for a moment before letting out a soft sigh.

"Then perhaps we should talk."

We carried our lemonade to a picnic table beneath the oaks. The drink was colder than I expected and sharp with real lemon and sugar. Children laughed somewhere behind us, and a dog barked once in the distance.

I was still trying to process the fact that Augusta Bloom, the author whose books had filled half my childhood, was sitting across from me.

And that she might also be the anonymous writer behind our movie.

"You and Rafe had a thing," I said.

She lifted an eyebrow. "A thing?"

"You were involved when he was adapting your books. I figured maybe you told him about Blue's murder and he promised to make a film about it."

"In a fit of passion?" she said dryly. "You do have a flair for dialogue, Noah. Rafe mentioned that. But no—I didn't tell him about Blue."

I wasn't convinced.

"You're not denying the two of you were involved."

"No."

"And you're not denying that you've been writing our script."

A faint smile crossed her face. "Guilty."

Kate leaned forward. "Why keep it secret? Noah says the script is excellent."

"Rafe preferred it that way."

"He wanted a ghostwriter?" I asked.

"He had his reasons."

"Did he have a reason for leaving the script unfinished?" I said. "Right now it doesn't have an ending."

"I'm still working on the final scenes."

"And do those scenes name the murderer?"

She shook her head gently. "I think you've misunderstood the kind of movie Rafe wanted. He was making a love story, not a murder mystery. The ending won't name the killer."

"Then the movie is toast," I said.

Her fingers tapped thoughtfully on the table. "If you were writing it, how would you end it?"

"I'd name the murderer."

"Besides that."

I considered the story again, returning to something that had troubled me from the beginning.

"A good film needs emotion," I said. "Characters the audience cares about. Stakes that actually matter. We've already got all of that." I watched her for a moment. "You say Rafe was making a love story. If that's true, then what happened to the love between Charley and Blue? Why did Charley go off and join the Army if he loved Blue so much?"

"I think you're finally beginning to understand," Augusta said. "What would be your theory?"

"I think Charley told her he loved her, just like Jace."

"And you're thinking she turned him down?"

"Exactly."

"Unrequited love," she murmured. "And that drives him to enlist? I agree it's one possibility, but it's not what happened."

"How can you be so sure what happened?" I asked.

Augusta's gaze drifted past us toward the edge of the park, as though another time lay layered over this one.

"There's a difference between telling a story and remembering one."

"What do you mean?" I asked.

"The name you know me by—Augusta Bloom—is a pen name."

"That part isn't surprising."

"My real name," she said quietly, "is Augusta Snow."

Kate blinked.

The name struck me a moment later. Snow.

Augusta met my eyes steadily.

"I know why Charley joined the Army because I was there," she said.

A long silence settled between us.

"I'm Charley Snow's little sister."

30.

When night finally fell, Kate and I crossed the road hand in hand and settled onto the creaky boards of her porch. Fireflies blinked in the tall grass, and a warm breeze carried the distant sound of music from the fairgrounds. Then the first firework burst above the tree line, a sudden bloom of color that made the night sky gasp.

"Charley Snow's little sister," Kate said. "I guess truth is sometimes stranger than fiction, and now I'm all curious about the real reason Charley joined the Army."

"I don't want to think about the movie right now," I said.

"Oh?"

As the clusters of light rippled across her face, I found myself watching her instead of the sky. The glow caught in her eyes, turning them into something I couldn't look away from.

"You're staring at me," she said.

"That's because I never, ever want to look at anyone else. I never want to be with anyone else. I'm in love with you."

She was quiet for a long moment, long enough that the silence between us felt like another kind of light, softer, more dangerous.

"You just think you are."

"I've never felt like this before," I said. "I'd know if it were just a thought."

She smiled faintly, almost sadly. "It's the ribs," she said. "That special sauce is some of the best in the world. It messes with your head."

"You don't feel anything for me?" I asked.

"Oh, I do," she said, and shrugged, eyes returning to the fireworks. "But it's complicated."

"Complicated," I echoed. The word tasted heavy, like smoke that wouldn't clear.

"Let's just leave it like that," she murmured. "For now."

The next firework exploded overhead, scattering light across her hair. She didn't look at me, and I didn't look away.

Morning came too early. I woke up feeling a few more aches from all the walking, three-legged races, and baseball swings from the day before. I also woke up thinking about the coincidence of Augusta Bloom being Charley Snow's little sister, and what answers she had for me in the yet unwritten part of the script.

I heard a faint patter of rain on the roof—soft enough that I wasn't sure at first if I was imagining it. When I looked through the glass doors, the creek had vanished behind a wall of fog, thick and quiet, almost glowing in the muted morning light.

I took a long, hot shower, hoping it would loosen the stiffness in my legs. After drying off, I wandered back to the bedroom and sat on the edge of the bed, listening as the rain settled into a steady rhythm, wondering what kind of day it was going to be.

July fifth. My birthday. It felt old to me, a quarter of a century. People my age usually know what they're doing. They've finished college. They've started jobs and families. People of twenty-five have plans, savings accounts, and routines.

I was twenty-five and feeling slightly sorry for myself. I was in love for the first time, and she didn't believe me. I still wasn't sure if I had talent enough to finish Rafe's movie, and someone in the cast or crew might have murdered my father. Life was confusing.

When my phone rang, I had a feeling my day was about to get worse.

"You've been busy," Griggs said, his voice tight, brittle.

"Good morning to you, too," I said. "Are you calling to wish me a happy birthday?"

He was quiet for a moment. Even after giving me a watch, he had forgotten the date. "Yeah, happy birthday. You went behind my back and hired a lawyer. Why?"

"I told you I wanted to finish this movie."

"But the Butcher," he said. "You know what she's known for?"

"For fighting for her clients? I needed someone in my corner."

"I've always been in your corner," Griggs said. "I've always taken care of you."

"I'm going to finish Rafe's movie," I said.

He drew in a slow, steady breath. Part of me had hoped Rita was wrong, that he would snap at me, tell me to take a flying leap off a high bridge, let her conduct the audit just to prove it, and then throw me out for good.

But he didn't. His voice stayed calm, almost accommodating. "I guess I didn't understand how much this means to you," he said. "Maybe we could sit down and talk. You could come here."

"I'm going to stay here until the movie is finished," I said.

I could tell he didn't like my answer, but he took another deep breath. "Okay. I'll come out there."

"You know you hate to travel," I reminded him.

Except for Las Vegas, I said to myself.

"We need to discuss this," he said.

"There's no time for discussion," I said. "I need to finish the movie, and then we'll talk." I thought of something else. "Oh, and you need to call the person who claims you sold him the movie and tell him the deal is off."

He waited a few heartbeats before speaking again.

"I can do that. We'll talk when you get back. We'll decide together what to do going forward." There was a catch in his voice. "But we don't need that woman interfering in our business. Call her now and tell her we don't need any kind of outside audit."

I felt a tightness in my chest. Rita's prophecy was coming true. Griggs sounded conciliatory, but for one reason only. He was desperate to stop any kind of audit. It meant Rita was right. Griggs was stealing. Dull, dry, antiseptic Griggs was stealing from the company and from our investors, all to impress a woman.

"I think we'll go ahead with the audit," I said.

"It's not necessary," Griggs said.

"I believe it is," I said.

He muttered something crude under his breath and hung up.

It went through my mind that Griggs wasn't family by blood, but he was the last connection to my mother I had left. I had just burned that bridge, and it wasn't a good feeling.

Happy birthday, Noah.

Top of Form

Bottom of Form

The rain began to taper off, the steady rhythm softening into scattered drips sliding from the eaves. I finally pulled myself off the bed and dressed: jeans, a soft T-shirt, and tennis shoes.

The hallway outside my room smelled faintly of coffee and something warm, cinnamon, maybe. The fog outside the windows was lifting in slow strips, like someone peeling gauze from a wound.

I stepped into the dining room and found an explosion of noise and color.

Balloons bobbed against the ceiling in wild clusters, silver, cobalt, and a few that shimmered with iridescent glitter whenever they caught the light. Banners swooped across the walls, each one hand-painted or hastily scrawled, all of them shouting some variation of HAPPY 25TH, NOAH! in bold, joyful strokes. Someone, Sparks probably, had even rigged a string of tiny LED lights to blink in rhythmic bursts, as if attempting to dance along with the chaos in the room.

Most of the cast and crew had managed to squeeze themselves around the dining room, chairs dragged from every corner of the house to accommodate the crowd. A few latecomers followed me in.

Then they started singing.

The cramped dining room was no place for so many voices to sing Happy Birthday, especially when so many were off-key. One person, I suspected intentionally, sang an octave too low. Someone else clapped on the wrong beat, loud enough to rattle the windows. But the energy was enough to make the floorboards tremble. Laughter wove through the melody, and by the time they reached the final stretched out "YOUUUUU!" the building felt like it might lift off its foundations.

The last note finally collapsed with cheering, applauding, and slapping me on the back, a few of them hitting harder than necessary. I had a feeling I was going to be bruised from where Dylan hit me.

"Silence," Kate demanded, and the room grew quiet. "It is the tradition that the birthday person gets their wish for breakfast, anything with reason." She held up a hand. "And before you ask, anything within reason includes anything that is currently in our pantry."

"An omelet," I said.

"Your wish is the chef's desire," Kate said

I desired the chef with every fiber of my being, but I was smart enough not to say it out loud.

I was huddled into a seat where Ann put a paper crown on my head, and Elly Wright put a luscious-looking blueberry muffin on the table with a single candle.

"Figured I owed you one," Elly said.

I blew the candle out, and both Elly and Ann bent down and kissed me on both cheeks while a half-dozen people took photos on their phones.

I had a feeling I would be getting texts with that particular photo for the rest of my life. I didn't mind.

31.

A sound woke me. I was not generally a light sleeper, but I think I was half-hoping Kate actually would come knocking on my door. I had considered knocking on hers, but I was sure she'd only give me a look of sad amusement and slam the door in my face. Or call for her father to bring his shotgun. No, I thought. Kate would not need her father. If there was any shooting to be done, she'd handle it herself.

I still wasn't sure what awakened me, but I listened for a moment and then rolled over and tried to go back to sleep.

Just as Cassie Rhodes started screaming. Again.

High, panicked, blood-chilling.

Please, I thought, heart already hammering, not another bear.

I was out of bed and halfway into my pants before my brain even caught up. No shirt, no shoes, no clue what time it was. Just adrenaline, cold air, and the sound of chaos barreling through the hallway like a freight train.

Someone was shouting. Something heavy crashed. A table, maybe. Or a chair. The lodge echoed with the sharp slap of movement and panic.

I stumbled out of my room, still barefoot, heart racing. Just ahead, near the lobby, a struggle was unfolding. Frantic. Violent.

Someone stood at the door of the editing room, dressed all in black, with a stocking mask distorting his features. He carried a bunch of script scenes in one hand and Rafe's laptop computer in the other.

I had a moment of panic myself. Though I had started saving everything on a RAID disk for transport to Los Angeles, I still hadn't finished. There was important information still on that laptop.

Cassie was on the floor, crouched around both his knees like some tiny, furious wolverine. Her arms gripped with a desperation that made it clear she wasn't letting go voluntarily. He kicked out savagely, trying to dislodge her. She bit him just below the knee, and he screamed.

I didn't hesitate. I charged toward him and hit him square in the chest hard enough to knock him stumbling backward, straight into the editing room doorframe. And, naturally, Cassie came along for the ride. She clung on like a tiny, screaming burr, her arms still wrapped around him. I was proud of her.

Our intruder staggered, swinging the laptop in a wild arc that slammed into my shoulder with a sharp thwack but did little real damage. I snatched it out of his hands, only to be shoved backward as he rammed his shoulder into me.

I was already off balance, wobbling like a drunk tightrope walker, doing a comical two-second dance to stay upright and trying not to step on Cassie. My bare foot snagged a cord, and gravity won. The laptop slipped from my grasp, and our intruder grabbed it up again.

I caught myself on the edge of a swivel chair that broke my fall. I hit my rear pretty hard, but it was a lot better than face-first.

Cassie squealed as our intruder finally broke free of her and headed for the front door.

"Who's making all the noise?"

Sparks stepped out of his room. One look was all it took for him to understand what was happening. He charged the intruder with far more strength and determination than I'd managed. Unfortunately, Cassie was trying to get to her feet, and most of his momentum sent her spinning across a nearby couch.

Sparks and the intruder locked together, with the intruder still desperately holding both a handful of scripts and the laptop. Sparks grunted, shifting his weight, trying to drag the man down. The stranger must have been stronger than he looked, because he twisted violently, nearly breaking free.

I heard more voices—people waking up, coming out of their rooms to see what all the noise was about.

The guy bolted toward the front door, bare feet slapping against the wooden floor, still clutching everything like they were winning lottery tickets and he was five seconds from cashing in.

Sparks lunged after him and, with a burst of effort, managed to grab hold of the man's leg. They both went down hard, the thud echoing through the lodge. Sparks clung to him, trying to drag him back, but the man twisted and lashed out, kicking Sparks square in the face with the heel of his foot.

The intruder scrambled upright again, just steps from freedom, one hand already reaching for the doorknob.

I heard a yell from the top of the stairs and looked up to see Roy Sterling. He waved two .22 pistols around his head like a cartoonish Tasmanian Devil, his eyes doing two entirely different things—one wide open, the other half-shut in a lazy squint.

He wore dark blue pajama pants, slipping halfway down one hip and threatening mutiny. His tank top sagged so low it could've doubled as a hammock, and across his belly bloomed a questionable red stain—wine? Barbecue sauce?

"I got this!" he yelled.

He pointed both pistols at the intruder. I silently thanked Sparks for taking all his cartridges just as the front entrance exploded outward in a spectacular crash of wood and glass. The intruder froze, as if simply touching the doorknob had triggered the apocalypse.

Then the would-be thief did the smart thing. He dropped everything in his hands and bolted, slipping past the shattered doorway into the night.

"Roy's got bullets!" I yelled at Sparks.

"Cartridges," Sparks corrected, diving behind a sturdy-looking couch.

"Great—cartridges. I'll make sure that's on my tombstone."

Roy was too drunk to notice the intruder had already escaped. He lurched down a couple of steps and fired again. I never saw where the bullets went, since I was busy trying not to die. One of the shots must have come close to Ann's room by the kitchen, because she shouted, "You drunken moron, stop shooting!" and then sensibly retreated inside.

He took another step down the stairway, pausing slightly.

"I'll shoot!" he bellowed, despite having clearly already done that.

I stood up in the editing room to yell at him. It was a serious mistake. I'd barely shouted, "The guy's gone, Roy!" when he spun toward me with both fingers on the triggers. I dropped to the floor again just as he fired, the pistols shattering the glass above my head.

My brain screamed, "Oh no, not again, stupid," but I still thrust my arms out to catch myself. My right wrist gave way like tissue paper. The world tipped violently. My nose met the floor with a painful crunch, and I lay there blinking.

I scrambled around on the floor and realized my nose was bleeding and my wrist hurt like fire again. I met Kate halfway, also on her knees.

"Don't stand up," I warned. "He's still shooting."

Roy fired again. I could see the far wall behind the reception counter, and I saw Roy kill Walter Brennan. Brennan's glass-covered smile shattered into glittering shrapnel as the bullet tore through the lamp and into Brennan's autographed picture.

I saw Cassie had curled up behind a couch. Her eyes were wide with fear, and her face pale. I hoped Roy didn't shoot her. I hoped we all lived long enough for me to tell her what a great job she'd done saving the laptop.

I peeked at the staircase. At least Roy had stopped shooting. He stood only a few steps down from the top, but he was still waving those pistols around like a crazed Tasmanian Devil. I didn't stand up again.

I saw Peggy Marsh step out of her room at the top of the stairs, right beside Roy's. For a heartbeat, the world seemed to pause. I prayed Roy wouldn't turn around. She was only inches away, fully exposed, impossible to miss.

She took a single step. Roy must have sensed her presence because his shoulders twitched and he began to turn.

Peggy moved.

She rushed him like a Rams linebacker hitting the gap and slammed into him chest-high. The impact knocked the breath out of him and sent him reeling backward. His heels caught empty air.

Roy pitched down the stairs alone, arms flailing, pistols flying free as his body struck step after step. Bone cracked against wood. The railing rattled. His head snapped back hard enough to make me wince as he bounced, twisted, and finally disappeared in a violent heap at the bottom.

I thought he was dead. I heard a sickening sound as his head hit the bottom step, and he didn't move after that.

Peggy showed no remorse. "I hope I killed the fool."

Kate and Sparks rushed over and turned him onto his back. Like me, he was bleeding from the nose, but he was breathing. I doubt a sober man would have survived the tumble down the steps.

Cassie stood over him, hugging herself and seemingly unaware that her already transparent nightgown was getting even more transparent from the rain blowing through the doorway.

Not that I noticed.

"He's not dead," Kate said. "He's snoring."

"Fools and drunks walk away," Peggy said. "Everybody else pays."

Ann was wrapped in a quilted bathrobe and looking grim. She took one look at Cassie and snapped, "Go put some clothes on."

Cassie squeaked and vanished into her room.

"Don't be hard on her," I told Ann. "She might've just saved all our lives, plus our movie."

"Our movie?" Ann asked.

"He had Rafe's laptop when Cassie grabbed him."

A trail of damp script pages heading toward the front door was turning into pulpy confetti. Sparks found a heavy blanket, and I helped him pin it to the door to stop more damage.

"You're bleeding," he said.

"I think my nose is broken," I said. "And I'm sure my wrist is again."

"Did you recognize him?"

"I did."

"Ellis Dubois," Sparks said. "Even in that stupid mask, you couldn't mistake him."

Ann came out of the kitchen with a towel and a first-aid kit. "We should call an ambulance. Just in case. Roy hit his head pretty hard."

"Nothing can hurt that fool," Peggy said.

Ann knelt and gently draped a wet towel over Roy's face like he was a fallen soldier.

"I'll tell you one thing," Sparks said. "If he's not dead, he's not getting these guns back until we leave this place."

"Amen to that," I said.

I looked toward the autographed photo of Walter Brennan and the hole just above his right eye. Tough old bird—shot in the head, still grinning.

32.

By the time things finally settled, daylight was bleeding through the edges of the curtains. The living room looked like the aftermath of a war zone. Glass crunched underfoot with every step, furniture was skewed at strange angles, and the air still carried the coppery tang of blood, sweat, and adrenaline.

The paramedics were the first to arrive, their red-and-blue lights flickering across the walls like a broken nightclub strobe. Most of our attention had been on Roy and the purpling wound blooming across his forehead. They managed to rouse him briefly; he slurred something incoherent, but between the alcohol in his system and what was clearly a concussion, he was out cold again before they could finish checking his vitals. They strapped him to a stretcher and loaded him into the ambulance, promising to keep him under observation at the hospital.

Kate had managed to stop my bleeding nose, and the paramedics spent some time wrapping my wrist again and telling me to see a doctor as soon as possible. It was definitely broken. Again. At least my fingers were only sprained. They suggested aspirin for the pain. I was thinking amputation might be better.

An unhappy Paul showed up just as a young deputy entered the house. Despite the softness of the deputy's baby face, his expression had the hardened, quiet watchfulness of someone who'd seen too much, too young. He didn't speak much at first. Just observed. Took in the scene. The broken glass. The overturned coffee table. The blood on the carpet. The unease in our eyes.

Then the questions began.

Rapid fire. Clinical. Efficient. About the break-in, the shots fired, the gun, the contents of the desk drawer. Who owned what. Who lived where? Why were film scripts locked away like state secrets? Who would want to stop the movie?

More questions. Exactly how did my nose and wrist get broken? Who hit Roy in the head?

The last question made Peggy look uncomfortable, but we explained that it was either hit in the head or wait until Roy ran out of ammunition.

The officer seemed a little awed by Cassie. Perhaps he was a fan of the Winthrop Saga, but he questioned her a little more gently than the rest of us. All of us were praising Cassie for being a heroine, and I think it made her feel a part of things for the first time.

Cassie told her story. She'd been thirsty. She couldn't sleep, so she got up to get something to drink. Her room was in the hallway, directly across from the editing room. She'd opened the door and saw the thief in the editing room. She tried to stop him.

The officer's expression showed what he thought of skinny little Cassie trying to stop a thief, but I was proud of her. I could tell Ann was also, and she was in her mother-hen mode.

"And you, sir?" the young deputy asked me. "You were injured by the thief."

"He struck me, but I was hurt mostly from falling."

I didn't tell him that I broke my nose trying not to get shot by Roy.

"And you didn't recognize the intruder?"

I felt Sparks looking at me as I shook my head. We both knew it was Ellis. I'm not sure why I didn't tell him.

Paul offered a detailed layout of the property and listed who had been staying in which room. Kate hovered near the front doorway; her arms folded tightly across her chest like she was holding something in.

When the deputy finally closed his notebook, he gave us a long, unreadable look.

"Someone will be in touch," he said, then turned and walked out into the gray light of morning.

It was still too early for the caterers to arrive for breakfast. Too late to pretend we'd ever sleep. The house had gone quiet again, but the silence didn't bring peace, just the echo of everything we weren't saying. One by one, we drifted toward the dining room, drawn like survivors clinging to routine. Ann brewed coffee. We gathered around the long table, the mugs warm in our hands, the steam rising like lifelines in the cold morning air.

Cassie had stopped crying and was wrapped in a quilted robe, her hair sleep-mussed and her eyes red-rimmed. She looked smaller than usual. Fragile. And Ann kept fussing over her. It had taken almost getting herself killed, but Cassie had finally become a part of the company.

Kate slid into the seat next to mine.

She sat close, closer than she had to. Her leg brushed mine under the table. It might've been casual. Maybe even accidental. But the contact lingered. She didn't move, and neither did I. She wore leggings, an old college sweatshirt faded at the seams, and worn-out slip-on Skechers. Her hair was still tangled, matted from sleep, and her face was bare, no makeup, just soft shadows beneath her eyes.

There was something about her like that, unguarded, stripped of her usual armor, that twisted something in my chest. It wasn't exactly desire. It was quieter than that. Heavier. More dangerous.

I looked up and found Paul watching me.

He wasn't glaring. Not quite. But there was a tension behind his stare, a cold calculation, like a scientist watching a specimen react under pressure. He didn't look at Kate. Only me. And suddenly, he looked less friendly and more like a protective father.

Then, without breaking eye contact, he lifted his mug and took a slow sip of coffee.

"Why does that man want our movie so badly?" Ann asked, her voice flat but wound tight around the edges, like she already knew the answer and just couldn't bring herself to say it aloud.

The question landed hard in the room.

Chairs creaked. Mugs paused mid-air. All eyes turned to me.

Before I could speak, Sparks leaned forward, elbows braced on the table, his gaze fixed on Ann.

"It's been obvious from the start," he said. His voice was low and even, but it carried an edge, a sharpness just under the surface. "Someone doesn't want this movie made."

Ann blinked. "I don't understand. Why? What could be so dangerous about a film?"

"Good question," Sparks muttered, leaning back. He exhaled like he was tired of asking himself.

"And how does breaking into an office and stealing a few old scripts stop anything?" Kate asked. "Or even stealing the laptop? Isn't everything on Rafe's laptop backed up?"

"Normally," I said.

Everyone looked a little sheepish.

Kate looked at me. "What's different this time?"

It was Sparks who answered. He leaned back in his chair, taking a slow sip of coffee. "Normally, we've got backups everywhere. It's the three-two-one rule. We make three copies on two different types of media, and we store one copy off-site. The other two copies are in constant flux. The director, the assistant director, and the cinematographer all use those copies to edit."

"But Rafe didn't do it that way this time," I continued. "I was stunned in the beginning to find out he had only one copy on his laptop. If he was sending stuff off-site, he made no notations of where. He even kept Ann from looking at what was on digital, and he'd never done that before."

Kate blinked. "But that seems crazy."

"I think Rafe knew from the beginning that someone was out to stop this movie. I don't know why." I sipped my coffee with my left hand. My wrist ached, and aspirin wasn't helping. "And it gets even crazier."

"What do you mean?" Paul asked.

"When Ned and I got into our little scuffle, I said some things I shouldn't. About Rafe. I don't believe Ned was guilty of anything, but Rafe's plane was indeed sabotaged."

Ann inhaled sharply. "You can't mean—"

"Somebody murdered him."

Paul's expression didn't change, but his voice came out cool and precise. "That's a big presumption. I thought the investigators ruled it a pilot error."

"True, and I didn't believe it when I heard. But now I'm certain."

"How can you be certain?" Paul asked.

"There's a retired detective. He's been digging around, asking questions. He uncovered records. The plane was tampered with. And the rumors that Rafe was drunk? False. There was no alcohol in his system."

"I see," Paul said, his voice unreadable.

Cassie shook her head. "But... murder? That's insane."

"I don't believe it either," Ann added, her tone brittle.

"At first, I thought it was personal," I said. My voice dropped. I looked at each of them in turn. "I figured someone in the cast or crew might've had a reason."

"You mean... us?" Sparks asked, quietly.

"Yes," I said, bluntly. The word dropped like a stone in the silence.

Ann recoiled. "But why on earth would you think—"

"Because of you and me," Sparks interrupted, calm but weary. "Our history. People talked. Whispered about it. Said I was jealous of you, of Rafe. I'm sure the detective was thinking jealousy got the better of me. And I won't lie... I know engines. I know how easy it'd be to make something look like an accident."

The silence that followed was thick and awful, full of half-buried memories and things none of us wanted to name.

I nodded slowly. "All of that is true. The jealousy. The rumors. The opportunity. You looked like the perfect suspect."

"But there were others," I continued. "Ned wanted out. Roy threatened Rafe repeatedly. Loudly. Half the crew could testify to that."

"And let's not forget me," Cassie said.

"You?" Ann asked. "What possible reason...?"

Ann stopped, her face red, because she knew the reason. Everybody did.

"Just another of Rafe's castoffs," Cassie said miserably.

"But you've changed your mind," Sparks said quickly, his voice a little faster now. "You don't think it was one of us?"

I looked at the table. At the steam curling from the mugs. At the people around me—so familiar, and now... something else entirely.

"I never did, really," I said. "But someone's still pushing Griggs to shut this film down. They're trying to buy it. They're afraid of what the last few scenes will show."

Ann's voice was tight. "So, what do we do?"

I looked at her. At all of them.

"We finish it," I said. "As fast as we can. And before anybody else gets hurt."

33.

K ate drove me back to the clinic the first thing that morning and had my wrist x-rayed again and rewrapped. The elderly doctor wasn't happy with me. He told me that perhaps I should find a new line of work. Producing movies didn't seem to be a healthy way of living.

I was starting to agree with him.

On the way back to the campground, my phone kept buzzing with calls from an unknown number I refused to answer. I figured it was someone trying to sell me insurance. The last call came just as Kate pulled up to the lodge, and I was irritated enough to pick up.

"Is this Noah Sterling?" the man asked. His voice was low and direct.

Definitely not a robocall. And no insurance agent ever started that way.

"This is Noah Sterling."

"Mike Mitchell. Mitchell Stop and Go."

"I've seen your stores around, Mr. Mitchell."

A brief pause. Then—

"You probably know me better as Jace Whitfield."

I should have been shocked. Instead, the name settled over me like something I'd been expecting to hear. Not a surprise, more like recognition. As if I'd been edging toward this truth for a while now, and it had finally decided to step out into the open.

"Most people think you're dead."

"I didn't have much choice," he said. "After that book, Murder in the Swamp came out, everything changed. That cop, Treadwell, all but accused me of killing Blue. You try running a business when folks look at you like you're the next Jack the Ripper." He paused, his breath catching. "And... I won't pretend I'm innocent in all of it. What happened to Charley? There's guilt there. I've paid for that, in my own way."

"Not the way Charley did," I said.

"You don't know as much as you think," he said.

"You want to enlighten me?" I questioned.

"I don't want to be accused of killing Blue in your movie. I did bad things, yes, but I loved her. I would never have hurt her."

"A lot of men in prison say they're innocent."

He was quiet for a moment. "I want you to come see me."

"I'm a little tied up right now. I've got a new scene to film. You could come here instead."

"I never leave my home," he said, his voice tight. "Health problems. But I need to see you. I need to tell you the truth." There was a choking edge to his words.

Even though I kept protesting, I knew all along I couldn't turn down the chance to meet Jace Whitfield in person. He would have answers I needed, and perhaps an ending for my movie. And I couldn't help being curious as to what kind of man he had turned out to be.

"I live in Thalman, Georgia," Whitfield said. "I have a private airstrip next to my house. It's called Mitchell Airstrip on the map. You can rent one of those small planes at Charley Snow, and you could be here in less than an hour. You can walk from the strip to the house."

There was a great deal Whitfield wasn't telling me, but I knew I couldn't turn down the chance to meet him in person.

He hung up, and I sat with it a moment. I suspected he still wanted to buy the movie from me. It had to be Griggs who'd given him my name and number, A last, desperate attempt to pry the film loose.

My first obstacle came immediately, Kate wanted to go with me.

"You can't go by yourself," she said. "Not with your wrist hurting like that. You need someone there in case you pass out. And I don't like the idea of you meeting Jace alone. You need a witness." She stopped and grinned at me. "Besides, you can rent my plane a lot cheaper than you can rent any others."

"Your plane?"

"David taught me to fly," she said.

I gave in, and I think she knew I would.

We left early the next morning for the airport. Kate drove. By the time we arrived, her aircraft had already been pulled out onto the tarmac. It was a Luscombe 8A, a model I had never heard of, and it looked a little flimsy to me. Kate treated it with the kind of attention reserved for an old friend.

She circled the plane, checking the engines, peering into the cowlings, tapping here, nudging there. Her hands ran along the wings, inspecting the flaps and ailerons, listening for the faintest rattle or misalignment. She crouched to examine the tires, turned back to the fuselage, then moved to the cockpit, opening panels and checking the fuel lines. Each movement was deliberate and methodical, born of familiarity and respect.

I leaned against the hangar and admired her movements, especially in the western-style jeans she wore. Once she looked up and caught my eyes and grinned and shook her head.

"Engines look good, fluid levels are fine, no visible damage," she muttered to herself, jotting notes in a small notebook she carried everywhere. "We will warm her up before takeoff and run through the checklist again, but she is ready."

"Are you doing all this routine checking for my benefit?" I asked. "So, I think you are a real pilot?"

"I am a real pilot," she said and punched me in the shoulder hard enough to hurt.

Kate climbed into the cockpit first, sliding into the pilot's seat with practiced ease. I followed, settling into the co-pilot's side. The interior smelled faintly of oil and leather, a reassuring mix of machinery and familiarity. The control panel was filled with dials, switches, and gauges, each one flickering with life as she powered up the systems.

She ran through her preflight checks methodically, flipping switches, tapping instruments, and speaking each step aloud. "Fuel pumps on, check. Avionics, check. Flaps, set. Lights, operational." Her voice was calm and precise but carried a quiet excitement that made my chest tighten.

With the engines humming steadily, she pushed the throttles forward slightly. The twin propellers spun faster, slicing the morning air with a low, vibrating roar. The plane shuddered gently on its wheels, eager now, impatient to leave the tarmac.

"Strap in," Kate said, hands steady on the yoke. I tightened my harness and braced against the rising vibration beneath us. She gave a quick nod to the ground crew and eased the throttles forward. The plane rolled, gaining speed, and the concrete beneath us blurred.

Then, with a subtle lift and a smooth surge, we were airborne. The runway fell away, shrinking into the distance, and the engines roared with controlled power as we climbed. I pressed my forehead to the window, watching the airport fade beneath us, the early morning sun glinting off the wings.

Kate's hands moved with effortless skill over the controls. "Climbing to ten thousand feet," she said over the hum of the engines. I thought she handled the small plane far better than the ex-Air Force pilot I had flown with earlier.

The flight was quiet except for the steady hum of the engines and the occasional crackling over the radio. The only challenge was spotting the airstrip. Kate circled low over the property twice, scanning the dense tree line for the thin strip of grass. Finally, through a break in the pines, she spotted a narrow, perfectly mown ribbon of green tucked into the clearing, flanked on both sides by tall oaks. She eased the throttle back, guiding the plane with careful precision. The wheels touched the grass softly, rolling over the slightly uneven surface, and for a moment, the only sound was the gentle rustle of the surrounding trees. Kate exhaled; the tension of the flight melted as the plane slowed to a steady taxi toward the hidden hangar at the far end.

The house was within walking distance, just as Whitfield had promised, but it wasn't what I had imagined. I'd half-expected a hidden mansion tucked deep in the woods. Instead, a large, spacious log-cabin-style home came into view, its broad wraparound porch a bit resembling the cabins at Mossy Creek.

The woman who opened the door wore a pale gray uniform that looked like it hadn't seen a wash in days, and a cigarette dangled carelessly from one corner of her mouth. From somewhere inside, a television blared so loudly the walls seemed to vibrate with its sound.

"He's waiting in his study," she said, and she left us standing there. I saw her retreat to a room nearby, and I could see a couch and a television.

I followed the narrow hallway toward the study. The house felt close and airless, the air thick with a musty smell that suggested closed windows and too many unwashed days. Cobwebs clung to the upper corners where the walls met the ceiling. As I passed the kitchen, I caught a glimpse of a sink piled high with dishes and a trash can so full that the lid no longer closed.

The door to the study creaked as I pushed it open.

Jace Whitfield was waiting.

He had once been a huge man, but illness had hollowed him out. What remained was shrunken and pale, almost skeletal, slumped in a wheelchair beside an oxygen tank. Clear tubing ran to his nose, the soft hiss of compressed air breaking the heavy silence. His clothes looked slept in and none too clean, and when I stepped closer, I caught the sour, unwashed smell of someone who no longer cared much about appearances.

He lifted his head slowly. His body might have been failing, but his eyes were not. They were sharp and alert, studying me with a quiet intensity that made the room feel suddenly smaller.

The study itself was crowded but arranged with deliberate care. Papers were stacked in neat piles across the desk, leather-bound books with cracked spines filled the shelves, and dusty, expensive knick-knacks lined the walls as though they had once mattered very much to someone.

"You," he said, almost spitting the word.

There was recognition in his eyes, though I knew we had never met before. I would have remembered.

"Excuse me?" I said.

"I wish to buy your movie."

He quoted a price that took my breath away, but I still shook my head.

"It's not for sale," I said.

"Why?" he asked. "Because you think you owe your father something? You owe him nothing. From what I hear, he never claimed you as a son and made your life a living hell."

"The movie is not for sale," I repeated.

He didn't like that answer. Even shrunken and filthy, he carried the air of a man who had rarely been denied anything. Power still clung to him, along with something darker—cruelty, maybe.

Whitfield studied me for a moment, then his gaze shifted to Kate. His lips curled into a faint, unpleasant smile.

"And you must be... Kate," he said, his voice raspy but deliberate. His eyes lingered on her a fraction too long.

The look made my stomach turn. I felt like drop-kicking him, wheelchair and oxygen tank included.

Still staring at her, he said, "I was told you were easy on the eyes."

"Ellis Dubois told you," I said. "He must have told you a lot if you know people think Rafe was my father."

Whitfield shrugged. "Ellis does odd jobs for me sometimes, but he's mostly useless. Always has been. That's why I asked you to come here. I still want to buy your movie."

"Then this has been a wasted trip," I said. "I don't care how much you offer."

He smiled and named another figure—bigger than my mother's entire trust fund. I even heard Kate gasp. If it had been Griggs sitting where I was, he'd have been salivating.

But I wasn't Griggs.

Not that I wasn't tempted. I was. Still, meeting Jace Whitfield—Mike Mitchell, or whatever he called himself these days—had convinced me I wanted nothing to do with him.

I shook my head.

"I'm finishing the movie," I said.

"Griggs told me you were hard-headed," Whitfield said. "He said you wouldn't sell. I didn't believe him. Every man has his price."

"How do you know Griggs?" I asked.

"I didn't until your father showed up at the Swamp Lily Motor Court planning to make a movie about Blue. I couldn't allow that to happen."

"So you sent Ellis to make Rafe an offer."

"I did."

"And when he refused, you sent someone to sabotage his airplane."

"No," Whitfield said calmly. "I didn't do that. I won't deny I'm capable of something like it, but I didn't."

"Why not?"

"I have reasons you wouldn't understand."

"Why do you want to destroy the movie so badly?" Kate asked.

"I'm dying," he said. "I don't want it hanging around after I'm gone."

There was a dangerous edge to his words, a simmering intensity that made the air feel heavier.

"That's not it," I said. "You're afraid of something."

"And you don't strike me as the sentimental type," Kate added. "I doubt you care much about what happens after you're dead."

He didn't answer.

"Tell us about Blue," Kate said quietly.

Something about the way she said it reached him. With me, everything felt like a challenge. With Kate, his eyes softened.

He leaned back in the wheelchair. For a moment, I glimpsed the boy he must once have been—the boy who loved a girl.

"You loved her, didn't you?" Kate said gently.

"I loved her," he said. His voice had lost its edge now, softer, almost fragile. "I loved her more than anything. I thought... with Charley gone, she might love me back."

His hands twitched faintly on the arms of the chair, as though reaching for something that wasn't there.

"And she turned you down," I said. "Flat."

If he'd been able to stand, I think he would have come at me.

"Get out of my house," he snapped.

"I don't understand why you asked me here," I said. "You didn't really believe I'd sell the movie. Something's bothering you. You want it out in the open. What happened? Did you try again? Did you lose your temper when she turned you down and kill her?"

"No," he said.

"They say confession is good for the soul," Kate added.

"I lost mine a long time ago," he growled.

"Then why bring us here?" I asked again.

"Because of her," he said.

His frail hands gripped the sides of the wheelchair, and his body began to tremble.

"Because of Blue. Because she won't leave me alone."

34.

Kate assured me there was enough fuel for the return trip, but she still went over the plane carefully before takeoff, just as she had back at Charley Snow Airport. I watched her move methodically through the checklist, touching gauges, scanning the wings, making sure everything was exactly right.

While she worked, she glanced over at me. "Do you think Whitfield killed her?"

"After meeting him," I said, "I'm pretty sure he did."

She checked another item off the list, then paused. "What do you think he meant when he said Blue wouldn't leave him alone?"

"It seems obvious," I said. "His conscience is finally catching up with him."

"He said he didn't have one of those," she said.

"Well, I'm not believing the ghost of Blue has been visiting him."

"No doubt you're right," she said.

When we returned to Mossy Creek Campground, Augusta Bloom was in the front room of the lodge, talking to Paul Deerfield. She looked up as I entered, her eyes sharp and questioning.

"It's true? Jace Whitfield is still alive?"

"News travels fast," I said. "Yes, he's alive. But he's miserable and broken, and I'm not sure how much time he has left."

"And is he rich? That's what he wanted above everything."

"Rich enough," I said.

"Then he got exactly what he deserved," she said, her voice cold. "In this life... and may the next be no different."

My eyes landed on a blue folder on the end table beside the couch.

"The final scenes?" I asked.

She nodded. "The end of your movie."

"Rafe's movie," I corrected.

"He started it," she said, "but I think it's yours now in more ways than you might ever understand."

I spent half the night in the editing room, reading the script. My coffee went cold. Each word twisted my stomach tighter, each sentence a knife I couldn't pull free. What had been done to Charley made my skin crawl. The pages didn't just tell me what happened—they shoved me into it, made me live it all through Charley's eyes.

Maybe it didn't answer who had killed Blue. But despite Jace Whitfield's denials, I was now certain he did it, and the audience would leave feeling the same.

Because Whitfield was a monster of the worst kind.

It took us a full week to set up the next scene. With help from Charlton County Fire Rescue and the sheriff's department, we tracked down an old, abandoned house buried in the pines just off a forgotten stretch of two-lane highway. It looked as if time itself had abandoned it—half-sunk into red clay, swallowed by weeds and creeping kudzu. A place you'd pass once and never notice again.

It was a single-story frame house, its roof bowed like a tired spine, the clapboard siding bleached gray and splintering from decades of neglect. No mailbox. No driveway. Just a dirt pull-off scabbed with tire ruts and pine needles.

Under Spark's direction, and with a small repair crew from Valdosta, we coaxed the place back to life. Not enough to make it pretty, just enough to make it believable. Too much polish would betray the mood we were after. We weren't building a set. We were resurrecting a ghost.

We patched the sagging porch steps, reinforced the front door so it wouldn't collapse mid-take, and brushed a thin coat of faded green paint over the worst of the rot, matching it to reference photos from county archives. The result wasn't pristine; it was perfect, as if someone had once cared, and then slowly stopped.

The house had no power, of course. The nearest utility pole stood a quarter mile down the road, wires dangling like brittle cobwebs. We hauled in a rented generator, loud, temperamental, heavy as a gravestone, and tucked it behind the house beneath a tarp. Every time the cameras rolled, it buzzed like a nest of angry hornets, but it gave us the light we needed to cut through the darkness inside.

We were only shooting on the porch and in the front room. Two setups. Both short scenes. But we wanted the kind of authenticity you can't fake on a soundstage.

We dragged in furniture from a local flea market: a sunken armchair that smelled faintly of mildew, a couch with cigarette burns, and a scarred coffee table. An old box television that actually worked.

By the end of the week, the house felt lived-in again. When the last prop was placed and the generator coughed to life, the crew went quiet.

One camera was on the truck as it turned off the highway, following another pickup, its occupants shouting and waving their arms. Another was inside the front room, where Charley Snow sat with his parents and younger sister, watching TV. The flickering screen cast shifting light across their faces. Evening shadows stretched across the dimly lit room, soft and quiet, as if holding their breath.

The exterior camera followed the truck as it barreled into the front yard, kicking up a thick swirl of dust and gravel. The tires skidded slightly before the vehicle jerked to a stop. Before the dust could settle, Dylan, as Jace flung open the passenger door and jumped out, shouting and waving a squat, ugly little pistol like it belonged to him. Two shots rang into the air, then a string of curses that echoed across the yard.

It was a part Dylan was born to play.

We had brought in two seasoned actors from Atlanta to play Ned's parents, both gray-haired, grounded in decades of local theater. Through the monitor, I watched them standing just inside the doorway, their faces drawn with the right mix of panic and helplessness as Jace sauntered toward the house, followed by two broad-shouldered extras who looked ready to throw someone through a wall.

The newest scene also revealed something surprising, or someone.

Ellis Dubois was mentioned in the script.

"Our Ellis Dubois," Kate exclaimed when she read the scene.

"Yes. He was directly involved. He only gave vague answers when he was interviewed for the book, but he knew a lot more. I don't actually know what Ellis was like back then, but I can imagine. Always playing the sycophant to Whitfield, running his errands, nodding at every word, making himself useful in all the little ways that keep a man in favor. Always in the background. Just fitting in. He's still doing it."

Kate brushed the back of my hand. "True, but what if there was another reason Ellis went along with Jace in terrifying Charley—something besides just kissing up?"

"What reason?" I asked.

"The consensus is that Blue was irresistible. Jace and Charley were both in love with her. What if Ellis also couldn't resist her?"

"You think Ellis loved her? But I thought he and Claire were always a thing?"

"We know they married eventually. But what if Claire was the rebound? What if Ellis thought that with Charley out of the way and Jace leaving for college, he'd finally have his chance?"

It was something I hadn't considered.

"If he was in love with Blue, and he told her his feelings..." I trailed off.

"And if she turned him down," Kate said, "he might have gotten angry."

"You're suggesting it might have been Ellis who killed Blue." I shook my head. "I don't think Ellis is the type to murder someone."

"Is there a type?" Kate asked.

Maybe Kate was making sense, but instead of clarifying anything, it only deepened the fog around her death. Motive could be twisted to suit almost anyone, and the timeline was elastic enough to stretch around whatever theory you wanted to believe.

It was more plausible that Jace killed her, but it could just as easily have been a stranger. An unseen presence slipping through the edges of the story. A random encounter. A wrong place, wrong time tragedy. The kind of explanation that offered no closure, no one to confront, no satisfying unraveling of motive.

We stopped the scene again for makeup, and then we started with Jace standing in the front yard, screaming for Charley.

The second camera cut to Ned as Charley. He curled in on himself, eyes locked on the front door like a deer in headlights. His body trembled. Ned nailed it. I thought this part might win him some awards.

The extra who played Ellis Dubois charged up the porch steps. His cue was to kick open the door and force his way inside. But during the first take, he slipped, stumbled, and went spinning off the edge of the porch, crashing into the side of a nearby stump.

We cut immediately. Crew members rushed in. He was fine, already laughing it off, and we reset the scene.

Second take, it was clean. The extra shoved open the front door and stormed inside, followed closely by Jace and Ellis.

"Cut," Ann called.

We couldn't run it straight through because of camera angles, and we had to be careful with continuity. Elly Wright made digital photographs of where everyone had been standing.

Ned, as Charley, backed into a corner. His eyes darted around the room, searching for an exit that didn't exist. Jace and his crew moved in fast. They grabbed him by the arms and shoulders and began dragging him toward the door. He struggled, yelling, but there was no escape. As they crossed the threshold, one extra was supposed to swing at Charley's face, sending him sprawling into the dirt.

The extra knew the move, but I saw blood on Ned's face.

"Cut," Ann called.

"You okay, Ned?" I asked.

"Marvelous," he said, with a bitter look toward me. "I'll be glad when we're done with this mess."

The makeup team rushed in. They added more blood to the corner of Ned's mouth, a smear of dirt on his cheek, a quick mist of sweat.

Back to positions.

"Action."

The rest of the scene was brutal, and made even worse because I knew we were watching an echo of what really happened.

I could hear the curses ring out, sharp and bitter. The dull thud of fists landing was almost worse than the shouting. The man playing Charley's father tried to stop it and was thrown aside like he weighed nothing, his body crumpling like a discarded coat.

We rehearsed carefully, walking the line between raw panic and theatricality. The helplessness had to feel real. Every beat had to come from truth, not spectacle. I kept asking myself where the line was between emotional realism and gratuitous violence, and how close we were to crossing it.

Even on set, surrounded by lights and cameras, I wasn't sure we hadn't already gone too far.

But I wanted the audience to feel it, to sympathize with Charley, to feel his fear.

I pulled Dylan aside. "You have one chance to stop Charley from taking the woman you love. Show me the jealous monster in you."

The girl playing the sister was local, picked from a Saturday casting call. Small part. No lines. But it felt a lot more personal for me now, since I had actually met Augusta. I was trying to separate truth from fiction in my mind, but a heavy part of me knew this had happened exactly as written. I had already started to suspect who our scriptwriter was.

A lot of people came out that evening to stand on the highway and watch us shoot the scene. One of them I recognized as Augusta.

At the last moment, I changed one detail.

"Put her in the doorway," I told Ann. "No lines. Just... let her see."

The crew paused. Subtle, but I felt hesitation in the air. A glance here, a hand held a second too long on a lens. No one said a word, but I knew what they were thinking.

Was it too much? Maybe. But I knew what I wanted.

Lights adjusted. Blocking tweaked. And when the camera rolled again, Jace and the others were dragging Charley Snow to the car, shouting, struggling, the last frame we held wasn't them.

It was her.

The little girl, barefoot in the hallway, framed in the doorway like a ghost. A white nightgown hung loose on her small frame. Hair tangled from sleep. A stuffed rabbit clutched to her chest like a shield. Tears streaked her cheeks, catching the light.

She didn't speak. Didn't move. Just stood there, wide-eyed and still, as her brother disappeared into the night.

And that was the moment.

Not the violence. Not the chaos. Not the lines we'd rehearsed a dozen times.

Her silence.

That was what landed.

Then Ann called, "Cut," and the moment shattered. People exhaled, moved, murmured. The little girl blinked, wiped her face, and looked up at me. Still silent. Still holding that rabbit.

I looked up at the hill at Augusta, and she lifted her hand to me.

And I knew we had it.

35.

I had thought the first part of Ned's kidnapping was uncomfortable, but the scene on Billy's Island turned out even worse.

The worst part was that I felt I had to be there, and my one day on the Laviolette Homestead with Kate had not endeared me to the swamp.

Getting all the equipment out there by boat was a nightmare. The day hung low and overcast, and there seemed to be more alligators in the water than usual. By the time we began shooting, the sky had deepened into a bruised gray. The low cloud cover gave the swamp a damp hush, and the wind barely stirred the Spanish moss hanging like tattered ghosts from the cypress trees. Perfect timing, Ann said. It didn't feel that way to me.

The swamp made me nervous even in daylight. At sunset, every shifting shadow felt like a threat.

We'd staged the boats on the dark water, lit faintly by battery-powered lanterns that cast orange halos and barely touched the gloom.

"Action," Ann called.

The camera picked up Dylan/Jace and the extras hauling Ned/Charley through the underbrush, his feet dragging, mouth taped, hands loosely tied for effect. When they reached the small clearing scouted earlier that morning, Jace tore the tape off with a theatrical flourish.

"You know this place?" he asked, voice low and menacing. "You know where we are?"

Charley whimpered, wiping at his mouth. He stared toward the trees, wide-eyed. They hadn't even started acting yet, but he already looked like a man losing his mind.

I was impressed.

"We'll come back for you," Jace said. "Maybe."

As the crew pulled back for the wide shot of the boats leaving, Kate sat in the bow beside me, watching the lantern-lit trees fade behind us. Her voice was quiet but carried well across the water.

Kate took my hand. "Take a breath, will you?"

I tried to relax.

"You know this island used to be a logging town?" she said. "Company town. Had a hotel, a post office, and even a school. All gone now. Nothing left but ghosts and gators."

I looked at her.

"If you're trying to make me feel better, it's not helping."

"It really bothers you, doesn't it? Being out here?"

"It does," I said. "I guess I'm just not a swamp person."

"You didn't have to come this time. Ann could have finished."

"I had to," I said. "I need to see this through, and I don't know why."

"Facing your demons," Kate said.

"I suppose that's it," I said.

"Bring it in again," Ann called. "Close-up."

Back on the island, Charley had collapsed to his knees, fists clutching the hem of Jace's jacket.

"Please," he begged, the pretense gone. "Don't leave me here. I'll do anything. You want money? I'll get you money. I'll disappear. Just, please don't leave me here overnight."

It was humiliation of the worst kind, humiliation dredged up from the inner soul, the place where terrible fears and nightmares live. I didn't want to look at it. I couldn't stop looking at it.

"They're off script again," Ann muttered.

"Let it run," I said.

Jace stood over Charley. "If you love her, at least act like a man."

Ann frowned at the monitor.

"You can't have her," Charley snarled. "It won't matter what you do to me." Tears mixed with fake blood ran down his cheek. "Even if I go away forever, you can't have her."

"Shut up," Jace snapped.

"She thinks you're a backwoods redneck," Charley yelled. "She will never love you!"

Jace hit him, and it wasn't staged. The blow smashed Charley's nose. He went down hard, and for a moment something mad flickered in Jace's eyes. The extras stepped between them; Ann was shouting "Cut!" over and over while Elly Wright and Kate knelt beside Ned, trying to stop the bleeding.

"Have you lost your mind?" Ann screamed at Dylan—Jace—who stood there looking strangely confused.

"We'll leave that scene as it is," I told her. "Then go straight to the time lapse."

"If we can stop his nose from bleeding," she said.

In the movie, the screen would go black, and the audience would hear Charley Snow crying.

Then light again: a long, lingering time-lapse of Charley spending the night huddled against a tree. The shot itself took only half an hour, but I would stretch it in editing. We circled him with handheld cameras. The lantern flickered, then died. Mosquitoes swarmed in hungry clouds.

"I wish somebody could tell the mosquitoes we're making a movie," Sparks muttered.

"Cut," I said.

We brought the boats in quietly, engine noise falling away as we reached the dock. We tied up without much talk. There was a heaviness to the group, an unspoken sense that we were nearing some end. Maybe it was the long days in the swamp catching up with us. Maybe it was the knowledge that whatever rhythm we'd found out here was slipping away.

Dinner was trout caught that morning, crisp fries, and a simple salad. We ate around the table, subdued, the clink of forks louder than any conversation. Everyone looked tired in that deep, bone-hollowed way that has nothing to do with sleep.

But for me, there was something else. I kept glancing at Kate across the table, trying to read her face, the way she moved or didn't. Being in love isn't easy, especially being in love with someone who has no intention of living in California. I didn't really want to leave her here, but I wasn't sure I could stay either.

What do I do about Kate? What will she do about me?

No answers came, only the sounds of the night settling in and the gentle movement of the crew cleaning up and drifting toward sleep. I fell onto my bed like a stone into water, no dreams, just darkness.

Then, too soon, the alarm.

Still half-asleep, I dressed, and Kate drove us out to the park. I wish I could say I had gotten used to the feel of the place, but I felt the same uneasiness climbing into the boat.

The sky was the color of peach and blood as the sun rose. Mist drifted over the water like smoke. Ned stepped out of the boat while the makeup artist recreated the bruises on his face. He settled into the same position we'd left him in the night before.

Sam had one camera set up, tracking Jace as he brought his boat to shore and approached Charley. Jace kicked him awake.

"You're lucky I came back," he said. "Next time I won't. Listen, I'll take you back, but you're leaving Folkston. Forever. Go to Alaska, join the Army, I don't care. Just leave. Or I promise the swamp will get you."

Another kick.

Charley didn't respond. He shook, lips moving silently, eyes locked on the tree line. Even after Jace hauled him into the boat, he kept glancing over his shoulder, as if something watched from the trees.

"Cut," I said.

We shot one more scene that day. The scene had already been shot once, but it was one of the few I didn't like. Sparks had found exactly what we needed: a restored train station in Jesup, Georgia, only a couple of hours away. After lunch, we set up to film Ned's departure scene.

"Scene 27 — Outbound — Take 2."

Slate clapped.

"Rolling."

"Sound speed."

"Camera speeds."

I nodded. "Action."

The camera drifted in from a wide, static shot, then began a slow dolly push. We framed the station so the platform stretched long and lonely behind him. His duffel sat at his feet. No uniform yet—just jeans, boots, and a button-down. Nineteen years old. Fresh-faced. Trying hard to look older.

The train was coming. Not visible yet—just felt.

Behind him stood his mother, father, and little sister. The girl clutched a red fleece jacket, her hair in a messy braid. I'd told costuming to leave it frayed at the ends—real. The mother's arms were folded tight as though holding herself together. The father kept his hands in his pockets, face unreadable, all expression contained in his posture.

Charley turned to them. No lines—just a long look.

The sister stepped forward. We'd rehearsed it loosely. She wasn't supposed to speak unless she felt it. And she did.

"I don't want you to go," she whispered. Off script. Better than anything on the page.

He smiled at her, barely. The actor was good. Subtle. My gut tightened watching him.

The train pulled in behind them, the real Amtrak Silver Meteor—wrong for 1968, but fixable later. We only had one clean pass. The brakes hissed, metal groaned.

He hugged his mother. She held too long and let go too fast.

His father just nodded. One silent, heavy gesture meaning everything: Be safe. Be brave. Come back to us.

The doors opened. A single beep.

The boy picked up his duffel, hesitated for one heartbeat, then stepped inside.

The doors closed. The camera held on the family as the train pulled away. His mother wiped at her eyes without realizing. The sister gave a hesitant wave. The father didn't move at all.

We held our silence until the train was gone.

"Cut."

A wrap.

36.

The final scene of a movie is a little like running a long-distance race, and finally reaching the end, or scoring a final touchdown, or knocking the ball over the center field fence. With Ann helping, I still had weeks of editing ahead of me, grueling, eye-watering hours in a windowless room where time dissolved and I'd forget what day it was.

But that was the future, and for now, I stood there watching the actors hugging each other, the crew exchanging high-fives, someone crying for reasons I didn't understand, and I felt... hollow, mostly. Hollow but relieved. Like I'd been holding my breath for forever and finally let it out.

I didn't have all the answers. I didn't know who killed Blue. I still suspected it had been Jace, and meeting him in person hadn't changed my mind. But I could only hint at my suspicion, just as the book had done. I couldn't put it in the movie. The audience would have to draw its own conclusion after knowing it was Jace who had driven Charley away.

Rafe used to say finishing a film shoot was like surviving a ship-wreck: you were glad to be alive, but you also looked around at the soggy wreckage and wondered how many pieces of yourself you'd lost along the way. He wasn't wrong.

It didn't take long for the final cast party to get underway. "Party" might be too generous a word. It was more of a chaotic, smoky, half-planned barbecue. Someone had dragged out the leftover Fourth of July ribs, three giant catering pans' worth, that had been occupying half the freezer for the past week. Beth had made two kinds of potato salad and something with fruit and nuts, and put out plenty of bread.

Someone else brought a bowl of what they called "queasy fingers," which turned out to be cocktail sausages floating in a bright-red glaze that looked like transmission fluid. People ate them anyway.

Music was playing from someone's Bluetooth speaker, old classic rock muddled with newer stuff, the kind of playlist built by committee and doomed to please no one. The smoke from the grill hung low, trapped by the heavy, humid evening, giving the place a sort of dreamy haze. Or maybe that was just exhaustion.

Ned McDonald didn't stay for the party. In fact, by the time we got back from the last location, he was already gone. Or close to it.

I caught a glimpse of him dragging his suitcase across the gravel, shoulders hunched, his ballcap pulled low. His Uber driver idled right behind him, trunk open. By the time I walked over to say goodbye, the trunk slammed shut.

He didn't turn around.

I wished him the best anyway. I still thought he was a nice guy, and he had done a fantastic job acting in Rafe's movie. I hoped he found the dream role he searched for. So many actors didn't.

The long picnic tables filled quickly, plates stacked with ribs and salads. The smell of smoke, charred meat, and home-brewed sweet tea syrup drifted through the air. Somebody had found some booze, probably Roy, who was well on his way to la-la land, and I don't mean California.

I took a seat at the end of one table, mostly to watch. I didn't need to be in the middle of anything. The evening had that loose, frayed feeling you get when everyone is too tired to behave. Someone laughed too loudly. Someone else cried on someone's shoulder and then switched to laughing. A few of the makeup girls had stacked plastic cups into a pyramid taller than the apple crate they were using as a table.

And then there was Roy.

I saw him perched on top of a cooler, attempting to tell a story with hand gestures so big he nearly punched a light stand. The story wasn't clear, something about a coyote, or maybe a cat, or maybe an actor he mistook for a coyote or a cat, but the point was lost because he kept interrupting himself with loud, theatrical hiccups.

At one point, he tried to dance. Not well. And not with the music, because the music wasn't even playing; a commercial had come up on the playlist. He danced anyway.

I was glad Sparks had hidden his guns.

He would regret all of this in the morning. Or tonight. Or right now, judging by the way he suddenly sat down like the ground had given out from under him.

But everyone laughed, not unkindly. It was that sort of night—everyone too relieved to be annoyed.

I was feeling pretty good myself, although I was just drinking tea. Unburdened. Like I just put a weight down. I was taking a sip of tea when my phone rang.

"Noah?"

I recognized the voice. "Augusta. You wrote a good ending."

"Then you're happy with it?"

"It's not perfect, but I think I can tweak it enough so the audience will be satisfied."

She was quiet for a moment. "Then you'll be leaving soon?"

I thought of Kate, and my throat tightened. "I suppose so."

"I want you to come see me before you go. It's... important."

"We're packing. I'll be busy," I said.

"Rafe made me promise something," she said, her voice wavering. "I hated it. I didn't think it was fair to you."

"Something about the movie?" I asked, curiosity prickling.

"No. Something else. Something you need to know now, even if I break my promise. Come see me."

Before I could answer, she hung up.

I stood frozen, phone in hand. I knew I couldn't refuse.

I went in search of Kate and asked her to come with me. Regardless of what Augusta might share, the day would be better if Kate went along.

"I sense hesitation," I said.

"Not so much," she replied. "It's just that your movie is over."

"Yes. I'd like to talk about that."

"I'm not sure there's anything to talk about," she said.

I felt uneasy. "Of course there is."

"I wouldn't be happy in California," she said. "And I'm sure you could never live here, away from the life you've known. You're not built for it—not for the heat, the bugs, or the quiet. You'd start climbing the walls."

It wasn't criticism. And I was afraid she wasn't wrong.

"But I love you," I said.

"And that's what makes it complicated," she said.

37.

K ate agreed to go.

We started early the next morning. Not sunrise-early, but early enough that the mist still clung low to the ditches and the air smelled damp and leafy. Kate drove. She said she knew the way, which might have been true, but I suspected her decision had less to do with convenience and more to do with control, specifically, keeping me from making any stops for impromptu make-out sessions.

I wasn't sure if she didn't trust me... or if she didn't trust herself. Part of me hoped it was the latter.

We didn't talk much. Augusta's address was in Camp Pinckney, which was just outside Folkston, and it was hard to tell where the town ended and Camp Pinckney began. We passed a modern-looking convenience store with mirrored windows and bold red letters:

Mitchell Stop and Go.

"Well, that explains all the receipts I found from that Stop and Go," I said. "Rafe must have been coming out here, meeting with Augusta, going over the script."

"That must be it," Kate said.

"You've been kind of quiet," I said. "Is there something else bothering you besides the fact that I love you, and you don't want to move to California?"

She punched me in the shoulder. It hurt. "That's at the top of the list, but I still have some questions about the movie."

"Such as?"

"For one thing, I'd never heard of Carol Treadway's book. I mean, I'd heard about Simone's murder and her ghost haunting the swamp. That was just a scary story we told around the campfire in Girl Guides. But I never knew Carol Treadway had written a book. I stopped by the library and found out they once had a copy, but it disappeared."

"I have their copy," I said. "At least it says so in the back of the book, where the little envelope used to hold some sort of library card."

"Then someone from here stole that book and sent it to your father."

"It looks that way."

"And it wasn't Augusta."

"She claims not." I glanced out at the passing scenery.

She was quiet for a moment. "One other question, and I'll shut up. Do you think Whitfield sabotaged your father's plane?"

"Whitfield has money and power," I said. "He could certainly have hired somebody to do it."

"Like Ellis?" she asked.

"I wasn't exactly thinking of Ellis, but he's a possibility."

"You know, I felt sorry for him."

"Whitfield?" I asked disbelievingly.

"Yes. He's in a wheelchair. He's near death. He's miserable. It was hard not to feel a little sorry for him, but then the more I learn about him, the less sorry I feel."

"I know the feeling," I said.

Camp Pinckney wasn't much more than a cluster of homes, a handful of roads, and the low white church that served as its center of gravity. The church looked like something out of a postcard: white, gleaming, and well-maintained. So was the cemetery behind it.

Kate turned onto the road just beyond it, and we followed it until we found the right address: a single-story brick home with gray shutters. Neatly trimmed hedges. A flowerbed so carefully tended it looked like someone knelt beside it every morning to apologize to the petals for existing too close.

"This is it," Kate said softly.

We sat in the car longer than we needed to. The engine was off, but the heat from the morning sun made the interior feel like a slow oven. I didn't really know Augusta. I'd met her only twice, briefly, and yet there was some connection I couldn't yet understand.

I also couldn't shake the images of the little girl standing in the doorway, watching her brother being dragged away. And the same little girl at the train station, silent, almost lost in the crowd.

"I don't want you to go away."

I found myself thinking about it, or maybe hearing it. It wasn't Augusta's voice, not really. It was like a line delivered by a talented young actor. Words improvised on the spot, and yet somehow fitting.

I reminded myself: the movie was just a movie. Fiction. Performance. But the real Charley Snow existed outside of any script. A hero. A Medal of Honor recipient. A man who had died saving others.

Maybe to somehow make up for his cowardice at leaving Blue, at being afraid of the swamp.

"I guess we shouldn't keep her waiting," I said. My voice sounded louder than I intended.

We stepped out and started up the short path to the house. Gravel crunched under our feet. I glanced at Kate. She wasn't looking at me.

I hesitated, caught somewhere between the need for reassurance and the fear that words might break whatever fragile equilibrium we had.

"Before we go in..." I said, my voice lower this time. "I just want to say—"

She cut me off gently, not unkindly. "Let's not talk about things right now."

Her eyes met mine briefly, then slipped away, as if afraid of what might happen if she lingered.

I gave a small, resigned smile. "Yeah. Complicated. I know."

Whatever this was between us, it would have to wait.

The front of the house burst with color: marigolds, purple salvia, pink zinnias in tidy beds. Two ceramic rabbits stood guard near the steps, their ears chipped with age.

The door opened before we reached it. Augusta stood framed in the doorway, posture straight, expression reserved. She stepped aside and let us in.

If this had been a movie set, her home would have been perfect for an author and artist: warm, orderly, and quietly alive with creativity. The air carried a soft hint of lavender, mingling with the faint, comforting smell of old paper.

Dozens of photographs lined the top of a piano that took up half the room, their frames overlapping in a cluttered but deliberate display. Augusta appeared again and again through the years: a striking young woman with bright eyes and a confident, almost defiant smile; Augusta in Sunday finery, surrounded by children clinging to her skirts; Augusta at a long, crowded table, relatives leaning over plates of food and laughter.

There were family portraits, holiday gatherings, and snapshots of noisy dinners, the kind of warm, crowded life Norman Rockwell might have painted and one I had always envied.

Near the center stood a wedding photograph, slightly larger than the rest. Augusta, radiant in lace, looked poised and self-assured, her smile calm and certain. Beside her stood a ruddy, awkward man who seemed far more at home driving a tractor than posing in a tuxedo. He held himself stiffly, as if unsure where to put his hands, his expression caught somewhere between pride and discomfort.

"Mr. Bloom?" I asked.

She half-smiled. "No. He hated being called that. I picked the name Bloom before I met Edward. That's Edward J. Tynell of Tynell Hardware in Waycross. We had a good life together. He passed about eight years ago."

"I'm sorry," I said.

Augusta inclined her head. "Thank you. Would either of you like coffee?"

"Coffee sounds good," I said, and Kate nodded.

Augusta disappeared into the other room and returned a moment later carrying a silver tray with delicate china cups.

"I so seldom get to entertain anymore," Augusta said as she set the tray down. "At my age, every year I have fewer friends."

"It seems you have a large family," I said.

"Oh yes, scattered everywhere. I do have several grandchildren in the area, and a couple of them even like my books."

Perhaps it was because I had loved her books so much, but I felt a strong connection. I realized I had felt it from the first moment we met at the 4th of July celebration.

I took a deep breath. "Okay, when you called, you told me there was something else I needed to know. Another secret that Rafe made you promise not to tell, but you decided it was unfair to me. Are you ready to tell me now?"

"Yes. But let's walk up the street first. To the cemetery."

We left the house and walked up the quiet path to the shaded, picturesque cemetery behind Camp Pinckney Baptist Church. The trees arched overhead, draped in long, silver strands of Spanish moss, their shadows shifting gently in the breeze.

She led us to a far corner where the ground sloped slightly, wilder and less tended than the rest. I found myself liking the place. It was small, peaceful, and well-shaded, as if time moved more slowly there. As Thomas Hardy wrote, it was truly far from the madding crowd.

Beneath a towering oak, Augusta stopped in front of a small, square cement tombstone, its surface etched with faded impressions of deer and an alligator. I paused, taking in the simple words carved into stone:

Simone Bleu Laviolette

Loved. Taken too soon.

I had never known her, and yet I felt the force of her presence. People had not forgotten her because there were dozens of memorabilia, a vial of swamp water, tiny stuffed alligators, wildflowers, pennies and dimes, silver charms, and a Girl Guide handbook.

"You were right about Rafe and me having a thing," she said, "but not in the way you meant. We were not lovers. I can't even say we were friends. The Rafe I met in California was a harsh man, unforgiving. Different."

"Different how?" I asked, puzzled.

"Different than who he used to be."

She opened her purse, took out a photograph, and handed it to me.

"My brother Charley," she said.

The photograph was old and faded, edges curled and yellow. A lean man stood in front of a bunker, his face tanned and tense under the harsh Vietnam sun. He was shirtless, brawny, deeply tanned, with dog tags taped together hanging around his neck.

I studied the photograph for a long moment, wondering if I was seeing something that wasn't really there. There was a familiarity in the way he held himself, in the curve of his jaw and the look in his eyes, something indefinable but unmistakable. The thought formed in my mind, and I dismissed it at once. Then certainty settled in. I had not spent so many years around Rafe Cardoc without knowing the way he carried himself. His sister said it was Charley, but I knew better.

The man in the photo was Rafe Cardoc, young, unscarred, undamaged.

38.

Kate leaned over my shoulder. "If there was ever any doubt, there isn't now. Before the injuries, before the surgery, that's you."

"You do resemble him, as a young man," Augusta said quietly.

I kept my eyes on the photograph. "But how?"

Augusta took the photo back. "Rafe told me that he did indeed jump on the grenade, not out of heroism but because he didn't want to live after I wrote to him that Blue had been murdered. When he woke up, his face was wrapped up, and they were calling him by a different name. He never corrected them, and after two years in the hospital and a half-dozen plastic surgeries, he came out of the hospital a different man, someone named Rafe Cardoc."

"And the real Rafe Cardoc was buried with military honors at Arlington," I said. "Under the name of Charley Snow?"

Augusta nodded.

"But Cardoc must have had a family somewhere."

Augusta shrugged. "If so, they never tried to contact him."

"Wait," I protested. "An uncle, I remember meeting. I remember the uncle telling everyone Rafe was injured in a car accident when he was a toddler."

Augusta shrugged. "Probably an actor. Someone he hired."

"What about DNA? Wouldn't they have checked?"

Kate explained. "While we knew about DNA back in the sixties, nobody started real testing until the late seventies and the eighties. The military started using it to identify men and women killed on the battlefield in the nineties. Nobody would have tested Charley's DNA back then. Or Rafe's." She shrugged. "I learned all that in school."

"Fingerprints then?" I protested. "And aren't there dental records?" I was remembering all the old crime show investigations I'd ever watched because I didn't want to believe it was possible.

"I don't know all the particulars of how he kept his secret," Augusta said. "But Rafe was Charley. He couldn't fool me. I knew him the moment I saw him in California."

Her voice tightened. "I was so angry with him. How could he stay away from the people who loved him? Our parents went to their graves believing he died in Vietnam."

She looked down at the photo for a long moment. "He said they died believing he was a hero. That it was better that way, because the Charley they loved died that night in the swamp."

"And he made you promise not to tell me you were my aunt," I said. "He wanted me to go back to California without knowing I had a family."

"Yes," she said. "And I did promise him. I'm ashamed of that."

"But why would you make him a promise like that?"

Augusta shrugged. "Because when you were in his presence, he was very compelling. It wasn't easy to say no to him."

"Few people could," I agreed.

We walked back to Augusta's tidy little home. Kate and I sank into the couch while Augusta took the piano bench. My eyes drifted to the photographs lined up across the piano, and I studied them more carefully than before.

I had come in thinking I had no family. Now I had an aunt. Cousins somewhere out there. Roots I hadn't even imagined.

Augusta, though, didn't look entirely at ease. It wasn't that our connection was a terrible secret, just that she was the sort of woman who believed promises were sacred. And she had broken one she'd made to Rafe.

"I think he'd forgive you," Kate said softly.

I glanced at her, surprised she'd picked up on the same unease I had sensed in Augusta.

"Would he?" Augusta asked.

"Rafe might not," Kate admitted. "But Charley would have understood."

Augusta considered that, then nodded slowly. "I think you're right."

"And it wouldn't have been fair to Noah," Kate added. "People need to know about their kin."

The quiet stretched, and I shifted the conversation.

"You said you knew Rafe was Charley the first time you met him," I said. "Even with the disfigurement."

"Yes," she replied.

"Could Ellis and Claire have recognized him?"

"Possibly. But I doubt it. I was his sister, remember. What was obvious to me might not have been obvious to anyone else. But they must have realized who Rafe was when you showed up. They would both have recognized you as a young Charley. Why do you ask?"

"No reason," I said, though my thoughts drifted to Claire. "I just noticed her looking at me strangely a couple of times. I wondered… maybe she could have recognized Rafe as Charley from a magazine, or a talk show, or something else."

Augusta's gaze lingered on me.

"You're thinking about the book, and the postcard," she said.

"What book?" Kate asked. "What postcard?"

"Someone from here sent Rafe a book stolen from the library, and a postcard addressed from the Laviolette Homestead post office."

"No such place," Kate said.

"There was writing on the back of the card," I said. "It reminded Rafe he should keep his promise."

"You're looking at me as if I sent those things," Augusta said. "I didn't."

"Then either Ellis or Claire must have known who Rafe was."

"I doubt it."

"Then who do you suggest?"

"You wouldn't care for my answer," Augusta said, a gleam of amusement in her eyes.

"I admit I'd prefer an answer that wouldn't land us both in the loony bin. I don't believe a dead woman from the swamps is responsible."

Augusta half-smiled. "Rafe always said you were practical, even as a little boy."

"How would he know what I was like as a little boy?" I said resentfully.

"I understand your feeling the way you do, but Rafe did care for you. In his way. He talked about you."

"I'm sure it wasn't anything good."

"You'd be surprised. Of course, he was a very private, deeply wounded man. I told him he should claim you as his son. He said it was better for you to think of him as a boss, not a father. Fathers were supposed to be good examples, loving, caring. He never felt he could be those things. He said that, except when he was creating or directing, when he was in that world, he was mostly dead inside. Hollow. That part of him, the part that could have been a father, was gone."

"It wasn't like he ever tried," I said, startled by the bitterness in my own voice. I had thought I had worked through all my feelings about Rafe. A creative genius, yes. Sometimes even a maniac. But a father? No. That had never been part of the picture. And I did not think I had missed it or even needed it.

Except maybe I was wrong.

Kate reached over and took my hand, a quiet anchor. I let her hold it, feeling the warmth seep in, letting myself breathe for a moment.

"When you are finished editing your movie," Augusta said, "you should come back here. You should meet your family."

I nodded. Kate squeezed my hand again. I could not trust my voice.

"I think that is a wonderful idea," Kate said for me.

39.

Kate drove us back to the campground. We wound along the narrow road to Mossy Creek, light flickering through the trees like a broken film reel, stuttering between shadow and sun.

My life had changed in just a few moments. Everything I thought I knew had shifted. Tilted. Collapsed.

"He cheated me," I said.

Kate nodded. She understood.

"I only knew Rafe as an angry director. I never once glimpsed the young man underneath. I think I would have liked Charley. The bookworm, the dreamer, the romantic. I would have liked him a lot better than Rafe. Rafe was only happy when he was breaking things or yelling."

Kate eased the car through a curve; gravel whispered under the tires. She was quiet for a long time, then said, "The fathers have eaten sour grapes, and the children's teeth are set on edge."

"That's not Shakespeare," I said.

"It's the Bible," she said. "I do read the Bible. And I go to church. It is part of who I am. I am not just a pretty face."

"Not just pretty," I said. "Striking."

"You flatter me," she said, "and you are changing the subject."

"That is because I do not want to sound stupid, and I have no idea what that grape thing means."

"It means that what a father does, what he hides, what he refuses to face, his inner anger and past sins, still reaches the children," she said. "Even if he never admits anything. Maybe especially then. Later verses talk about individual responsibility, but I think that one applies to you."

Her eyes stayed on the road, her voice steady with conviction.

I let it settle. She was right. My father's anger was not just his; it had shaped me. When Griggs offered me the job back in Culver City, I had once again been tempted to follow the path of least resistance. Instead of standing up for myself or taking risks, I had learned to stay small, to keep my head down, afraid to disturb the fragile peace I had convinced myself was enough.

Kate pulled in front of the lodge and parked. "I know this will be hard for you to understand, but you need to forgive him."

"What?"

"Forgive your father. Let it go. What is done is done." She offered a faint smile. "I would tell you, like people always do, to remember the good moments with him, but from what you have told me, I am not sure there were any."

"I hated him," I said. "And I loved him."

"Of course," Kate answered. "And now you must forgive him. Totally. Completely. Why? Because it will make you a better man. A more loving man."

"I'd like to love you. Here. Now."

She unhooked her seat belt and turned toward me. "I know my timing is atrocious, but I cannot wait any longer to say this. I have been thinking about it ever since the hospital. I care for you. Truly. But deep down, I know we would never fit. We would be wrong for each other. We come from different worlds. I dream of a little veterinary hospital, of mornings filled with animals and evenings scented with woodsmoke, of campouts and church socials and fish fries with people who know my name. You dream of something dazzling, of movie stars and bright city lights and a life that would swallow me whole. I cannot marry you, Noah, not when I know loving you would mean giving up everything that makes me who I am."

"We could make it work," I said, though even I heard the doubt.

I leaned back. She leaned closer and brushed her lips against mine. It was brief, just a touch, but it lingered longer than it should have, like the echo of something neither of us could fully name. Complicated, I thought. Always complicated.

"You will be leaving soon," she said. "I will miss you, but it is better this way."

She stepped out of the car and walked toward the lodge, her stride quick and purposeful. I hesitated, watching her go. I wanted to follow her, to love her, to marry her, to take her away from all this, but I knew leaving was the very thing she did not want.

I climbed out after her and closed the door quietly. The knot in my chest tightened. I could not face the people in the lodge, so I walked toward the brush, for once not considering bears or alligators or any other wildlife. My mind was full of Kate.

Only a few steps into the dark, I ran into a man with a gun. In a stocking mask.

"Do not make a sound," he said. His voice quivered. He sounded more scared than I was, which was saying something. The mask distorted his voice a little, but not enough to fool me.

"Not again," I said. "Are you kidding? This is the dumbest thing you have done yet, Dubois. Holding me up? It's insane. It'll get you nothing but jail time."

I could not tell through the mask whether he was upset that I recognized him or if he simply did not care. Either way, his hand shook, and the pistol looked much bigger than the ones Roy Sterling carried.

"You are coming with me. No shouting. I want the movie. Your computers. Your notes. Everything."

"Whitfield did not send you, did he?" I said. "He is not that stupid. This is your idea."

His gun twitched, a tiny, irritated jerk, and I knew I had hit a nerve. "Get moving."

Lights from the lodge spilled across the lawn in long yellow rectangles. Everything felt strangely quiet. Only one white van remained in front of the lodge. The others had been turned in. Most of the cast and crew were gone.

I lifted my hands slightly, not in surrender, but more in disbelief. "You want me to walk you in there at gunpoint, wearing that mask? There are still a few people around. You think nobody will notice? It will be worse than when you tried to steal it in the middle of the night."

"Get moving," he said, voice tight behind the fabric.

He did not sound confident. He sounded strained and shaky. Up close, his hand trembled even more. Dubois was not a criminal. He was not even especially brave. He was someone who had made one terrible decision after another, and then let it snowball into something worse.

"You were fired," I said, understanding. "Whitfield fired you. Is that what this is? A last-ditch effort to get back in his good graces?"

Laughter drifted from the lodge. A door slammed. Someone shouted something unintelligible. Life was happening thirty yards away, loud enough to drown out reason but not loud enough to save me if Dubois panicked.

I took a slow breath.

"Dubois," I said quietly, "you are not built for this."

His jaw clenched beneath the mask. The gun twitched again.

"Move," he said, almost pleading. "Just move."

Instead of backing away, I stepped closer. His knuckles went white. The gun looked too heavy for him, as if even it was not sure whether it wanted any part of this.

"Think about it," I said. "You walk into the lodge with a gun and a stocking mask. There are at least a dozen people there. One is drunk. One is probably armed. Another will assume it is a prank and hit you with a barstool."

"I want the movie," he said, his voice cracking. "I have to have it."

"Alright. Let us say you make it through the door. Someone gets nervous. Someone yells. Someone trips over a cooler. Even if you are not tackled, one shot will set off the whole place. You will have every angry actor, PA, and ex-stuntman swarming you like bees at a picnic."

"Shut up!" he barked, louder now.

But his finger hovered near the trigger, not on it. He seemed more afraid of the gun than I was. He did not want it. That was my opening.

"You are not going to shoot me," I said, folding my arms like I was waiting for a bus. "Not here. Not tonight. You would go down in criminal history as the dumbest guy alive. You would be the punchline at every bad dinner party."

I was pleased with the line. It deserved applause. Burton, Nicholson, or Clint Eastwood could not have done it better. I thought about taking a bow.

Right up until he shot me.

40.

I came to half-submerged in cold, black water, the taste of mud and blood thick in my mouth. Every breath rasped like sandpaper. The air stank of rot and rain and something older that had been waiting a long time to pull someone under.

It was as dark as midnight. Rain was a thin, steady drizzle that tapped the leaves overhead like a thousand small fingers drumming on a coffin lid. My coffin. I was pretty sure I was dead or soon would be.

The drops slid through the branches, found my face, and stung when they hit. Beneath that gentle rhythm was another sound, a low pulse, a slow, living heartbeat. The swamp itself breathed around me.

"Somebody pinch me," I said.

I closed my eyes. It had to be a dream, a terrible, fevered dream. My skull throbbed, my chest burned, and it took a long, blurred moment before I remembered the gun, the flash, Dubois's shaking hand.

He shot me. The idiot had shot me. Didn't the fool know he was going to be charged and put in prison, and he would lose his license to practice law, and Jace Whitfield would never pay him a dime? The thought of him being punished gave me surprisingly little comfort.

So, why wasn't I dead? He had a big pistol, and I was standing close. He couldn't have missed at that range.

I opened my eyes again. Still there. Still half-submerged in about a foot of black, silty water. My shirt clung to me, heavy and cold. My legs refused to move. The world tilted, swayed, then steadied with the steady drip of rain.

No, not dead. Not yet. Just hurting, everywhere.

I lifted my head, and pain flared brightly behind my eyes. The trees loomed like sentinels, their moss hanging low and gray, and something rippled nearby, too close to tell if it was a fish or something larger.

The truth hit hard and cold: my worst nightmare wasn't that I was dead.

It was that I was alive, shot, bleeding, and dumped somewhere in the swamp.

My head throbbed with brutal insistence, each pulse sending a fresh jolt of fire through my skull. The ringing in my ears wasn't ringing anymore; it was a full industrial symphony, a dozen hammers pounding steel inside my brain. I was dizzy, disoriented, caught somewhere between pain and panic.

Then my wrist screamed. Oh man, not my wrist. The pain was sharp and electric, like someone driving nails through bone. Broken again. Worse than before. What was the old saying? Third time's the charm. Well, the fourth was no picnic.

Panic came fast and merciless. It slammed into me like a wave, stealing my breath and crushing what little calm I had left. My chest tightened. I gasped, choking on swamp air thick as soup.

The water around me felt alive, closing in, black and cold and endless. Shadows wavered at the edges of my vision: dripping moss, twisted cypress roots, the ghost shapes of trees bending closer as if to watch me drown. Something hissed nearby, snakes or the sound of snakes, which was almost worse. A twig snapped in the dark, followed by the heavy, deliberate slap of an alligator's tail slicing through the water.

I remembered what Atkins had told me, back when this was still a story, something to laugh about. "No official record of anyone ever being eaten by an alligator in the Okefenokee," he said. "I read it online."

Small comfort now.

I was about to make history.

I was trapped in the belly of the Okefenokee, in the dark and the rain.

A fragile creature in a silent, breathing world that didn't want me here.

My chest tightened again, my heartbeat thudding so loud I thought it might burst free from my ribs. I couldn't move, couldn't think past the overwhelming flood of raw fear clawing up my throat. I was a wild, unthinking animal fighting for escape where none existed.

I yelled for help, stupid, more instinct than thought.

The sound shocked me back, breaking the tide. My voice, human and real, cut through the thick air and cracked the invisible wall of dread pressing down on me. I knew nobody was coming.

Slowly, I forced my body to obey.

Breathe. One slow, trembling breath.

Then another.

I closed my eyes and focused on the rain, the cold drip steady and real. It grounded me. I focused on the pain in my wrist, sharp and fiery, reminding me that I was still alive.

I was here.

I was breathing.

I was alive.

The water was shallow enough to stand, but I couldn't see anything except the black mirror around me. I fought the urge to panic again. Panic wouldn't help. Panic would get me killed. An alligator or a snake under the surface would get me killed. Everything around me would get me killed.

Or maybe I was already dead, and this was purgatory. It smelled like it.

I knew two things for certain. One, walking would probably get me bitten by a snake, alligator, turtle, or bullfrog. The list seemed endless. Two, I was certain to die if I stayed where I was.

Some choice.

I took a slow, careful step forward, feeling the muddy bottom squish beneath my loafers. The water barely reached my knees, but the darkness beneath the surface was a void, hiding whatever waited there. Every snapped twig or rustle in the thick swamp brush set my nerves on edge. I tried to focus on my breathing, slow, steady, pushing down the tightening coil of fear in my chest.

Man, I was scared.

The air felt heavy, and the scent of decaying leaves mixed with the sharp, metallic tang of blood and something alive and watching. Shadows shifted in the murky water at the edge of my vision, but when I looked directly, there was nothing but blackness. My heartbeat thundered in my ears, louder than any croak or splash.

I moved with the caution of prey, reaching out to steady myself on a gnarled root or a moss-covered branch as I navigated the uneven swamp floor. Each step was deliberate, careful enough to avoid disturbing whatever lived beneath the surface, yet desperate enough to keep me moving forward.

In the distance, a faint glow of dying light flickered through the tangled canopy. I hesitated. It couldn't be sunlight. Not at midnight, or somewhere near it. I had no idea how long I'd been unconscious.

It might be a lantern held by a long-dead woman who wanted to take me as her lover. And drown me.

"Stop it," I said aloud, my own voice startling me.

Maybe it was a lantern, or whatever else it wanted to be, but it was a direction. I clung to that hope, even as the swamp seemed to close in tighter.

Panic pressed at me again. It's hard to describe sheer terror unless you've felt that sense that the whole world wants you gone. I tried to keep my mind off the black water I was wading through. I thought of Kate and the way she made me feel different from anyone I had ever known. I thought of movies I'd watched, of John Wayne stomping through a swamp and scaring every creature away.

I was no John Wayne. I wouldn't have even made a good sidekick.

I wasn't much of a churchgoer, and I seldom prayed, but I found myself praying now. With every step, I whispered please, and it was every prayer anyone had ever said, rolled into one word.

Through the dense curtain of moss and mist, I could see nothing but blackness and that single light in the distance, flickering, moving ahead of me, always just out of reach.

I passed a twisted cypress, ancient and bent, its roots clawing out of the water like fingers reaching for salvation. I recognized it. Kate had stayed close to it on our boat ride.

Her boat had seemed fragile then, barely able to float.

If only I had it now.

41.

W here was a Girl Guide when I needed one?

In the darkness, something touched me.

Not a branch. Not a drifting weed. Something else. Something slimy.

At that moment, I might have walked on water. I know I ended up at a good distance from where I started.

Breathing hurt. I was tasting blood, rain, and something like copper with every breath. The taste clung to the back of my mouth like those terrible fish tacos. My feet were in mud, and it sucked off one of my hand-stitched Italian leather loafers. Next time, I was getting boots. Something built for the long haul. I remembered a commercial like that, or was that a truck commercial?

It didn't matter. There probably wouldn't be a next time.

A few minutes later, I lost the other loafer.

"Please," I whispered. Not to anything in particular. Just... out there. To the trees. The fog. The thing that had touched me.

But the swamp said nothing. My prayer vanished into the sodden hush like a breath on glass, unheard, unwelcome, and utterly alone.

Whatever had touched me didn't follow, or maybe it did, just out of reach, just out of sight. Close enough that I could feel it pressing against the edge of my mind, a whisper of presence like a shadow you can't quite catch.

I kept moving. Or tried to. The mud clung to my feet, thick and greedy, sucking at each step as though it wanted me to stay. One of my socks was gone. I didn't even remember losing it. Cold, wet filth oozed between my toes, seeping into the cracks of my skin, and the sensation was so vivid, so real, that it almost broke through the fog of panic. It squelched when I lifted my foot, a slow, obscene sound that made me shudder.

I had no idea where I was or where I was going. The darkness felt alive, shifting and breathing around me. Only the light ahead offered any direction, a trembling promise of escape or doom. I followed it because there was nothing else to do.

The ooze worked its way deeper with every step, slick and clinging, a reminder that the earth itself didn't want to let me go. I could feel tiny pebbles and unseen things moving against my skin, trapped with me inside that cold embrace.

I might be walking into my own death, but it didn't matter anymore. Death felt clean compared to this. Death didn't crawl between your toes or whisper from the dark.

At some point, I lost my other sock. By then, it hardly mattered. I didn't need socks anyway. My feet weren't all that cold. Was there a commercial about heavy socks? I bet there wasn't. If I could think of a good jingle or tagline about heavy socks, I could make a fortune. Something like if you're ever stuck in the swamp, don't take a chance on being barefoot, buy the heavy socks, guaranteed to protect against insect bites, alligator teeth, and slush between your toes.

Guaranteed. I said it out loud and drew out the syllables like good old Justin Wilson with his wine, hot sauce, and Cajun cooking. I wasn't all that fond of Cajun cooking, but I was getting hungry. Beggars can't be choosers.

I saw a flicker of light again, just ahead of me.

Are you there, Simone? Are you waiting on me? I doubted it was Simone. A reflection off the water, maybe, or one of those bugs that lit up. What did they call them? Bugs that light?

At the cemetery, I'd said I would have liked to meet her, but not like this. My brain fed me ghost stories, dredging up every whispered legend I'd ever half-listened to. I kept telling myself I didn't believe in any of it. I didn't believe in her.

But there was definitely a light up ahead.

It flared once, sharp and sudden, then dimmed to a faint, trembling glow. Could be a camper, I told myself. Someone might have been spending the night on one of the old docks, maybe fishing, maybe just looking for quiet. Someone real.

It certainly wasn't Simone Laviolette, risen from the black water, calling out for the lover who never came back. That was just a story.

The light flared again, brighter this time, too bright to be a lantern, and then faded into the mist. The air around me grew thicker, colder. The boards beneath my feet gave a low groan, like something breathing just below.

I swallowed hard, trying to convince myself to keep moving.

Just a camper.

Just a light.

Just a story.

Well, if Simone were calling, I guess I would meet her. My choices were dwindling.

The light returned, swaying now, unsteadily, as if it were being carried by an unseen hand. It no longer moved aimlessly. There was purpose in its motion. And worse, it moved like it knew I was watching.

It pulled at me. I felt it in my chest, like a thread winding tighter with every step. Not painful, but inescapable. Like a hook through the ribs, gentle but sure. I didn't resist. I don't think I could have, even if I wanted to.

I don't know how long I followed it. The ground clung to my feet, thick with mud that made every step an effort. My legs throbbed with fatigue, and my throat burned from the damp, heavy air. Every time I slowed, the light drifted ahead, and fear would crawl up my spine until I moved again.

I kept telling myself there had to be a reason. I remembered something I'd read once about strange lights in marshes. Natural phenomena. Swamp gas. Phosphorescent fungi. Something scientific. Something real.

Not Simone. Maybe?

I held onto that idea like a rope in deep water. I needed to believe there was an explanation, even as the light slipped between the trees, always just far enough ahead, always moving forward, as if leading me somewhere I was meant to go.

I kept going, one exhausted step at a time, following that faint, flickering light and trying not to think about the muck squelching between my toes. Every breath was shallow and ragged, the air heavy with damp earth and decay. Branches scraped against my arms as if the forest itself was trying to hold me back.

Then I bumped into something solid. Hard. I stumbled back, heart pounding. In the dim light, a shadow took shape, different from the hunched silhouettes of trees around me. It had edges, angles, and straight lines that did not belong here.

Not natural.

Manmade.

My heart hammered in my chest, louder than the rain. For a moment, I thought I was imagining it, some trick of the storm or my own desperation. But then, through the pounding rain, a faint glow flickered just beyond the edge of the trees, like a candle flame caught in the wind.

A deck. A dock.

I felt the edges, wood slick and worn but unmistakably real. The planks stretched out into the darkness, leading somewhere beyond the black water's edge. I stumbled forward, one shaky step, then another. My legs buckled, and I nearly dropped to my knees, not from relief but from sheer, shaking exhaustion.

I clawed onto the bottom step like a half-drowned thing, dragging myself up with numb fingers. The wood was slick with rain and algae, but it held. Solid. A rare certainty in a shifting world.

I collapsed on the bottom step, shivering and gasping, breath ripping in and out like I'd been running for hours. Water streamed off me in thin, cold rivulets, soaking into the cracks of the dock. My limbs trembled, cold and fear and raw effort making them feel alien, as if they belonged to someone else.

The world tilted, shuddering at the edges of my vision. I knew I was hallucinating, had to be, but that knowledge did nothing to dull the terror clawing through my chest. The spectral shape hovered just ahead, a wavering smear of bluish light that pulsed and shimmered as though alive. Its outline kept shifting, human then not, its form dissolving into mist before reforming, faintly luminous against the night.

I could see eyes within it, or thought I could, glaring and pitiless, burning through the dark. They weren't made of light, but of absence, two black holes rimmed with the faintest silver glow. They fixed on me, and something in their gaze beckoned, wordless and relentless.

Hysteria rose in my throat, hot and wild. I wanted to run, to scream, but instead I crawled, slow and desperate, drawn by the shape's silent summons. A presence brushed against my thoughts, cool and electric, as if invisible fingers were threading through the fabric of my mind. Up, it whispered without words, and I obeyed.

The dock loomed before me, slick with rain and shadow. My fingers dug into the rough, splintered wood. Every muscle in my body trembled with the effort. The boards were slick beneath my palms, but they held. My teeth clenched, breath coming in ragged bursts as I pulled myself upward, inch by inch, the bluish glow above growing brighter, closer.

When I finally dragged myself onto the dock properly, I collapsed against the boards. They groaned beneath me but did not give way. The spectral shape hovered a few feet ahead, wavering in the night air, almost transparent now.

And then, just like that, it disappeared, gone in the blink of an eye, leaving only the empty dock, the steady rain, and the thick, enveloping darkness. Deep down, I was certain it had been nothing more than a trick of my mind. Hysteria mixed with the pounding adrenaline in my veins had twisted reality into something unreal. There was no ghost, no shadow lurking, just the rain, the night, and my own restless thoughts playing cruel games. I forced myself to believe it, convinced that fear had painted pictures where there were none.

And yet...

42.

I t was unfair.

Things were bad enough. I had enough to contend with, but I had learned the lesson a long time before.

Never, ever, believe it can't get worse.

The rain got hard, almost angry that I escaped the swamp. I was shivering. My teeth were chattering. And I have to be honest. I don't care what anyone says about preserving flora, fauna, wildlife, or the so-called "wonderful experience" of canoeing in the wild; I will go to my grave despising the swamp.

Every inch of it. The thick, suffocating humidity that clings to your skin like a wet blanket. The relentless stench of decay and damp earth seems to seep into your very soul. The heat is a heavy, oppressive force that makes every movement feel like a battle. And then there are the bugs, the monstrous, relentless insects the size of fists, buzzing mercilessly around your head, diving straight for your exposed skin like they've got a personal vendetta.

I was no backwoods survivalist. I didn't thrive on the wild; I belonged in civilization, preferably somewhere with air conditioning humming quietly in the background and a coffee maker ready to brew a fresh, steaming cup at a moment's notice. Somewhere clean, controlled, and free of the endless swarms of biting, irritating bugs. Absolutely no bugs. Because in the swamp, bugs aren't just a nuisance; they're an assault on sanity.

I spent the night curled in a trembling knot on the splintered wooden platform, sweating even though my clothes were soaked through and the rain kept falling. Bugs were in my face and probably in the hole I feared a bullet had left in my head. Every creak of the trees and rustle of leaves jerked me awake and made me think I was about to meet something with too many teeth.

With the first fragile light of dawn, the relentless rain finally began to slacken. All night long, it had poured from the sky in blinding torrents, smudging the outlines of trees and water into a single formless smear, as if the world had been painted with a reckless hand and left to drip.

I sat hunched in the middle of the weathered platform, knees pulled to my chest, arms curled tightly around them. The thick, humid air clung to my skin like a wet shroud, damp, heavy, suffocating. Cold seeped through my soaked clothes, crawling deeper by the minute, sinking into my bones. The night had been a brutal pendulum, swinging between shivering fits that wracked my body and feverish waves of heat that flushed unevenly across my skin.

I had found by accident where I had been shot, a deep groove over my right ear. It hurt to touch it. The wound was raw and crusted over, and touching it had made it bleed again. I tried not to touch it anymore.

I needed food. I needed shelter. I needed warmth. None of those things was likely to be found.

And whenever the rest of me wasn't hurting severely, my wrist ached.

All around me, the Okefenokee stretched into the dim, mist-laced gloom, a desolate sprawl of dark, glassy water, curtains of hanging vines, and tangled, half-submerged roots that looked more like claws than trees. The place didn't feel indifferent—it felt hostile, like it resented my presence.

I tried to stand. Bad call. A wave of nausea surged through me—violent, overwhelming. I doubled over and vomited up a thin, bitter slush—mostly rainwater and bile. My stomach clenched, empty and aching.

I tried to clear my head. Thinking only made it worse. The swamp was unnervingly quiet, blanketed in a heavy stillness broken only by the soft patter of leftover drizzle and the distant, muffled croaks of unseen frogs. But there was something else, too, low and deep, like a rumble buried beneath the earth. A growl, maybe. I'd heard it a few times the night before, threading through the rain. I told myself it was thunder. Just thunder. But I wasn't sure. And the last thing I needed was one more predator I hadn't met yet.

I knew for certain I wasn't about to risk another step into that black, sucking mud. I'd stay put until help arrived, or until hunger and thirst consumed me. The idea of starving seemed less terrifying than braving the swamp again.

Or maybe I could build a boat. People did that, right? I'd read that Native Americans made canoes from trees. But how? I had no clue where to start. They also supposedly made fire by striking rocks together. Even if I knew how, I lacked energy.

I realized I was stuffed full of trivia gathered from watching endless movies, none of which actually taught me how to survive.

In a movie, the hero would have already started a fire, trapped a bear for clothing, and cleared the area to begin building his cabin, all while resetting his own wrist, stitching the wound on the back of his head, and fashioning a weapon from whatever happened to be lying around. Somehow, in the middle of all that chaos, he'd have rescued a lost, half-dressed maiden with perfect hair and makeup, who would shower him with gratitude.

I looked around. No beautiful half-dressed maidens in sight.

I shifted wrong, and pain lanced through my wrist—sharp and insistent. I hated looking at it. The skin was puffed and mottled, a sickening swell of purples and blacks blooming beneath the surface like rot.

I also realized I wasn't going to have to worry about my expensive watch being ruined. It was no longer on my wrist.

I found a slightly less painful position to sit in and closed my eyes. Time blurred. I don't know how long I stayed like that—minutes, hours. Maybe I passed out. Everything was heavy and quiet, except for the noise in my head.

I thought of Kate.

Her face when I kissed her. How her lips trembled, just for a second, before she smiled. That small, stunned laugh, like she couldn't quite believe it was happening. Like joy had snuck up on her. I held onto that moment like it could keep me tethered to the world, something real and warm and human in the face of everything unraveling.

Then, out of nowhere, food. Vivid. Almost absurd in its clarity.

Porcini mushroom tagliatelle from that cramped little Italian place in Culver City, the sauce silky and earthy, the kind of flavor that made you close your eyes and just sit with it.

Or Fred's taco stand outside the office, tacos so greasy they disintegrated the moment they hit the paper, but you didn't care. You just grabbed a stack of napkins and dove in. King crab legs, steaming and sweet, cracked open with bare, dripping hands. A bowl of beef stew that tasted like January—tender chunks of carrot and potato, broth thick with comfort. Greek salads with briny olives, juicy tomatoes, and feta crumbled like snowfall. A collage of tastes, textures, and memories, little feasts that made life feel rich, abundant, worth living.

And then, always, back to Kate and things I liked about her.

I liked everything about her.

I was struck, with painful clarity, by how unfair it would be to die now. Now, when I had finally found someone I wanted to share all of it with, the flavors, the quiet moments, the laughter. The ordinary days that suddenly mattered because she was in them.

Images flickered behind my eyes like the last, shaky frames of an old film reel.

I saw Rafe. My father. A ghost, really, someone I'd never truly known. I saw Walter Griggs and realized I hadn't known him either.

Then more faces, flickering, urgent.

I saw Roy Sterling, waving his guns like a man unhinged, eyes wild, teeth gritted. I saw Ned swinging his fist at me, Elis Dubois pointing a gun. I saw Cassie becoming someone else, becoming Blue.

And then, a different kind of clarity hit me.

A vision. I was somewhere else. No, I wasn't just somewhere else, I was inside it, breathing it. Directing a scene? No. Watching it unfold. I could feel a different kind of tension in the air. It was real. The people in it were real. I knew them, or at least I thought I did.

Blue was there. Always Blue, calm in the storm, a steady presence I could cling to. And then another face, familiar, impossibly familiar. I shouldn't have been surprised. I knew I shouldn't. And yet, when my eyes met theirs, a jolt ran through me. My stomach knotted. Recognition twisted with disbelief. How could I have missed the truth?

I saw it happen—the figures struggling, the sharp crack of the gunshot reverberating through the quiet swamp, and the face that turned back toward me, eyes wide with shock and fear. Time seemed to slow, each second stretching painfully, and in that instant, I knew Simone had shown me who her murderer was.

43.

I made it through the night and somehow through the next day. At some point, I couldn't say when, I finally managed to stand. I walked the length of the dock. Well... "walked" might be generous. It was more of a shuffling, awkward stumble, like a newborn colt with a concussion. But I was upright. I was moving.

But not for long.

The far end of the dock led to a narrow trail that pushed only a few yards into the brush before ending abruptly at more dark water, as if the swamp had simply changed its mind about having a path there.

If I had known then that I was going to spend the rest of the day and another whole night on that dock, I might've just waded back into the black water and let whatever creatures lived beneath the surface finish the job.

The second night was no better than the first. Worse, maybe. My sleep was broken into pieces; I kept jolting awake every several minutes, shivering enough to make my bones feel like they were shaking. Once or twice, I stood to stretch, but my body fought me, stiff, swollen, uncooperative. Each movement felt like it scraped along the inside of my skull.

And the dreams... those were the worst.

Terrible, full-color dreams that played like old film reels melting in the projector. The Laviolette homestead flickered in and out of darkness, its windows glowing like open eyes in the night. Blue was there, running across the yard, her hair streaming behind her like a banner, her face twisted toward something I couldn't see. Then someone stepped out of the shadows.

Dreams were supposed to end. But that one didn't. Every time I dozed off, it came back, unspooling the same way, beat for beat, as if my brain had forgotten how to tell a story that moved forward.

The same person kept killing Blue, and I kept watching, unable to do anything, over and over and over.

Just after dawn on the second day, a voice dragged my eyes open.

For a second, I thought I was hallucinating again. Maybe Simone had come back. Maybe my brain was finally peeling away from reality like wet wallpaper. My vision blurred and shimmered at the edges, like heat waves rising off asphalt, except there was no asphalt and no warmth left in the world.

Darkness was creeping in again, not from sunset but from somewhere deeper inside me. The rain had come and gone in relentless bursts, soaking the dock, the trees, and me all the way down to the bone. At some point, I'd stopped caring.

My body felt fused to the boards beneath. Too cold to stand, too tired to try. Each limb was a sandbag. Each breath was an argument I didn't have the strength for. My clothes clung to me like a second, clammy skin. The chill had seeped farther than the flesh; it had numbed thoughts, blurred the line between exhaustion and surrender.

A real hero would've fought. Pushed. Crawled. Something.

But I wasn't a hero.

I wasn't even sure I wanted to be saved.

Slipping into unconsciousness sounded like mercy.

Mercy was all I craved.

But then, the voice again.

"Hey! Hey, mister, are you okay?"

I jolted, or thought I did. Hard to tell. The voice was too young, too normal, too real to be part of my hallucinations. A kid's voice.

Footsteps followed, a whole scatter of them. Feet slapping wood. Shadows shifting. Flashlights bobbing like fireflies.

I blinked hard until shapes came into focus, small forms in khaki shorts, bright patches, sashes. One kid had glasses too big for her face.

"We found him," one whispered. "It's him. It's really him."

"Is he alive?"

"I think so! He's breathing!"

I tried to speak, but the sound that came out tasted like gravel.

An adult voice, firm and feminine, steady, cut through the scramble.

"Blankets."

The kid with the oversized glasses crouched next to me, eyes huge.

"Don't move, mister. We're Girl Guides."

Girl Guides. I might've laughed if I'd had the strength. Dying on a rotted dock in the middle of the Okefenokee, and my brain had conjured Spielberg extras to retrieve the body.

But then, hands. Warm, dry, real hands. Wrapping blankets around me that smelled of plastic and pine. Something cold pressed against my temple.

"Hey, man, he stinks," one kid muttered.

A boat engine rumbled to life. A spotlight flared, slicing through the mist. Voices rose—radios crackling, orders shouted across the water.

"Call the sheriff's office."

They lifted me, and pain detonated in my skull so sharply I nearly blacked out.

I don't remember much of the ride back, just flashes: the slap of water against the hull, the hum of the motor, the endless blur of cypress and moss leaning in like spectators.

But I do remember the ambulance waiting at the dock, its lights strobing silently in the humid dusk.

The paramedics worked quickly, their voices distant, muffled, like they were speaking through cotton. The stretcher rattled beneath me as they loaded me in. The siren wailed. Somewhere between swamp and asphalt, I passed out again.

When I next surfaced, I was in a hospital bed. The lights above me swirled into starbursts each time I blinked. The monitor beeped steadily, annoying and comforting at the same time.

I reached up and found stitches running along the back of my head. My wrist was encased in something that felt like concrete, heavy and unforgiving.

"You're lucky, Mr. Sterling," a voice said.

Very matter-of-fact. Too cheerful. A doctor's version of bedside optimism.

"I don't feel all that lucky."

"Oh, but you are. A linear skull fracture from where the bullet hit you. Less severe than it could've been, truly lucky. It's a miracle you made it to that dock at all."

"That miracle came with hallucinations," I muttered.

"Not surprising," he said. "You were severely dehydrated, infected, bitten half to death, and your wrist... well, you may never get full use of it again. But your head, that's the good news. I stitched the wound neatly. Once your hair grows back, no one will know. Actors appreciate that."

"I'm not an actor," I said.

He blinked. "Oh? But your mother—Patricia Alden—"

"She was. But I didn't follow her. I'm a director."

The words felt solid. True.

Like I'd finally stepped into the right skin.

"Oh, any films I might've seen?"

"Not yet," I said. "But you will."

When I drifted awake again, two men were standing at the foot of my bed—detectives, by the look of them. I answered some questions. Or didn't. I wasn't sure. Everything slipped through like water.

The next time consciousness found me, Kate was there curled up in a chair, legs tucked under her, a book open in her lap. She looked small and tired and... beautiful.

My voice came out sandpaper rough.

"Hey."

She flinched and glanced up. Her eyes sparkled with relief and fear tangled together.

"Noah," she whispered. "You're awake."

"Barely." I swallowed. "Feels like a fever dream. Except... you're here."

"Ann and I have been taking turns," she said softly. "We didn't want you waking up alone."

"I want to marry you," I blurted.

She froze. "That's just the drugs talking."

"Maybe," I said. "But when I thought I was dying, I kept thinking about you. And food. But mostly you."

Her expression broke, just a fraction.

"I knew," I said, quieter now, "that if I made it through this, I wasn't going to waste another minute. I want the rest of my life with you."

"Noah..."

"I mean it."

She leaned forward slowly and rested her forehead against mine. Her breath was warm, carrying the faintest tremor, and for a moment we stayed that way, suspended. When she finally spoke, her voice was low and careful, as if the words themselves might break.

"We'll talk about it," she whispered, "when you're not half-drugged."

"Promise?"

She touched her fingers to her lips, then to mine.

"Promise."

And for the first time since the swamp, I felt warm.

44.

I sat on the edge of the hospital bed, the paper-thin mattress groaning beneath my weight. The room smelled of antiseptic, and something sour I couldn't name—something that clung to the back of my throat no matter how shallow I breathed. The air was too clean, too bright, humming faintly with fluorescent light.

Ann had brought me a new pair of soft slip-ons, the kind that didn't need laces or buckles or effort. Just a weak tug and they were on. She'd thought ahead. Even though my right wrist was wrapped so solidly, the smallest movement sent dull, electric pain running up my arm. Lacing anything was out of the question.

She'd also brought clothes from the campground: jeans, a shirt, a belt. They were clean, at least. Folded neatly at the foot of the bed. The denim smelled faintly of detergent and pine smoke. I stared at them for a while before reaching out.

My hospital gown rustled when I moved, and even the slightest movement reminded me how bruised I still was: shoulder to ribs, ribs to hip. I could feel the tight pull of stitches when I bent, the dull throb behind my skull where bone had cracked, and skin had been sewn back together.

The nurse had left a plastic bag on the rolling tray. My "personal effects," she'd called it. Inside: a wallet, a keyring, and some soggy dollar bills.

My original clothes were gone, shredded, half burned, stiff with dried blood. They'd cut them off me in the ER and sealed them away, out of sight, out of mind. I never asked to see them. There wasn't anything worth salvaging.

And nothing from that night I wanted to remember.

Except I couldn't stop remembering. I'd be fine one moment, and then the shivering would start, that same terrible, ugly fear tightening its grip around my throat.

Getting dressed took longer than I expected. Every movement felt like it belonged to someone else's body—slow, clumsy, unsure. My head throbbed beneath the stitches: tight and hot, as if something alive pulsed just under the skin. It wasn't pain anymore, not exactly. Just pressure. Constant. Relentless.

I'd asked how many stitches there were. No one had given me a number. That probably meant too many.

The hospital room was hushed, still holding its breath between night and morning. Pale light leaked through the blinds, striping the floor in narrow bands of gray. Somewhere down the hall, a cart squeaked, followed by the soft murmur of nurses starting their shift.

It was early. Quiet.

I thought of Paul Deerfield. I wondered what he'd say when he found out I wanted to marry his daughter. Probably laugh first. Then go quiet. Then give me that long, level look of his that said he was measuring whether I deserved her.

A soft knock at the door pulled me back.

"Come in," I said, though my voice came out rough, more gravel than sound.

The door opened just enough to let in a sliver of hallway light. The nursing assistant stepped in, tall, thin, with big brown eyes behind round glasses that made her look even younger than she probably was. Her name tag read NAN in neat block letters.

We hadn't talked much. Maybe she was uneasy around me. The first few days, my room had been crowded with detectives and uniforms. They'd stood in the corners, murmuring, taking notes, asking questions. Nan had seen all that. Maybe she hadn't decided yet whether I was the victim in the story, or the cause of it.

I wasn't sure either. It was easier in old westerns when the bad guys wore black hats and spat tobacco in front of the schoolmarm.

"They arrested Mr. Dubois," she said.

"Oh?"

"They found him at the Atlanta Airport, trying to get on a plane to Mexico City. It's in all the papers." She hesitated, as if she wanted to ask something more but thought better of it. "Are you ready?"

"As I'll ever be," I said.

Nan nodded and rolled the wheelchair closer. I told her I was capable of walking and even tried to stand on my own, but she pushed me down.

"Hospital policy," she said with a shrug. "Liability stuff."

I didn't argue. My legs felt hollow anyway, like someone had scooped the marrow out while I wasn't looking. The cast on my wrist tugged uncomfortably as I settled into the chair, the vinyl cold through my clothes.

As she steered us toward the elevator, Nan glanced down at me.

"So... are you really one of those movie people?"

"I suppose I am," I said.

Her face brightened. "Do you know Austin Butler?"

"Never met him."

The light dimmed a little in her eyes. I didn't mention the ones I had met, directors, screenwriters, a few character actors who'd probably played someone's shady uncle in a Netflix limited series. Names she wouldn't recognize. Or worse, she'd pretend to.

The elevator chimed. We stepped in. The ride was quiet, just the soft whir of machinery and the low, humming buzz of fluorescent lights overhead.

When the doors opened onto the lobby, the space felt suspended in that early morning lull. A few vinyl chairs sat empty, lined up like forgotten passengers in a bus station. A plastic plant leaned in one corner, dusty and tired.

Through the wide glass doors, I saw Sparks behind the steering wheel of one of the vans, a ball cap pulled low.

Ann stood on the sidewalk, arms crossed tight over her chest, her weight shifting from foot to foot. Her face was pale, worn down to the bone by leftover worry. She'd slept, but not well.

"We were so worried about you," she said.

"I was a little worried myself at times," I admitted.

Nan slowed to a stop just before the threshold.

"You want me to wheel you all the way to the van?"

"No," I said quietly. "I've got it from here."

She gave me a small nod, stepping back. "Good luck, Mr. Sterling."

"Thanks," I said. "And it's Noah."

The doors hissed open.

I stood slowly, bones creaking, knees unsure. For a second, I thought I might fall. But I didn't.

Outside, the air smelled like morning dew and motor oil. The world was still waking up. And I was still trying to decide if I was ready to join it again.

A familiar Dodge Ram truck pulled to the curb, roof stacked with fishing gear. Retired detective Tobias Atkins got out of the passenger side. I wasn't surprised. I'd expected him sooner. I'd even rehearsed our meeting like an actor preparing for a role. He noticed everything, and I couldn't let him see what I was thinking. One slip, one hint, and I'd never be free of him until he uncovered the truth.

You're looking better than when I saw you last," he said.

"Oh?"

"I was at the hospital when the paramedics brought you in. You were waterlogged and half-dead, but at least you still had all your body parts. You hadn't provided any snacks for the local critters."

"It feels like the mosquitoes ate half of me," I said.

"And did you run into Simone's ghost out there?" he asked.

As much as I had prepared myself, something must have shown on my face because his eyes grew suddenly suspicious.

"No ghosts," I said. "If she was out there, she left me alone."

He was quiet for a moment, as if sensing something off-kilter in my answer. I was reminded that he was a former detective, a good one, used to hunting half-truths and lies. I wasn't lying, but I was hiding something, and he knew it instinctively.

"You know about Dubois being caught?" he finally asked.

"Yes."

"He's not exactly a master criminal. They even found the gun he used on you stuffed underneath the front seat of the car he left at the airport. A Ruger LCP."

"I don't know about guns," I said.

"It's a little pocket pistol. Not all that effective. Lucky he didn't pick something more powerful, or he'd have taken your head off standing that close."

"Lucky," I said.

"He's doing a lot of talking," Atkins said. "He admitted Jace Whitfield was his client, and that Whitfield wanted the script. They sent a detective to question Whitfield. He confirmed he'd tried to buy it, through Griggs first, and when that didn't work, he sent Dubois to make another attempt. Whitfield swears he never told Dubois to steal it, and definitely not to come after you with a gun."

"You believe him?" I asked.

Atkins exhaled through his nose. "Dubois's is a loser, a small-town lawyer who always wanted to be somebody bigger than he was. Talking to him, yeah... I think I do believe it. And I also suspect there was a little bit of hero worship involved. From what I gather, Dubois looked up to Jace even back in high school. I think he believed if he got that script, Whitfield would have finally appreciated him."

"I doubt it. I've only met Whitfield one time, but he didn't strike me as the type who appreciated people."

"You're probably right. Ellis claims that shooting you was an accident. The gun just went off. And when he saw how much you were bleeding, he panicked. He was sure you were dead. Head wounds will do that. He says he never would have dumped you in the swamp if he'd realized you weren't dead."

"Considerate of him," I said.

"He also had your watch."

"Excuse me?"

"I noticed your watch when I first talked to you in the restaurant. Expensive. Dubois figured you wouldn't need it anymore, being dead and all, and he didn't think it should be ruined in the swamp water."

"Considerate of him," I said again.

"And sort of stupid. He was wearing it when they caught him, so it was hard for him to deny seeing you, especially when Kate said you had it that very night. You'll get it back eventually, after all the legal stuff is done."

I wasn't sure I wanted it back, or anything ever from Walter Griggs.

The conversation spun around me like heat haze. I was suddenly lightheaded, the ground shifting just enough to remind me I was still healing. Ann must've seen it. She opened the truck door, and I climbed in slowly.

Atkins followed, stopping beside the open door. "One other thing," he said. "I found out from Dubois that it wasn't Jace Whitfield's idea to mess with your father's plane."

My heartbeat quickened. "No?"

"You remember the argument I mentioned between Dubois and your father at the Okefenokee Restaurant? I think that's when Dubois made the original offer to buy the script, and your father told him to take a hike. Whitfield made his disappointment clear, and Dubois figured he'd blown his chance to impress him. Maybe Whitfield mentioned, offhand, that if your father weren't such a stubborn man, he could deal with someone else and get the movie shut down. It gave Dubois ideas."

"What are you saying?"

"Dubois used to be a pilot," Atkins replied. "He even used to have an airplane at Charley Snow Airport. As soon as I found out, I asked the sheriff if I could talk to him about that. Dubois eventually admitted he was the one who tampered with your father's plane."

So stupid, I thought. So many lives messed up, ruined because of what...greed...ambition, loyalty to a nasty, crippled, unhappy man in a wheelchair?

"I talked to the sheriff and the county DA," Atkins continued. "They're just trying to figure out what they're going to charge him with. Murder, attempted murder, and they've even dug up some financial problems. Apparently, he wasn't honest with his clients. Dubois will never get out of prison."

I drew a slow breath. "So that's it, then? You and your friend can go fishing."

"We can go fishing," he agreed, but he didn't look all that happy.

"What?" I asked.

"I'd still like to know if one of them, Jace or Ellis, or someone else entirely, killed Simone Laviolette. I hate leaving mysteries unsolved."

I didn't tell him that I knew.

45.

By the time I rolled back into Mossy Creek, the place looked like it had been evacuated overnight. It even felt empty. I was surprised to see Cassie Rhodes sitting out front of her cabin, talking on the phone. I would've thought she'd be the first to leave.

I was glad to see her. What I had in mind could have been done without Cassie. I could have staged it artfully, keeping everything in shadow, letting another actor stand in for her and sell the illusion. But it would work far better if we showed her face.

"Cassie is riding back with us," Ann said. Sparks is driving one van. Peggy Marsh is driving the other van that has all the costumes. Elly is riding with her. We'll turn in the vans and all the rest of the stuff in Atlanta, and then grab a plane out."

"We'll need a couple of hand-held cameras," I said.

Ann gave me a wary look. "Why?" "

"I want to do one more scene."

"No." She shook her head firmly. "This movie is done. You said it was done. Everybody's gone. No people, no lighting. The experts are gone."

"I have you and Sparks and Cassie, Peggy and Elly, and me. That's enough to shoot another scene." I took a sharp, sudden breath as I moved my head wrong and felt close to blacking out.

"Look at you," Ann said. "You're a mess. You're barely standing up, and you want to do another scene?"

"It's just a short scene. We can do it this afternoon, but we have to go back out to the Laviolette Homestead."

Ann shook her head and went to gather the others while I walked toward Cassie. She saw me coming and hung up.

"Why are you looking at me like that?" she asked.

"Like what?"

"Like you've made a decision I'm not going to like."

"One last scene."

Her eyes narrowed. "Please tell me you mean a pickup shot of a tree blowing in the wind. Or a hand turning a doorknob. Something I can do without getting stung, bitten, or emotionally scarred."

"It's the murder," I said.

She froze mid-blink.

"I thought it was never going to be a filmed murder," she said. "It was supposed to be implied. Atmospheric. Off camera. Like the book."

"I know." I tried to smile; it probably looked worse than a frown. "But I can see it now. Exactly how it should look. I just need to capture it."

Cassie stared at me, waiting for the punchline. When none came, she raked a hand through her hair and muttered something that sounded suspiciously like a prayer.

Ann returned, rounding the corner of the nearest cabin, Sparks behind her, looking like he'd swallowed a lemon. Peggy Marsh was right behind him, and Elly was only a few steps behind.

"I miss my babies," Peggy said. "I'm not hanging around here one second more than necessary. You told us this movie was done."

"Just one short scene more. It's important."

"No more important than my babies," she said, "and besides, you don't look healthy enough to direct another scene. Possibly you could star in another episode of The Walking Dead."

"I'm fine. And we have to do this."

I was surprised by how steady my voice sounded.

I glanced at Sparks. " I also need a firearm. A pistol."

"Roy's gone," he said. "He took his guns with him."

"Something that looks real. A toy. We can add the sound later."

Sparks nodded. "I can probably find something like that."

Ann folded her arms. "This is nuts."

"Look," I said, "it won't take long. I wrote the scene while I was lying in bed. It's mostly action, not much dialogue. We just need a few costumes and a drive to the Laviolette Homestead. We can do it this afternoon. Just a couple of hours."

Kate came out of the lodge just then, keys in hand, hair tied back. "What's going on?"

When she heard, she gave me a look that suggested she wasn't entirely convinced my head wound hadn't scrambled something.

She sighed. "All right. But I'm coming. And if you pass out, I'm dragging you back to bed."

She blushed a little at the implication of her words, and I was tempted to pretend to pass out on the spot.

"I guess I'm going to have to unpack the costumes," Peggy said.

"No," I said. "I've got something specific in mind."

It took longer than I wanted, but Peggy drove me into Waycross in my rental, and the two of us went through a half-dozen clothing stores and ended up finding what I needed in a Salvation Army store.

I needed a simple cotton blouse, pale in color and soft with age. I needed a light blue cardigan with military-style buttons. I needed something that passed for khaki pants, and I found them hanging in a back corner. Not quite Cassie's size, but close enough. The look matched what I had seen in my vision.

I found the rest of what I needed, and as we were turning to leave, something tugged at my memory. I doubled back to the table where they'd laid out the jewelry, rows of cheap imitation pieces glinting under the lights, and there I found a small gold locket on a chain.

Up until then, I hadn't remembered the locket, but now I saw it being torn from Cassie's neck in the struggle, and I knew it was an important piece of the visual.

"I've picked costumes with producers before," Peggy said on the drive back, "but never with one so obsessed over exact colors and cuts. What's that about?"

"If I tell you, you'll think I'm crazy."

"I already think you're crazy."

"I saw the scene in a hallucination out in the swamp."

"Ah," she said after a beat. "I'm right."

"About what?"

"You're crazy."

In the afternoon, we caravanned to the Laviolette Homestead. Kate drove me with me in the Nissan. Sparks, Cassie, and Ann rode in the van. We were lucky to find no tourists at the site.

I waited until everyone was together to hand out the scripts.

Up until that moment, nobody had guessed what the ending would be, and now they all looked at me with shocked faces.

"I want to start with Blue on the porch," I said. "She has just learned that Charley was killed in Vietnam, and she's come here because it's her place.

When they started to ask questions, I gave them no explanations, just a short "let's do it."

We got it on the first take, and I was thankful. I wasn't sure I had the energy to run the scene more than once.

The hand-held cameras moved perfectly, capturing the strange, dreamlike quality I wanted. In moments, Cassie became Blue again, more intensely than ever.

We followed her into the woods, toward the water, when a figure emerged from the shadows. Sparks had come up with a plastic gun that looked real, and now the figure pointed it at Blue.

For a heartbeat, nothing moved. The trees stood rigid, the surface of the water dark and glassy beyond them. Instinct took over—Blue turned to run—but the ground betrayed her. Her foot slid on mud near the water, and she went down hard, the impact knocking the air from her lungs in a sharp, helpless gasp.

She tried to push herself up, fingers clawing at the mud, but her arms shook too badly to hold her.

The scene unfolded exactly as I had seen it in the swamp—every movement, every second falling into place with a terrible, unchangeable certainty.

Blue looked up, horror widening her eyes as the figure stepped over her, blotting out what little light filtered through the trees. Slow. Certain. Inevitable.

A hand reached down and seized the chain at her throat.

It snapped with a thin, metallic crack.

"He gave that to you."

The locket was flung into the undergrowth, vanishing into shadow with a soft rustle. Blue lay trembling on the damp earth, her breath shallow, uneven. Her vision blurred at the edges, the world dimming and swimming. Somewhere to her right, the locket caught a sliver of faint light, half-buried in the leaves—glinting weakly, as if trying to be seen.

Her attacker straightened and pointed the weapon again. The swamp seemed to hold its breath. Even the water nearby stilled, its quiet lapping gone, as though the world itself had paused—waiting.

Watching.

For a moment, everything stretched thin, suspended between one second and the next.

Then the figure said, " Bang."

The sound of the gunshot would be added later, but I could hear it in my soul by just watching the eerie ballet of violence.

"We're done," I said.

Nobody spoke. Nobody moved until I walked over to pick up the piece of jewelry with the quick clasp that I'd purchased and found something else beneath the wet leaves. At first, it looked like a mis-shapen stone. When I brushed the leaves' aside, it glimmered faintly.

The locket was old. Not bright, polished, cold, deep, swamp-soaked cold, like something that had slept in the dirt for years. My fingers sank into the grime; the metal felt rough, pitted, like old bone left out in the weather. A smear of mud slid off, revealing a sickly flicker of gold. The metal was dark, bruised, and mottled with green-black corrosion around the hinge.

I rubbed away more dirt until the inscription appeared:

To Blue, from Charley.

46.

We got back to Mossy Creek Campground just after sunset, too drained even to pretend otherwise. The sky shifted from deep purple to pale gold, thin light threading through the Spanish moss, but none of us paid attention. We walked like the newly shell-shocked, hollowed out by something that had taken more from us than we ever meant to give.

"Are you sure about the ending?" Ann asked.

"I'm sure," I said.

Later, I helped Sparks, Ann, Cassie, Peggy, and Elly pack the last van. Ann and I spent the rest of the afternoon packing up the editing room. I spent the rest of the afternoon packing up the editing room. We finally moved all the scenes onto backups, and I put Ann in charge. I kept the laptop.

That evening, we shared one last simple meal, vegetable soup, and freshly baked bread. Afterward, I sat with Kate on the balcony. The rain had returned, soft and steady, darkening the surface of Mossy Creek. Each drop spread into widening circles, dissolving the reflections of the trees. A blue heron moved along the bank, cautiously stepping and probing the water, searching for whatever the creek might offer.

"I'm still taking pain pills to sleep for my wrist," I said.

"Oh?"

"But the pills are not all that strong. I'm in my right mind."

She gave me a look. "That's debatable."

"You did promise we'd talk about it."

She sighed. "It's complicated."

"You've said that before."

"This is my home, Noah. And I don't just mean Mossy Creek Campground. I mean a way of life where people still respect authority, where we show the flag, where we go to church, and keep our vows. It's not exciting. It's not Hollywood."

"Everybody in Hollywood isn't insane. We got to church. We respect the flag. Well, some of us."

"It's also my dream, Noah. I want to finish school and set up a veterinary office here. I want to work with real farm animals as well as dogs, cats, and rabbits."

"We have rabbits in Hollywood. And cows. And as for dogs? Talk to Peggy. She has a multitude. She could keep you in business with just her animals."

"You already have a return flight," Kate said, still looking at the water. "A studio waiting. Projects lined up. Your whole life points west—toward things I'm not sure I'd ever want to be part of. And I'm... rooted here. In this muddy, beautiful nowhere. In cypress trees and quiet churches. In a life that probably seems impossibly small to someone like you."

"That's not—"

"Isn't it?" She turned to me, eyes bright. "Be honest, Noah. Can you really see yourself staying here? Building a life in a place where the biggest excitement is a church fish fry? Where everyone knows everyone else's business going back three generations?"

I wanted to say yes. I wanted to tell her I'd stay anywhere she was. But the words wouldn't come. She was right. My whole life was three thousand miles away. I desperately wanted Kate to share it, but I couldn't bring myself to say I was willing to live in Folkston.

"It is a long commute, I admit," I said, "but maybe we could find a way."

She nodded, as she'd expected it. "It's just not going to work, Noah."

"What if I could promise to stay here?" I asked, too quickly.

"Could you?" Her voice held no malice, only tired truth. "Could you walk away from everything you've built? Could you be happy here when the novelty wears off, and it's just... this?"

"I don't know," I said again.

"That's what I thought." She smiled sadly. "I can't build my heart around I don't know. No matter how I feel."

"So you do feel something?"

She gave a small, watery smile. "Of course, idiot. I don't go parking with boys I don't like."

"I love you," I said again. "I want to marry you."

She closed her eyes as if the words hurt. "Don't."

"It's true," I said. "I know the timing's awful. I know there are a hundred reasons this shouldn't work. But I love you, Kate. I love your strength. Your mind. Everything."

When she opened her eyes, they were glassy with tears. "That makes it worse."

"How?"

"Because I have to break both our hearts instead of just mine." She stood, holding her book tight to her chest. "I can't do this, Noah.

Please go. Your movie's done. We had a few good moments. I'll remember them."

Then she left me alone.

I stood there, staring at the boards, half-tempted to follow, half-tempted to plead, or pick her up and carry her to my bed. But this wasn't a movie, and I wasn't Rhett Butler.

And she was right. In a week, I'd be back in Culver City, pulled under by meetings and edits and fast-talking people chasing things that didn't matter. Kate would still be here, rooted in this quiet place that had shaped her.

Maybe that was love, too, knowing the difference between what you want and what's possible, and letting both truths stand.

I guess that's maturity, but it's highly overrated.

The rain came harder. Down below, the big blue heron planted its long legs in the shallow water, then slowly spread its massive wings. With a strong push, it lifted into the mist and rain, growing smaller with every beat until it vanished into the gray haze.

47.

I had one thing left to do, something that required confrontation and accountability, but I couldn't bring myself to do it. Not yet.

I couldn't convince Kate to leave with me, either, though I tried for days. We walked in the woods and talked at length about the future, about commitments, about compromises. In the end, neither of us could bend far enough.

I wasn't giving up. I knew I'd be back.

I was leaving something undone.

The freeway spit me out into Culver City just after dusk. The sky was bruised and heavy, an odd color I couldn't ever remember seeing before.

The sign over Venice Boulevard flickered as if it were considering surrender. Half the letters were dim, the rest buzzing with a tired electric whine. I slowed at the light and stared at the low buildings crouched along the street, their stucco facades stained darker than I remembered, windows reflecting nothing but the sagging purple-gray sky.

Culver City used to feel open. Sun-bleached. Easy.

Now it felt like something had been drained out of it.

Or maybe it was just me.

Getting out of the taxi at the condo, I froze for a moment. An unnatural bluish light flickered near the entrance, and my heart jumped, as if Simone had followed me from the swamp. The fear clutched at my chest until I realized the light was nothing more than a reflection from a neon sign across the street, glinting off the glass doors. Even so, the moment left a chill crawling up my spine.

"Get a grip," I told myself.

I met with Rita Boucher and her investigator, Harold Keene, in Rita's office in LA, perched atop a glass tower downtown. The city sprawled beneath us, a glittering maze of streets and light.

Dark walnut bookshelves lined the walls, packed with leather-bound law books, glossy magazines, and a few abstract sculptures. A black leather couch faced a polished oak desk, nearly bare except for an ornate penholder and a glass of water that caught the sunlight streaming through the floor-to-ceiling windows.

Framed degrees, certificates, and awards hung in precise alignment, some modern, some classical, all silently declaring competence. Above the couch, a muted painting of a stormy coastline lent the room a quiet gravitas. Its blues and grays deepened the air of calm authority.

Rita sat behind the desk in a high-backed leather chair, legs crossed, laptop open, fingers steepled beneath her chin. She wore a sharply tailored gray pinstripe suit, heels reinforcing a posture both exacting and deliberate. The faint scent of expensive perfume lingered in the air, mingling with the soft hum of the city below.

Harold Keene looked more like a professor of economics than a private investigator. He was a small man in a rumpled suit with no tie and glasses.

"Yesterday at three o'clock, Rafe's will was processed through probate," he announced.

"And?"

"Rafe left five percent of his shares of Sweet Angel Pictures to Ann Girodana, and the remainder he left to you. With the shares you inherited from your mother, you are now the top shareholder."

I shook my head in disbelief. "Why would Rafe leave me his shares?"

Rita looked at me evenly. "He was your father."

"He never claimed me, and I don't think he liked me much."

"He told me once that you reminded him of who he used to be. He also said he resented you because you constantly reminded him of a promise he hadn't kept."

For a moment, I could almost feel Rafe's presence, watching from the edge of the shadows. I shook off the thought. No more ghosts for me.

I looked at Rita. "And you're certain Walter's been messing with the books?"

"As certain as I can be," she said.

Harold Keene explained, "So far, he hasn't let us look at his books. But we know he's been spending like there's no tomorrow, and he follows Lucy Delight around like he's her personal assistant with a credit card."

"Lucy Delight?" I asked. "Seriously?"

"Her real name is Lucy Wizoski, but she took Delight as her last name when she was dancing for the Elixir 77 Club."

"Exotic dancer?" I asked.

"You guessed it."

"I think that young woman has made Griggs a little crazy," Rita said.

Poor Griggs, I thought. A poor, miserable man who loved my mother so terribly that it nearly destroyed him when she died, and who had spent a lifetime buried in financial ink until another woman came along and made him feel young again.

Lucy Delight. It was hard to believe.

I nodded. "If there's anything I've learned in the past few weeks, it's that love can make you do some insane things."

Rita studied my face with the intensity of a lawyer who had someone on the stand and was about to pounce with the question that would change the outcome of a trial, or my life. "Have you been bitten by Cupid, Noah?"

"Either that, or I picked up some kind of nasty bug during my couple of nights in that swamp."

"Are you going to do something about it?"

"She doesn't want Hollywood," I said.

Rita nodded in sympathy.

"And what are you going to do about Griggs?" she asked. "He says he won't let anybody near the books until he talks to you face-to-face. I think he believes he can talk you out of it."

"Not this time," I said.

"We should probably go to the police with what we suspect," Rita argued.

"I can't do that."

Rita let the silence stretch, then stood and moved to the cabinet behind her desk. She poured two fingers of something dark into a cut-glass tumbler. She didn't offer me any, knowing how I felt about it.

"If he keeps spending money on Ms. Delight, you'll be flat broke by the time you finally decide to act," Rita warned.

"I believe Griggs thought he was in the clear until he found out that Rafe had changed his will and left his shares to you," Harold said. "In panic, he delayed the reading of Rafe's will. At first, he thought that if the movie could be finished, he could recoup some of the investors' money and save himself. Then he sent you off to finish the movie, removing you from the picture while he scrambled to cover his tracks. He was desperate to replace the missing money and make the books look clean again."

"One of his last-ditch efforts," Harold added, "was entertaining that offer to sell the movie. It would have solved all his problems. But you stood in his way. You fought him, and then you hired us. Once the word audit got thrown around, he lost it."

"I hate to say this," Rita said, "but it occurred to both Keene and me that Griggs might have had something to do with crashing your father's airplane. Maybe he hired somebody."

"No," I said. "He didn't intentionally send someone to wreck Rafe's plane, but he was indirectly responsible. A man named Dubois did the actual act, and he might have had more than one reason."

"This was the same person who dumped you in the swamp?"

"Yes."

"And you're sure Griggs didn't tell him to do that?"

"I'm sure."

Harold Keene shook his head a little disgustedly. "You're a trusting soul, Noah."

"Not so much anymore," I said sadly.

48.

In the time I'd been gone, the front office in Culver City had been remodeled. Griggs now had an outer reception area, where a trim, attractive receptionist with a welcoming smile sat behind the desk. Her nameplate read Abigail Morris, but I had already figured she was far too young and innocent-looking to be Ms. Delight.

"Welcome to Sweet Angel Productions," she said.

"I'm here to see Mr. Griggs."

"He's in a conference, but I'll ring him when he's off. Do you have an appointment?"

I went past her, ignoring her protests, and walked into Grigg's office like I owned the place. I did.

The moment I stepped inside, I froze. Griggs lounged in his chair, a plump, blond woman straddling his lap. Her blouse was half-unbuttoned, and she laughed too loudly at something he had said.

It took them both a moment to notice me, and then the woman jumped from Griggs's lap as if she had been burned.

"Noah," Griggs said.

"I love what you've done with the place," I said.

He reddened. The woman, whom I assumed was Lucy Delight, casually buttoned her blouse and walked out of the room. The door slammed behind her, and I heard her snapping at the receptionist. I felt a little sorry for Abigail Morris. I felt a little sorry for both of us.

"Noah," Griggs said again. "I wasn't expecting you so early."

"Obviously," I said, letting the words hang in the air.

I could see he was close to losing his temper, but his face snapped into that familiar polished smile he reserved for investors: perfectly white teeth, perfectly empty warmth.

"But since you're here," he said, his voice tight, like he was scolding a misbehaving stepson, "maybe you can explain why I'm getting frantic calls from Mays and Daws. They're saying you—"

"Fired them," I said. "Rita Boucher's firm will handle all our legal matters."

"You can't just fire our legal firm on a whim," he snapped.

I shrugged. "But I did."

"We need to discuss major changes to the firm."

"You mean like you've been doing? Spending time in Vegas. Remodeling, spending money you've been claiming we don't have?"

He licked his lips. "I can explain."

I slouched in a chair in front of his desk.

"I don't think so, Walter, and I don't care to hear your explanations. Rita Boucher is going to audit this company, and there's something you should be aware of. She has every receipt for the luxurious hotels you stayed at with your girlfriend, every receipt for wine, food, shows, and gambling expenses: every breadcrumb."

He started to say something, but ended up gulping like a fish.

"This wasn't how I wanted things to go," I continued. "You may not have been the best stepfather, but you were still more of one than

Rafe ever was. You were there after my mom died. You stepped in. You didn't have to. But you did. And I owe you for that."

Something flickered in his eyes. Regret, maybe. Guilt. Or the memory of the man he once was.

"That's why I'm letting you walk away," I said. "Maybe you should be charged. Maybe there should be a trial. Maybe you should go to prison. But I can't bring myself to send you there."

Griggs shrugged and half-smiled. "How long would I last?"

"That's true," I said.

"Can we make some sort of arrangement?"

"You mean like paying back the money you've stolen in installments or something?"

"Something like that. We could still work together and make this company successful."

"No," I said. "I don't think so."

"You said you owe me."

"And I could forgive you almost everything except for trying to buy your way out by killing Rafe's last movie. That was contemptible."

Walter rubbed his mouth, then the back of his neck. He looked smaller than I remembered.

I pulled a folded document from my coat and handed it to him. "This document transfers all of your shares in the company to me," I said. "Everything. For one dollar."

His eyes narrowed. A flicker of the old businessman sparked back to life. "You can't possibly think I'd—"

I cut him off.

"We're going to audit the books down to the last penny. If you don't agree, we'll go to court, and I'm going to sue you. Even if you're not found guilty of anything criminal, which you probably will be, a lawsuit will take every dime you have. You'll be on the streets, Walter, and I doubt your girlfriend will still want you around without money. This is your once-in-a-lifetime chance to walk away before everything gets nasty. Rita would prefer you not to take it. She'd like to humiliate you in court. I admit a part of me wants just that."

Griggs stared at the paper. His silence stretched, heavy and final.

"I built Sweet Angel Productions," he said.

I laughed sourly. "You're a paper pusher, Griggs. You built nothing. My mother and Rafe built the studio. You were hired help, a numbers cruncher. Someone who polished the nameplate on the door."

I didn't like myself much at that moment, but I knew if I showed any sign of weakness, Griggs would fight me. After a long moment, he picked up the pen and signed. The ink moved slowly as if he wanted to drag it out, make it hurt.

It did, maybe more for me than him.

He slid the document back to me. I folded it and tucked it into my coat. It felt heavier than steel.

"Please believe me when I say this," I told him. "If I hear your name associated with Sweet Angel Productions again, even once, the whole story goes to the police. Every receipt. Every lie. I don't care how old you are or how crippled."

He studied me for a moment and nodded. "You've changed. You're harder."

"Not long ago, I had a few nights of unwanted self-reflection," I said.

Walter nodded, small and defeated. He turned to leave, and I told him to remember to take Lucy Delight with him.

49.

Ann and I spent the next few weeks editing the film, and during that time, I spoke with Kate often on the phone. She was back in school, and sometimes her voice sounded distant. It was not only the distance between us. Something else had crept into our conversations, something I could not quite name.

I had the uncomfortable feeling that I was fouling things up somehow, that if I was not careful, I might lose her entirely. The thought troubled me, but I could not see any clear way to fix what seemed to be slipping out of my hands.

Late in August, I called Paul Deerfield and asked if I could have my old room for a night.

"Kate's not here," he said after a moment, his voice almost apologetic.

"I know," I told him. "There is just one thing left to do about the movie. Something I left unfinished. I think it is time for a little closure."

He did not understand what I meant, but he told me I would be welcome anyway. When I drove into the yard that evening, he and

Beth were waiting for me. I was not the only visitor. A tour bus from Savannah stood beside the cabins that had once housed my movie crew, and the place had the comfortable bustle of tourists settling in for the night.

I slept well. The next morning, I shared breakfast with Paul and Beth, thanked them for their hospitality, and then got back on the road.

It was only a short drive.

Through Kate, I had been hearing occasional news about the Swamp Lily Motor Lodge, so I already knew the place had closed. When I pulled into the gravel lot, I saw the "For Sale" signs planted out front. The restaurant windows were boarded up. The whole place looked tired, as if it had simply given up.

I parked and walked around back toward the apartment.

The day was much hotter than it had been in June, but the heat did not bother me the way it once had. Perhaps I had simply grown accustomed to it. Perhaps something else had changed.

Even then, I could not have explained exactly why I felt compelled to come. I was not a vengeful man, and confrontation had never been something I enjoyed. It usually left a metallic taste in my mouth that lingered long afterward.

Still, there are moments when something must be faced.

Claire opened the door before I reached the porch.

She wore a loose Hawaiian muumuu and held a glass that carried the sharp smell of whiskey. Her hair was unkempt, and her eyes had the dull heaviness of someone who had not slept well for a long time. In the months since I had last seen her, she seemed to have aged twenty years.

"You," she said.

"Like a bad penny," I replied.

"What do you want?"

"I thought we might talk."

"I had nothing to do with what my husband did," she said immediately. "He always was a stupid man."

"I am not here to talk about Ellis."

She studied me for a moment, then turned and walked back into the apartment. I followed her inside.

She dropped onto a sagging couch and poured more whiskey from the open bottle on the coffee table.

"Want any?" she asked, lifting the glass slightly.

"No."

"More for me, then."

I sat down across from her.

"Kate told me you are selling the motel."

Her eyebrows lifted. "You still talk to her? I thought you had gone back to California."

"We talk whenever we can."

She took a slow sip of whiskey.

"Where will you go after the sale?" I asked.

She considered that before answering. "Florida. My sister lives there. She lost her husband a few years ago, and she has been asking me to come down. It is something I probably should have done a long time ago. I am leaving this place behind."

"It must be difficult," I said. "Leaving the town where you grew up."

Her shoulders rose slightly in a dismissive shrug.

"And Ellis?" I asked. "Have you seen him since everything happened?"

She shook her head.

"No. And why should I? He nearly killed you. The man was always an idiot. I suspected as much even when I married him, although back then, he seemed like he might amount to something. A law degree can make a man look promising."

"But the way things turned out was not entirely his fault, was it?"

Her eyes narrowed slightly.

"I'm not sure what you mean."

I set my laptop on the floor beside my chair. She only glanced at it, uncaring, her gaze lingering on it for a moment before returning to my face.

There was that familiar look again, the same curious scrutiny I had seen from her before. For the first time, I understood it.

She was searching my face for traces of someone else.

"Augusta told me something interesting," I said.

Claire did not answer.

"She said that when she first met Rafe in California, she recognized him immediately."

Claire shifted slightly on the couch but said nothing.

"Of course she would," I continued. "She was Charley's sister. Blood recognizes blood even after a long time."

Claire lifted her glass again.

"But Augusta also said something else," I went on quietly. "She told me she doubted anyone else would recognize him after all the surgeries. Not you. Not Ellis. Too many changes."

Claire's hand paused halfway to her mouth.

"Ellis certainly did not recognize him," I said.

I waited.

"But I believe you did."

She lowered the glass slowly.

"That awful man was not Charley," she said sharply.

"I wonder what the moment felt like when you realized who he was," I said. "Did you tell him right away? Did you welcome him home?"

"You are talking nonsense."

"Perhaps. Still, it must have been a shock to see him again after all those years."

She stared down into her drink.

When she spoke again, her voice had softened slightly.

"I told him I loved him," she said.

The admission seemed to cost her something.

"I told him I had always loved him."

Her mouth twisted.

"He said he did not care. He called me a dried-up old woman."

I let the silence settle between us.

"And after that," I said quietly, "you told Ellis who he really was."

She did not answer.

"Rafe hurt your feelings," I continued. "Ellis rushed out to defend you, the way a knight might charge into battle for his lady."

Her fingers tightened around the glass.

"He told the police he sabotaged the plane because he wanted to stop Rafe from making the movie," I said. "Perhaps that was partly true. But it was not the whole truth."

I leaned forward slightly.

"He did it for you."

Claire's laugh held no humor.

"Everyone thinks Ellis ruined your life," I continued. "Poor Claire. She could have done so much better."

Her eyes lifted toward mine.

"But you never wanted to do better after you thought Charley was dead."

The glass left her hand before I could react.

I had been expecting it, but it still missed me by only a few inches before striking the wall and shattering, whiskey splashing across the faded paint.

Claire stared past me as if she were looking at someone standing in the doorway.

"Wonderful Blue," she murmured. "Lovely Blue. The most perfect girl you could imagine."

Her expression hardened.

"But she was not so perfect. Not really. She led every one of those boys around like they were toys. Charley. Jace. All of them. She played them like fiddles and never looked back."

"Everyone tells me she was a kind girl."

"Everyone was wrong," Claire snapped. "She made him love her when he should have loved me. Do you understand that? She took him from me. She sent him away, and she got him killed."

For a moment, the room was quiet except for her breathing.

Then I said softly, "I know what you did, Claire."

She looked up at me.

"I know what happened," I said

I lifted the laptop onto the coffee table and opened it.

Claire leaned forward slightly.

"You're going to show me your movie?"

"A little piece of it. The ending. I think you'll find it interesting."

I pressed play.

The strange footage began to move across the screen, distorted shapes and drifting colors captured from impossible angles. It looked almost dreamlike, yet the details were unmistakable. I thought Elly did a good job standing in for the killer. Maybe she had a future as an actress.

Claire watched without blinking.

At first, her expression remained calm.

Then small changes began to appear.

Her jaw tightened. Her breathing grew uneven. The color slowly drained from her face.

When the clip ended, she whispered, "How could you know?"

I closed the laptop but left it on the table.

"There was nobody there," she said, her voice rising. "Nobody. Just me and her. Do you understand that? Even the clothes, the jacket, the dress. How could you know those things?"

I did not answer.

She tried to stand but had to steady herself on the arm of the couch.

"It was not fair," she said hoarsely. "Blue had them all. They adored her. Charley. Jace. Even Ellis. They all adored her, and she crushed the souls out of them. And then she sent Charley to die."

"You're wrong about that."

"She made a fool of him. She pretended to love him, and then she turned him down. That's why he left."

"No."

"Elis told me what happened," she insisted.

"Ellis lied."

I told her then what had really happened, how Jace and Ellis had taken Charley into the swamp and left him there overnight, humiliating him and frightening him badly enough that he ran from the town the first chance he had.

Claire listened in silence.

When I finished, she shook her head weakly.

"No."

But I could see she believed me, and I was certain if she had ever suspected the truth, Ellis Dubois would not have lived long enough to sabotage Rafe's plane.

I picked up the laptop and slipped the strap over my shoulder.

"How could you know?" she asked again.

Instead of answering, I reached into my pocket and pulled out the small locket.

I dropped it into her lap.

She stared at it as if it had appeared out of thin air.

"Blue told me," I said quietly. "She asked me to give that back to you."

Her face went pale.

I turned toward the door.

Behind me, I heard a drawer slide open.

I spun around.

Claire stood beside the couch holding a pistol.

"I will not allow you to show that in your movie," she said.

The weapon looked strangely familiar. I had seen its shape before in the strange visions that haunted my nights in the swamp. Later research had given it a name.

A Steyr-Hahn M1912.

Simone's autopsy had mentioned the unusual bullet, and after enough digging, I had eventually found photographs of the weapon online. When Germany annexed Austria in 1938, the Germans inherited warehouses full of those pistols and distributed them among police and reserve troops.

The one Claire held had likely come home with her father after the war.

The pistol looked older than the conflict that had made it famous. Heavy steel, blunt and stubborn, built to outlast the men who carried it.

And now it was pointed directly at me.

I knew Claire might still have the gun. I knew perfectly well she was capable of pulling the trigger. I had even considered the possibility that she might be tempted to shoot me. I decided it was not that great a risk.

Sometimes I wonder how I've lived to the age of twenty-five

Her finger began to tighten.

Then something strange happened.

At first, it was only a small flicker in her expression, a faint tremor passing across her face like the ripple of wind over still water. Her arm jerked slightly, and the gun dipped before rising again.

For an instant, I thought I saw a faint blue glow around her, soft and cold, the same color that had haunted my dreams in the swamp.

Claire's breathing became ragged. She got the same strange, puzzled look in her eyes that I had so often seen in Cassie's. It was the look of someone struggling against something rising inside their own mind.

The pistol wavered in her grip. Her arm trembled violently. She tried to force the pistol back toward me, but it twisted in her grasp as though guided by some other will.

I wanted to move, to knock the weapon aside, but my body refused to obey. Some unseen force seemed to hold me where I stood.

Slowly, almost gently, the barrel of the pistol turned. Claire gasped as the muzzle came to rest beneath her chin. For one terrible moment, it seemed certain that she would pull the trigger. Then suddenly all the strength drained from her arm. The gun slipped from her hand and clattered to the floor.

I could move again. I stepped forward and picked up the pistol. The metal felt cold, as though it had been lying in ice.

Claire collapsed onto the couch and began to sob.

I left her there.

Rain had begun to fall outside, turning the sky a dull gray. I drove slowly away from the motel, the windshield wipers scraping rhythmically across the glass. The pistol lay on the passenger seat beside me like a coiled snake.

For a while, I considered taking it to the police. It was clearly the weapon that had killed Simone. Claire should be held accountable. It would also mean hanging around and answering a lot of questions from unhappy policemen.

So, what was I going to do with it? Leaving it stuffed under the seats of my rental seemed a bad idea.

The swamp was the obvious answer, but that wasn't going to happen. I had promised myself I would never go back there again. It was strange, then, that I somehow found myself turning onto the narrow access road that led to the Laviolette Homestead when I could have sworn I was heading in the opposite direction.

I parked in the visitor area and spent ten minutes arguing with myself. I lost the argument. I picked up the gun, got out of my car, and walked down to the spot where Simone had been murdered. Somewhere nearby, something splashed, followed by a deep rumbling sound that reminded me of a motorcycle starting. During my nights in the swamp, I'd heard that sound often, and Kate told me later it was the throaty roar of a bull alligator.

I was glad I had not known that then.

Fear twisted in my chest as I stepped closer to the dark water. It was a feeling I suspected I would never completely escape. I hurled the pistol as far as I could and watched it vanish instantly, swallowed by the quiet, indifferent depths.

I felt proud. I didn't run back to my car.

Okay, I might have hurried my steps a little, but it was raining.

50.

B lue was released that October.

In the beginning, I hated the movie's title, but I decided not to change it. It made sense. Blue had weighed heavily on the consciences of many people, including my father, Jace Whitefield, Ellis, Claire, and Augusta. In different ways, Blue changed all of their lives.

Even mine, maybe especially mine.

I spent long, tedious hours in the editing room until I finally had a movie I thought would work. Ann helped some, but I'd also sent her out to direct a comedy romance written by a new scriptwriter. It was a good script, and I thought the movie would do well.

I was right. It was successful, and near the end of September, Ann and Sparks were married in a small Vegas wedding chapel. Several people from Blue attended.

Meanwhile, I'd been calling Kate every day, running up a massive cell phone bill. I couldn't convince her to marry me, but I did finally convince her to attend the movie premiere of Blue in Atlanta at the Fox Theatre, along with her parents.

The Fox was a sprawling, gold-leafed cathedral with velvet seats and a ceiling painted like a night sky. We held hands the whole time, but we didn't talk about the future. I wanted to badly, but something in her manner held me back.

She laughed and cried during the movie. Told me it was incredible. Watching it with her, I thought it was good, but not great. Her enthusiasm, I figured, came from growing up in Folkston, and a lot was familiar. Maybe, I hoped, some of it was also about me.

But my honest opinion? I could've done better.

Then something strange happened.

The critics didn't just tolerate Blue; they loved it. They called it haunting. Mature. Restrained. Brave, even. I read the words over and over in disbelief. Somehow, this strange little film set in the shadows and backwaters of Georgia had cracked something open.

And the public didn't stay away. People showed up, not in a polite trickle of film students and indie diehards, but in a steady stream. Crowds. Word spread. Scenes were shared, lines quoted, memes made. It became a conversation.

And it made money.

A lot of money.

Right after the premiere, I got a call from retired detective Tobias Atkins. He told me Micki was back home and that they both loved the film.

"Interesting ending, though," he said, always the cop. "I never would have thought of a woman killer. Did you have someone in mind?"

"I just used a little poetic license," I lied. "It worked in the movie."

"It did," he admitted, but I heard suspicion in his voice.

He phoned me again only a few days later.

"The Charlton County Sheriff called me," he said, "and for some odd reason I thought you might want to know. Claire Dubois disappeared. Her car was found abandoned at Stephen Foster State Park, where you were filming. One of their boats is also missing."

"You think she went into the swamp," I said. "By herself."

"The Sheriff's department is thinking suicide," Atkins said.

Full circle, I thought. Rafe gone, Jace Whitfield close to death, Ellis rotting in a prison cell, and now Claire. One by one, the players had left the stage. The act was done, the curtain finally lowered on a story that had taken decades to unwind.

"I guess she was broken-hearted over Ellis," Atkins said.

"Hard to believe," I said.

But I shuddered as I remembered the madness in Claire's eyes when she had held that gun on me. Had Blue really taken over, possessing her? Had Blue possessed Cassie, or was it all my imagination?

I knew there had been a light in the swamp, and I'd followed it. Was it Blue's lamp? If it was, she led me to safety. What if Claire had followed the same lamp with different results?

It was not something I wished to dwell on.

"Hope your movie continues to do well," Atkins told me, and I thanked him.

I waited for the backlash, the inevitable takedown. Some clever, scathing piece calling Blue just another "arthouse swamp noir with delusions of relevance." But it never came. Somehow, we'd slipped through the cracks. It wasn't labeled an indie darling, or a message movie, or even an accident. It just... was. And people accepted that. Maybe even needed it.

Rafe Cardoc's name was still on the credits as director. That had been baked in from day one. I didn't fight it. Told myself it didn't matter. At the time, I think I believed that.

Ned McDonald didn't get the part he wanted. The director said he wasn't believable as a villain, and Ned ended up doing a sitcom on independent television about a social worker in the inner city. I hadn't watched it, but I heard it was okay.

Because of Blue, Dylan Welch landed the role of Captain Matt Perry in Red Planet. He was good. Cassie got another soap opera role playing herself. I knew Blue would always be her best role.

A few weeks after the premiere, I heard Dylan let it slip to a director in Vancouver, the truth: that I'd done most of the editing, shaped the story in post, practically lived inside the footage until it felt like something real. Something that could make people feel.

Word spread.

By Christmas, a half dozen scripts had landed at Sweet Angel Productions in Culver City. Good ones. A few with serious talent attached, producers whose names carried weight. Actors I'd only dreamed of working with.

For the first time, people wanted to know what I wanted to make.

I should've been thrilled. And part of me was. I had clawed through unpaid gigs, student films, and coffee-fetching PA days just to get here.

But the other part, the bigger part, felt like it had been left behind in Georgia.

I was in the office late one afternoon, half pretending to read a script but really just staring out the window. The sun was slipping behind a bank of smog and palm trees, Culver City at its golden hour best: shiny and fake and sad.

Ann walked in without knocking. She never knocked. After all, she owned five percent.

She shut the door behind her, arms crossed, giving me a look that sliced through the fading light.

"You're not happy," she said.

I blinked. "What makes you say that?"

"You're wearing the same shirt you wore to the wrap party. You haven't shaved in a week. And you've ignored three calls from an Oscar-winning cinematographer."

"I need some time off."

"Take all the vacation you want," Ann said. "But that won't fix what's bothering you."

"What's bothering me?"

"It's that redheaded girl from Georgia."

She stepped closer, her tone softening. "You're in love with her."

"I am," I admitted. "And I'm miserable. I asked her again at the Fox Theatre to marry me, and she turned me down. She doesn't want any part of this city. Or me, I guess."

"No, that's not right," Ann said. "I've seen the way she looks at you. Maybe you should meet her halfway."

"How am I supposed to do that?"

"Move the studio to Atlanta. Or close to it. There's no rule that Sweet Angel Productions has to stay in Culver City. And you wouldn't be the first. The Walking Dead, Stranger Things, and The Hunger Games were all shot in Georgia. It's practically a tax haven for filmmakers. We've already got contacts at Trilith Studios in Fayetteville. Everything you need is there."

"My financing is here."

"Your finance people will follow you as long as you make good movies."

"And you think she'd marry me if I moved everything to Georgia?"

"I think it's worth a shot."

I went back to France for two weeks before we made the move to Georgia. I rented the same villa from the same suspicious landlady.

I walked the same beach, watched the fancy boats drift lazily in the harbor, and practiced my French with a new woman at the bakery.

A script had come across my desk that I liked. It wasn't one Rafe would have chosen. It wasn't dark, but it had strong, memorable characters and plenty of humor.

I needed a movie like that, something that could make people laugh and feel good about themselves.

One evening, after dinner, I wandered down to the harbor, thinking about casting. The golden glow of sunset spilled across the waves. The sky blazed with pinks and oranges, the colors melting into the horizon like someone had painted them just for that moment.

I started back toward the villa when I noticed a figure coming down the hill. At first, it was only a silhouette, framed by the fading light. My heart skipped. Then I saw the auburn hair, the familiar sway in her walk, and the same easy smile she'd worn that first day at Swamp Lily Motor Court, when I'd thought she'd look perfect in front of a Paris café.

"A crazy woman accosted me and told me I wasn't welcome anywhere near your villa," Kate said as she reached me. "Is she your girlfriend?"

"She's my landlady," I said, still catching my breath.

"She's a little scary," she said with a grin. "Aren't you going to kiss me?"

"I'm still a little shocked to see you here," I admitted.

"I called and talked to Ann. She says you're moving the entire studio to Georgia, which is great, but I want to be clear. I had already made up my mind before I heard."

"Made up your mind about what?" I asked.

"Well, honestly, Dad and Mom helped make up my mind. They said I was making everyone miserable with my moping around. And my grades were suffering." She stepped closer. "Dad said if I was so determined to be Dr. Pol, I could do it in California."

"Who's Dr. Pol?" I asked, smiling despite the lump in my throat.

"He's a vet who has a television show. Don't evade the question. Aren't you going to kiss me?"

I did, slowly, savoring the warmth of her lips, the certainty in her eyes.

"And the answer is yes," she said, pulling back just enough to look at me.

"What?"

"I will marry you," she said, her voice steady, soft, and final.

I laughed, almost in disbelief, almost in relief, and pulled her close as the sun slipped into the water, painting the harbor in gold and fire. In that moment, everything else, France, Georgia, the movies, the distance, seemed to fade away. There was only her, only us, only forever.

Not long ago, I paid to have Rafe's body exhumed and reburied in the Camp Pinckney Baptist Church cemetery.

While the workers dug his grave, I sat in the fellowship hall with Augusta's children and grandchildren, cousins I had never known. They filled the room with quiet conversation and the easy warmth of people who already belonged to one another. Faces I didn't recognize smiled at me, names were exchanged, stories begun and abandoned for better ones. For a little while, I felt myself pulled into something larger than I had ever allowed.

Afterward, we ate together, more homemade food than I had ever seen in one place. Tables sagged under casseroles, fried chicken, biscuits, pies, and dishes passed from hand to hand. The noise of it all, the laughter and the clatter of plates, softened something in me I hadn't realized was still hard.

Later, Augusta, Kate, and I walked alone out to my father's new resting place. It was a cold autumn afternoon, the light thin and colorless. Even the old cypresses seemed to bow under it. We laid him beside Simone. His tombstone was a white block, unmarked except for a small camera carved into one corner.

As the evening shadows deepened, Kate slipped her hand into mine, and we walked back to the church, leaving him behind with Blue.

AFTERWORD

Camp Pinckney Baptist Church is indeed a real church, and the shaded cemetery behind it has a quiet, reflective beauty that can easily spark a story—or at the very least, a mildly overactive imagination. Places like Camp Pinckney—still, dappled with light, and filled with names and dates on old headstones—have a way of making you feel as though you've just stepped into the opening scene of a mystery.

That said, Simone Laviolette and the entirely fictional Girl Guides exist only in the author's imagination. Visitors wandering through the cemetery won't find her grave there—no matter how carefully they look. The setting is real; the story simply takes a few creative liberties (as stories tend to do).

There is also a real Okefenokee Restaurant, and stopping by is a fine way to round out a visit—especially if you enjoy good Southern cooking. And yes, Okefenokee National Wildlife Refuge and Stephen C. Foster State Park are quite real as well. They're beautiful, peaceful, and—according to officials—safe.

In fact, in the 87-year history of the refuge, there has never been a documented alligator attack on a human there. And now you know it's true—because, naturally, it's on the internet.

ABOUT THE AUTHOR

In a city known as the Gateway to the Mountains, I write stories from a basement filled with memories, memorabilia, and far too many coffee cups—occasionally wondering what happened to my mind.

ALSO BY

RAVEN Detective Tobias "Swede" Atkins wakes from a year-long coma to a world that's moved on—his best friend is dead, and his body is failing. Retirement seems inevitable... until a child disappears on Kalanu Mountain, the one place he knows better than anyone. Racing against time through Georgia's wild terrain, Swede uncovers a deadly plot led by a man who believes he's a mythical Cherokee witch. No one else believes him, but Swede knows: if he fails, an innocent child will pay the ultimate price.

PAST SINS second in the series of Kalanu Mountain Mysteries. Retired detective Tobias "Swede" Atkins is in for a rollercoaster ride. Battling post-coma challenges, a perplexing ex-wife, and accusations of arson, his world spirals into a tangled web of suspicions and doubts.

As he navigates a town on the edge of chaos, a woman's desire to turn a restaurant into a battleground unravels a historic murder and concealed secrets fanned by the mountain's fiery whispers. Swede discovers the past haunts the present and truth is as elusive as mountain winds.

A GHOST TOO MANY Jodi Weathers was stunned when the mayor of Sandy Shoals offered her the job of police chief. She had grown up along the coast of Georgia and it would mean returning to an area she loved, but her first inclination was to refuse. She didn't feel qualified even when the mayor described her duties as writing reports and shaking hands. "The Sheriff's Department will take care of the real police work," he assured her. "You'll be handling public relations." At the time the mayor had no warning of the approaching hurricane, and he couldn't have foreseen finding a dead woman on the beach. To be fair, Jodi also didn't mention that she was seeing her ex-husband. Her dead, ex-husband. She knew he was dead because she had gone to his funeral. Jodi finally convinced herself that she wasn't crazy, and that what was needed to escape the ghost of her ex-husband was a change of scenery. But then the second ghost showed up, and that was a ghost too many.

FINDING CHARLIE "Finding Charlie" is a short story set during the Vietnam War, focusing on the experiences of Marines in First Platoon as they take positions on a high ridge near a river. The narrative emphasizes the tension, fear, and human moments of Marines in combat, highlighting the psychological and emotional aspects of war rather than large-scale battles. The story captures the uncertainty of survival and the personal experiences of those involved in the conflict.